THE HOUSE BEHIND
THE CEDARS

THE HOUSE BEHIND
THE CEDARS

BY

CHARLES W. CHESNUTT

FOREWORD BY

WILLIAM L. ANDREWS

BROWN THRASHER BOOKS
THE UNIVERSITY OF GEORGIA PRESS
ATHENS AND LONDON

Foreword by William L. Andrews
© 1988 by the University of Georgia Press
Athens, Georgia 30602
All rights reserved

The paper in this book meets the guidelines for
permanence and durability of the Committee on
Production Guidelines for Book Longevity of the
Council on Library Resources.

Printed in the United States of America

92   5   4   3

Library of Congress Cataloging in Publication Data

Chesnutt, Charles Waddell, 1858–1932.
The house behind the cedars / by Charles W. Chestnutt ;
foreword by William L. Andrews.
    p.   cm.
"Brown thrasher books."
ISBN 0-8203-1021-2 (pbk. : alk. paper)
I. Title.
PS1292.C6H68 1988
813'.4—dc 19
88-9999
CIP

British Library Cataloging in Publication Data
available

The House Behind the Cedars was first published in 1900
by Houghton Mifflin & Co.

CONTENTS

FOREWORD

JUST before the publication of his first novel, *The House Behind the Cedars,* in the fall of 1900, Charles Waddell Chesnutt confided to his editor at Houghton Mifflin in Boston: "I hope the book may raise some commotion, I hardly care in what quarter, though whether, from the nature of the theme it will, I don't know." The Cleveland author had to admit that he could not think of any part of the United States where "the subject of the book, bluntly stated as a story of a colored girl who passed for white," would be especially appealing. Still Chesnutt hoped his novel would sell "in spite of its subject, or rather, because of its dramatic value apart from the race problem involved." No one conversant with the popular fiction or social debates of late-nineteenth-century America could deny that the subject of Chesnutt's novel was, at the very least, controversial. But Chesnutt believed he could offer a new and virtually unique perspective on what had become by the turn of the century a recognizable tradition in American fiction—the novel of passing and miscegenation.

Chesnutt's commitment to the story of Rena Walden, the "colored girl who passed for white" in *The House Behind the Cedars,* was long-standing and deep. He had not drawn her from his imagination; she was, as Chesnutt remarked to a critic, of "mine own people." Her life and circumstances in post–Civil War eastern North Carolina had much in common

with his own youth. The acutely color-conscious
world of Patesville in *The House Behind the Cedars* is
grounded in Chesnutt's memories of Fayetteville,
North Carolina, where he grew up classed as a
"bright mulatto" easily capable of passing for white
himself. Rena's mother, Molly Walden, the mistress
of a white man in antebellum Patesville, is pat-
terned on Chesnutt's paternal grandmother, Ann
Chesnutt, whose unsanctioned liaison with Waddell
Cade, a prosperous white Fayetteville widower,
produced five mixed-blood children. The aspirations and frustrations of Rena Walden and her
brother John were all too familiar to Chesnutt. He
once hinted in a letter that he had aunts and uncles
who had taken Rena and John's path toward social
fulfillment—passing for white—as their way of escaping the restrictions of the color line. As a teen-
ager Chesnutt himself had toyed with the idea of
passing, but he rejected it because it required too
great a personal sacrifice for the apparent socioeconomic advantages gained. Still, as a writer Chesnutt
was determined to have his say on the questions of
passing for white and racial amalgamation, partly
for personal reasons but just as much, if not more,
for social, aesthetic, and moral reasons.

Early in his literary career Rena Walden's story
took hold of Chesnutt's imagination. His original
version of her life went through at least four revi-
sions between 1890 and 1899 while he labored dog-
gedly to produce a novel that would both represent

his unconventional views on color and caste and satisfy the demands of a conservative commercial publisher. A prosperous businessman, he had enough money to finance the publication of his manuscript out of his own pocket in a manner typical of many black writers of his time. But Chesnutt knew that self-published novels by Afro-American authors, regardless of their quality, rarely found readers outside the black community. He was therefore determined that Rena's story should be published, read, and reviewed by whites (though not to the exclusion of blacks) so that his message could reach those who needed most to hear it. At a time when only one other black writer, Paul Laurence Dunbar, could boast a well-established white publisher, Chesnutt shrewdly prepared the way for Rena's national advent by publishing two books of short stories—*The Conjure Woman* (1899) and *The Wife of His Youth and Other Stories of the Color Line* (1899)—under the auspices of the prestigious Boston firm of Houghton Mifflin. The favorable critical response to both collections convinced Houghton Mifflin to become the first major publishing house in the United States to underwrite an Afro-American novel. *The House Behind the Cedars* thus became the most widely reviewed and read Afro-American novel in American literary history up to 1900.

To his white audience Chesnutt hoped to present Rena Walden and those she represented not as a social problem but as sympathetic people, recognizably American people, with the strengths and weaknesses, goals and limitations of most nineteenth-century Americans. Rena and John Walden are not idealized in *The House Behind the Cedars*, but in acknowledging their faults, their creator refuses to blame their mixed blood, nor does he believe that their actions disqualify them from a sympathetic hearing in the court of public opinion. Trained as a lawyer, Chesnutt wanted very much to serve as a literary spokesman and public defender of the Waldens. At the same time, he did not wish to identify himself as an advocate of passing for white, since the trend of white and much black American literature in the nineteenth century opposed racial assimilation in any way that increased the likelihood of miscegenation. Well-known white novels of the era, such as William Dean Howells's *An Imperative Duty* (1892), Mark Twain's *Pudd'nhead Wilson* (1894), and Gertrude Atherton's *Senator North* (1900), differ widely in their moral judgments of mulattos who pass for white, but in none of these books is a miscegenate love affair allowed to come to fruition in the United States. Black writers like Frances Ellen Watkins Harper and Sutton E. Griggs took up novel-writing with the express intention of refuting the popular assumption that light-skinned Afro-Americans *wanted* to merge into the white race at any cost. Harper's *Iola Leroy* (1892) and Griggs' *The Hindered Hand* (1905) reject the idea that light-skinned Afro-Americans were so

selfish that they would sacrifice their duty to their
fellow blacks on the altar of merely personal advancement. In these novels, as well as in most
popular white fiction of the late nineteenth and
early twentieth centuries, the renunciation scene,
in which a high-minded mulatto, ususally a woman,
rejects the temptation to pass for white and marry
into comfort in the white world, became almost a
stock ingredient. These self-abnegating mixed-
blood characters act on a popular presumption that
the obligation of the light-skinned "Talented
Tenth," as W. E. B. Du Bois termed the largely
mulatto leadership of Afro-America, was to identify
their interests with that of black, not white,
Americans.

Well read in this fiction, Chesnutt knew that the
Waldens would be judged by what we might call the
ethic of renunciation in novels of passing and miscegenation. He knew that unless Rena and John refused the chance to pass for white, preferring instead a supposedly higher moral commitment to the
uplifting of black people, they would be subject to
nearly automatic condemnation. This partly helps
to explain why, in the latter half of the novel, Rena,
having failed in her attempt to pass for white, re-
nounces further offers from her brother to cross the
color line. Rena's emphatic decision to "'stay with
my own people'" echoes the ultimate choice of most
mulattos in both black and white fiction of Chesnutt's
time. Nevertheless, though Rena's decision seems

to endorse the popular stereotype of the duty-
conscious, self-effacing mulatto, her brother's behavior works at distinctly cross purposes to that stereotype. From his boyhood, John Walden refuses to
accept the idea that he is "a Negro," or that "his
people" are black. He justifies his identification with
the white world on the basis of his free birth and
background and his white paternity, but underlying
all else lies his simple appeal to an obvious fact, "'A
Negro is black; I am white, and not black.'" John's
argument is not lost on Archibald Straight, the antebellum judge who represents the soul of impartiality
and fair-mindedness in the novel. Indeed it is
Straight, a white man, an old-school southerner of
unquestioned probity, who confirms John's "'somewhat unusual privilege'" of "'chosing between two
races.'" Even after George Tryon, Rena's disappointed white suitor, learns of John Walden's heritage, he cannot help but admit, "I shall never be
able to think of you as other than a white man."

Why then, Chesnutt's novel seems to ask, should
people who look as white as "whites" and whose
cultural affinities and socioeconomic goals mirror
those of "whites" be automatically condemned as
racial imposters for simply *being* what to all appearances they actually are—white men and women.
Fair-minded southerners like Straight and Tryon
have trouble answering this question with a conventional knee-jerk appeal to racist categories. Back of
their difficulties stands their creator's fundamental

skepticism about any attempt to define or classify people according to race. "What Is a White Man?" Chesnutt asked point-blank in the title of his first published essay. With scathing irony, he went on to show that while every state of the former Confederacy had tried to legislate a definition of white and black identity in order to justify segregation laws, none of the states could agree on their own definitions. Labeling one light-skinned person "white" and another "black" was, therefore, a largely arbitrary act on the part of society. Yet the consequences of this arbitrary classification were, Chesnutt believed, enormous, inescapable, and almost always grotesquely unjust.

In an essay published in the same year as *The House Behind the Cedars*, Chesnutt argued that "it is only a social fiction, indeed, which makes of a person seven-eighths white a Negro; he is really much more a white man." It was just such a national "social fiction"—one that let a caste identity assigned to an individual take precedence over that individual's personal sense of identity—that Chesnutt's literary fiction was designed to expose. Chesnutt's aim in writing *The House Behind the Cedars* was not to say that persons seven-eighths white like the Waldens *ought* to consider themselves white or pass for white. Chesnutt never argued mixed-blood people like himself to take a step that he was unwilling to take. But he vigorously opposed any societal attempt to label as criminal or unnatural the taking of

such a step, especially in light of the discrimination
a person of mixed blood would suffer if he or she
acceded to membership in the Negro caste. In
short, Chesnutt was convinced that society had no
legal right to prevent those who could from crossing
America's color line.

As for the right to moral condemnation of such an
act, Chesnutt believed that a novel was the best
forum in which to argue that the ethics of passing
for white and miscegenation could be neither neatly
formulated nor absolutely maintained. It had always been Chesnutt's intent to tell Rena Walden's
story in the manner of contemporary realist novelists, so that instead of conforming to the conventional literary view of his subject, he could be free
to represent real life as he knew it. Chesnutt was in
sympathy with the realists' demand that readers
recognize that individuals generally do not dictate
their destinies; their choices are often restricted by
circumstances beyond their control. In the real
world, as depicted in classic realist novels such as
Howells's *The Rise of Silas Lapham* (1885) and Edith
Wharton's *The House of Mirth* (1905), morality is
rarely a simple matter. Few characters can be
evaluated according to a rigid standard; individuals
must be judged on individual bases, in light of the
social, economic, and psychological factors that
produce and shape them. In the domain of social
behavior, realist novelists suggested that the right
and wrong of an action are often relative, depend-

ing on the situation, the human consequences, and
the perspective from which the act is viewed. To
Chesnutt, the realists' pragmatic attitude toward social morality, along with their sympathetic view of
the individual inevitably implicated in a social context not of his or her making, made possible the por-
trayal of the mixed blood's situation in new and lib-
erating ways.

The first half of *The House Behind the Cedars* is
dominated by two realist perspectives: that of John
Walden and that of the narrator of his story, who
often seems to feel himself obliged to explain, if not
justify, Walden's thought and behavior. Clearly,
Walden's course in life, sustained by a pragmatic,
tough-minded, and largely self-serving attitude toward the future, can lead one to conclude that he is
hardly more than a young man on the make, with
little sense of responsibility to anyone or anything
aside from his own advantage. Almost always, as
the narrator of the novel points out, when John considers matters involving his own desires and his
rights to gratify those desires, he prefers to take
"the practical point of view." But in returning to the
house behind the cedars after a ten-year absence,
John displays an uncharacteristic lapse in the pragmatic self-regard that had enabled him to become a
success in the white caste. His motive in propelling
his sister into his adopted caste is neither selfish nor
calculating; he simply wants to help Rena attain the
same opportunity, prosperity, and respectability

that he has earned. His depiction of the acme of his
sister's prospects—"'a rich man,'" "'a fine house,'"
"'a carriage and a servant,'" and the right to hob-
nob with "'the best in the land'"—may seem a bit
crass. And John may be criticized for manipulating
his mother's guilt and naïveté in order to induce her
to let Rena follow him to South Carolina. But from
his point of view, these means are justified by the
end that necessitates them, the opening of social
doors to his beautiful and deserving sister.

Though one might condemn John for encouraging his sister to desert her mother and her past in a
bid for the status symbols of white middle-class success, Chesnutt insists that at the same time one
must grant the brother's altruistic motives in all this.
No one knows better than John that a man who
passes for white commits a serious error in holding
onto the past. As the narrator puts it, a man who
lives "by principles of abstract right and reason,"
especially when they are "at variance with what society considers equally right and reasonable,"
should "be careful about descending from the lofty
heights of logic to the common level of impulse and
affection." But because John does not exercise this
prudence, his return to his home to aid his sister
cannot be viewed as calculated. Though a prag-
matist about his own affairs, he reveals himself a
sentimentalist, a man governed more by his
"affection" than by his reason, in his familial rela-
tionships. Thus to the moral critic who would con-

demn John Walden for not being loyal to "his people," Chesnutt asks, are not Walden's family first and foremost his people? If so, can he be so easily denounced for acting on his affection toward his sister? Is it natural or realistic to expect a brother not to share with his sister the advantages of life that he has won for himself?

The problem of how far the mulatto may go in pursuing social and economic advantages arises again in Chaper 9 of *The House Behind the Cedars* when Rena must decide whether she is justified in not only passing for white but marrying a white man who has fallen in love with her. Does she have a moral right to conceal her past from him? Rena and her brother discuss the ethics of her marriage decision in a remarkably unconventional way. Neither gives any thought to the racist idea that by marrying the blue-blood George Tryon, Rena will be tainting his family's racial purity. To the conscientious Rena the only thing that can taint her marriage to Tryon is her failure to be completely honest, not her failure to be completely "white." On the other hand, John Walden thinks only the pragmatic side of the question is relevant. When Rena wonders, "'would he marry me if he knew?'" John replies, in effect, wouldn't he be happier, and wouldn't everyone be a lot less troubled, if he didn't know? No American novelist before Chesnutt had so dispassionately depicted the pros and cons of passing and miscegenation. Chesnutt the realist does not allow Rena the luxury of the conventional melodramatic renunciation scene based on a set of simplistic moral options. Should she opt for the absolute honesty of self-revelation, she realizes that she would also have to reveal her brother's racial antecedents, thus ruining his prospects, as well as those of her nephew, in the process of doing what seems to be the right thing. Compared with such dire consequences, the acknowledging of her racial heritage begins to look like a moral nicety to Rena. Besides, as John argues, does she have the right to "'involve all of us in difficulties merely to secure your own peace of mind?'" In this light, Rena sees keeping silent about her past as truly an act of "self-sacrifice." Thus what might seem at first "a sort of sin" to both Rena and the reader begins to appear "a virtue" as the total context of Rena's life, implicated as it is in the fortunes of so many others, impinges on her choices. Rena's eventual acceptance of Tryon's marriage proposal is presented as a thoughtful, even a conscientious, act. Without blinking the possibility of criticizing Rena's judgment, Chesnutt's narrator points out, with a realist's appreciation of the relativity of morality, "It was not the first time, nor the last, that right and wrong had been a matter of view-point."

Through the narrator of *The House Behind the Cedars,* the "view-point' of Charles Chesnutt comes directly before the reader. On the eve of Tryon's discovery of Rena as a Patesville "colored woman," the narrator pauses to make his most explicit plea in defense of the Waldens. "If there be a dainty reader of this tale who scorns a lie, and who writes the story of his life upon his sleeve for all the world to read, let him uncurl his scornful lip and come down from the pedestal of superior morality, to which assured position and wide opportunity have lifted him, and put himself in the place of Rena and her brother, upon whom God had lavished his best gifts, and from whom society would have withheld all that made these gifts valuable. To undertake what they tried to do required great courage." Here Chesnutt argues his realist perspective on the Waldens most forcefully by challenging any reader who feels morally superior to them to put himeself in their places and then consider the justice of their actions. Nor does Chesnutt ask that the understanding and sympathy for those entrapped by racial prejudice be applied only to the "black" characters in his story. One of the strengths of this novel is Chesnutt's attentiveness to the inner conflicts and genuine suffering that George Tryon undergoes in the latter half of the novel. Although it can be argued that Rena rarely deviates from the standard role of the "tragic mulatto" after her marriage plans fall through, Tryon's character actually develops and deepens as he becomes aware of what he has lost in Rena. Ironically, with John Walden permanently removed from the story, and with Rena firmly opposed to marrying outside her caste,

George Tryon's consciousness becomes the final arena in which the social proscriptions and emotional justifications of interracial love do battle. Ultimately, Tryon resolves this conflict between custom and love in favor of the latter. But by the time he can make up his mind to "give up the world for love," this latter-day Antony cannot save his Cleopatra.

The pathos and ironies of the outcome of *The House Behind the Cedars* are not unusual in Chesnutt's fiction. Often a Chesnutt protagonist undergoes an awakening to a more liberal and realistic moral perspective and a more sympathetic view of the racial "other" only after he is powerless to halt imminent tragedy. Nevertheless the fact that Chesnutt concludes this novel with a typical southern aristocrat, exemplary of the best people of his region, willing to put aside "the instinctive ready-made judgments of his training and environment" in favor of his love for a "black" woman, indicates an abiding sense of hope in Chesnutt. He seems to have maintained an almost willed belief in the capacity of white southerners to change their racial "view-point" toward Afro-Americans, despite the preponderance of evidence during his time that such change would be very slow in coming.

The House Behind the Cedars sold well enough to whet its publisher's appetite for a second race-problem novel from Chesnutt, this time about major sociopolitical issues of immediate concern in the contemporary South. In less than a year after his first book, Chesnutt gave Houghton Mifflin *The Marrow of Tradition*, a novel based on the Wilmington Race Riot of 1898, which its author hoped would become the *Uncle Tom's Cabin* of his generation. Though reviewed extensively, *The Marrow of Tradition* proved too controversial and perturbing to its readers and did not sell well enough to satisfy Chesnutt. Returning to his business as a legal stenographer, which he had briefly put aside to attempt to become a self-supporting fiction writer, Chesnutt put his novel-writing career in abeyance until 1905. In that year, his friend and advisor, Walter Hines Page, agreed to publish Chesnutt's third southern novel, centered on the efforts of a former Confederate officer to reform a depressed North Carolina town. *The Colonel's Dream*, however, failed to revive Chesnutt's flagging literary fortunes. When he died, in 1932, his fiction had been largely forgotten except in the Afro-American community, which never entirely lost sight of *The House Behind the Cedars*. In 1921 Oscar Micheaux, the first major black filmmaker, bought the rights to Chesnutt's first novel and produced a movie version of it, giving it a happy rather than tragic ending. A year later, the Chicago *Defender*, one of the most influential black newspapers in the United States, serialized *The House Behind the Cedars*, putting the novel back into print for the first time in more than fifteen years. Passing for white and miscegenation

continued as topics of concern among some of the
best-known writers of the Harlem Renaissance.
Few could deny that major Afro-American novels
such as James Weldon Johnson's *The Autobiography
of an Ex-Coloured Man* (1912) and Nella Larsen's
Passing (1929) owe much to Chesnutt's pioneering
efforts to depict sympathetically the dilemmas of
the "white" Negro. The central issues of *The House
Behind the Cedars* do not play as momentous a role
in more recent fiction as they did in the literature of
Chesnutt's day. Nevertheless, if most twentieth-
century American writers have liberated themselves from the condescending sentimentality and
simplistic moralism of the "tragic mulatto" fiction of
the past, the debt they owe to Charles Chesnutt's
pioneering work should not be forgotten.

THE HOUSE BEHIND
THE CEDARS

THE HOUSE BEHIND THE CEDARS

I

A STRANGER FROM SOUTH CAROLINA

TIME touches all things with destroying hand;
and if he seem now and then to bestow the bloom
of youth, the sap of spring, it is but a brief mock-
ery, to be surely and swiftly followed by the wrin-
kles of old age, the dry leaves and bare branches
of winter. And yet there are places where Time
seems to linger lovingly long after youth has departed, and to which he seems loath to bring the
evil day. Who has not known some even-tem-
pered old man or woman who seemed to have
drunk of the fountain of youth? Who has not
seen somewhere an old town that, having long
since ceased to grow, yet held its own without perceptible decline?

Some such trite reflection — as apposite to the
subject as most random reflections are — passed
through the mind of a young man who came out
of the front door of the Patesville Hotel about
nine o'clock one fine morning in spring, a few years
after the Civil War, and started down Front Street

toward the market-house. Arriving at the town
late the previous evening, he had been driven up
from the steamboat in a carriage, from which he
had been able to distinguish only the shadowy outlines of the houses along the street; so that this
morning walk was his first opportunity to see the
town by daylight. He was dressed in a suit of
linen duck — the day was warm — a panama straw
hat, and patent leather shoes. In appearance he
was tall, dark, with straight, black, lustrous hair,
and very clean-cut, high-bred features. When he
paused by the clerk's desk on his way out, to light
his cigar, the day clerk, who had just come on duty,
glanced at the register and read the last entry : —

"'JOHN WARWICK, CLARENCE, SOUTH CAROLINA.'

"One of the South Ca'lina bigbugs, I reckon
— probably in cotton, or turpentine." The gentleman from South Carolina, walking down the street,
glanced about him with an eager look, in which
curiosity and affection were mingled with a touch
of bitterness. He saw little that was not familiar,
or that he had not seen in his dreams a hundred
times during the past ten years. There had been
some changes, it is true, some melancholy changes,
but scarcely anything by way of addition or improvement to counterbalance them. Here and
there blackened and dismantled walls marked the
place where handsome buildings once had stood, for
Sherman's march to the sea had left its mark upon
the town. The stores were mostly of brick, two

stories high, joining one another after the manner of cities. Some of the names on the signs were familiar; others, including a number of Jewish names, were quite unknown to him.

A two minutes' walk brought Warwick — the name he had registered under, and as we shall call him — to the market-house, the central feature of Patesville, from both the commercial and the picturesque points of view. Standing foursquare in the heart of the town, at the intersection of the two main streets, a " jog " at each street corner left around the market-house a little public square, which at this hour was well occupied by carts and wagons from the country and empty drays awaiting hire. Warwick was unable to perceive much change in the market-house. Perhaps the surface of the red brick, long unpainted, had scaled off a little more here and there. There might have been a slight accretion of the moss and lichen on the shingled roof. But the tall tower, with its four-faced clock, rose as majestically and uncompromisingly as though the land had never been subjugated. Was it so irreconcilable, Warwick wondered, as still to peal out the curfew bell, which at nine o'clock at night had clamorously warned all negroes, slave or free, that it was unlawful for them to be abroad after that hour, under penalty of imprisonment or whipping? Was the old constable, whose chief business it had been to ring the bell, still alive and exercising the functions of his office, and had age lessened or increased the number of times

that obliging citizens performed this duty for him
during his temporary absences in the company of
convivial spirits ?   A few moments later, Warwick
saw a colored policeman in the old constable's
place — a stronger reminder than even the burned
buildings that war had left its mark upon the old
town, with which Time had dealt so tenderly.

The lower story of the market-house was open
on all four of its sides to the public square. Warwick passed through one of the wide brick arches
and traversed the building with a leisurely step.
He looked in vain into the stalls for the butcher
who had sold fresh meat twice a week, on market
days, and he felt a genuine thrill of pleasure when
he recognized the red bandana turban of old
Aunt Lyddy, the ancient negro woman who had
sold him gingerbread and fried fish, and told him
weird tales of witchcraft and conjuration, in the
old days when, as an idle boy, he had loafed about
the market-house. He did not speak to her, however,
or give her any sign of recognition.   He threw a
glance toward a certain corner where steps led to
the town hall above.   On this stairway he had
once seen a manacled free negro shot while being
taken upstairs for examination under a criminal
charge.   Warwick recalled vividly how the shot
had rung out.   He could see again the livid look
of terror on the victim's face, the gathering crowd,
the resulting confusion.   The murderer, he recalled, had been tried and sentenced to imprisonment for life, but was pardoned by a merciful

governor after serving a year of his sentence.   As
Warwick was neither a prophet nor the son of a
prophet, he could not foresee that, thirty years
later, even this would seem an excessive punishment for so slight a misdemeanor.

Leaving the market-house, Warwick turned to
the left, and kept on his course until he reached
the next corner.   After another turn to the right,
a dozen paces brought him in front of a small
weather-beaten frame building, from which projected a wooden sign-board bearing the inscrip-
tion : —

ARCHIBALD STRAIGHT,

LAWYER.

He turned the knob, but the door was locked.
Retracing his steps past a vacant lot, the young
man entered a shop where a colored man was employed in varnishing a coffin, which stood on two
trestles in the middle of the floor.   Not at all
impressed by the melancholy suggestiveness of his
task, he was whistling a lively air with great gusto.
Upon Warwick's entrance this effusion came to a
sudden end, and the coffin-maker assumed an air
of professional gravity.

" Good-mawnin', suh," he said, lifting his cap
politely.

" Good-morning," answered Warwick.   " Can
you tell me anything about Judge Straight's office
hours ? "

" De ole jedge has be'n a little onreg'lar sence

de wah, suh; but he gin'ally gits roun' 'bout ten
o'clock er so.   He's be'n kin' er feeble fer de las'
few yeahs.   An' I reckon," continued the undertaker solemnly, his glance unconsciously seeking a
row of fine caskets standing against the wall, — " I
reckon he'll soon be goin' de way er all de earth.
' Man dat is bawn er 'oman hath but a sho't time
ter lib, an' is full er mis'ry.   He cometh up an' is
cut down lack as a flower.'   ' De days er his life
is three-sco' an' ten ' — an' de ole jedge is libbed
mo' d'n dat, suh, by five yeahs, ter say de leas'."

" ' Death,' " quoted Warwick, with whose mood
the undertaker's remarks were in tune, " ' is the
penalty that all must pay for the crime of
living.' "

" Dat's a fac', suh, dat's a fac' ; so dey mus' —
so dey mus'.   An' den all de dead has ter be buried.
An' we does ou' sheer of it, suh, we does ou' sheer.
We conduc's de obs'quies er all de bes' w'ite folks
er de town, suh."

Warwick left the undertaker's shop and retraced his steps until he had passed the lawyer's
office, toward which he threw an affectionate glance.
A few rods farther led him past the old brick Pres-
byterian church, with its square tower, embowered
in a stately grove ; past the Catholic church, with
its many crosses, and a painted wooden figure of
St. James in a recess beneath the gable ; and past
the old Jefferson House, once the leading hotel of
the town, in front of which political meetings had
been held, and political speeches made, and polit-

ical hard cider drunk, in the days of " Tippecanoe
and Tyler too."

The street down which Warwick had come intersected Front Street at a sharp angle in front of
the old hotel, forming a sort of flatiron block at
the junction, known as Liberty Point, — perhaps
because slave auctions were sometimes held there in
the good old days.   Just before Warwick reached
Liberty Point, a young woman came down Front
Street from the direction of the market-house.
When their paths converged, Warwick kept on
down Front Street behind her, it having been
already his intention to walk in this direction.

Warwick's first glance had revealed the fact
that the young woman was strikingly handsome,
with a stately beauty seldom encountered.   As he
walked along behind her at a measured distance,
he could not help noting the details that made
up this pleasing impression, for his mind was singularly alive to beauty, in whatever embodiment.
The girl's figure, he perceived, was admirably
proportioned ; she was evidently at the period
when the angles of childhood were rounding into
the promising curves of adolescence.   Her abun-
dant hair, of a dark and glossy brown, was neatly
plaited and coiled above an ivory column that rose
straight from a pair of gently sloping shoulders,
clearly outlined beneath the light muslin frock
that covered them.   He could see that she was
tastefully, though not richly, dressed, and that she
walked with an elastic step that revealed a light

WHERE IS
THE
LIBERTY?

heart and the vigor of perfect health. Her face,
of course, he could not analyze, since he had
caught only the one brief but convincing glimpse
of it.

The young woman kept on down Front Street,
Warwick maintaining his distance a few rods
behind her. They passed a factory, a warehouse
or two, and then, leaving the brick pavement,
walked along on mother earth, under a leafy
arcade of spreading oaks and elms. Their way
led now through a residential portion of the
town, which, as they advanced, gradually declined
from staid respectability to poverty, open and un-
abashed. Warwick observed, as they passed
through the respectable quarter, that few people
who met the girl greeted her, and that some others
whom she passed at gates or doorways gave her
no sign of recognition ; from which he inferred
that she was possibly a visitor in the town and not
well acquainted.

Their walk had continued not more than ten
minutes when they crossed a creek by a wooden
bridge and came to a row of mean houses standing
flush with the street. At the door of one, an old
black woman had stooped to lift a large basket,
piled high with laundered clothes. The girl, as
she passed, seized one end of the basket and helped
the old woman to raise it to her head, where it
rested solidly on the cushion of her head-kerchief.
During this interlude, Warwick, though he had
slackened his pace measurably, had so nearly

closed the gap between himself and them as to
hear the old woman say, with the dulcet negro
intonation : —

"T'ank y', honey; de Lawd gwine bless you
sho'. You wuz alluz a good gal, and de Lawd
love eve'ybody w'at he'p de po' ole nigger. You
gwine ter hab good luck all yo' bawn days."

"I hope you 're a true prophet, Aunt Zilphy,"
laughed the girl in response.

The sound of her voice gave Warwick a thrill.
It was soft and sweet and clear — quite in harmony with her appearance. That it had a faint
suggestiveness of the old woman's accent he
hardly noticed, for the current Southern speech,
including his own, was rarely without a touch of it.
The corruption of the white people's speech was
one element — only one — of the negro's unconscious revenge for his own debasement.

The houses they passed now grew scattering,
and the quarter of the town more neglected.
Warwick felt himself wondering where the girl
might be going in a neighborhood so uninviting.
When she stopped to pull a half-naked negro
child out of a mudhole and set him upon his feet,
he thought she might be some young lady from the
upper part of the town, bound on some errand of
mercy, or going, perhaps, to visit an old servant or
look for a new one. Once she threw a backward
glance at Warwick, thus enabling him to catch a
second glimpse of a singularly pretty face. Perhaps the young woman found his presence in the

neighborhood as unaccountable as he had deemed
hers; for, finding his glance fixed upon her, she
quickened her pace with an air of startled timidity.

"A woman with such a figure," thought Warwick, "ought to be able to face the world with the
confidence of Phryne confronting her judges."

By this time Warwick was conscious that something more than mere grace or beauty had attracted him with increasing force toward this
young woman. A suggestion, at first faint and
elusive, of something familiar, had grown stronger
when he heard her voice, and became more and
more pronounced with each rod of their advance;
and when she stopped finally before a gate, and,
opening it, went into a yard shut off from the
street by a row of dwarf cedars, Warwick had already discounted in some measure the surprise he
would have felt at seeing her enter there had he
not walked down Front Street behind her. There
was still sufficient unexpectedness about the act,
however, to give him a decided thrill of pleasure.

"It must be Rena," he murmured. "Who
could have dreamed that she would blossom out
like that? It must surely be Rena!"

He walked slowly past the gate and peered
through a narrow gap in the cedar hedge. The
girl was moving along a sanded walk, toward a
gray, unpainted house, with a steep roof, broken
by dormer windows. The trace of timidity he had

observed in her had given place to the more assured
bearing of one who is upon his own ground. The
garden walks were bordered by long rows of jon-
quils, pinks, and carnations, inclosing clumps of
fragrant shrubs, lilies, and roses already in bloom.
Toward the middle of the garden stood two fine
magnolia-trees, with heavy, dark green, glistening
leaves, while nearer the house two mighty elms
shaded a wide piazza, at one end of which a honey-
suckle vine, and at the other a Virginia creeper,
running over a wooden lattice, furnished additional shade and seclusion. On dark or wintry
days, the aspect of this garden must have been
extremely sombre and depressing, and it might
well have seemed a fit place to hide some guilty or
disgraceful secret. But on the bright morning
when Warwick stood looking through the cedars,
it seemed, with its green frame and canopy and its
bright carpet of flowers, an ideal retreat from the
fierce sunshine and the sultry heat of the approaching summer.

The girl stooped to pluck a rose, and as she
bent over it, her profile was clearly outlined. She
held the flower to her face with a long-drawn in-
halation, then went up the steps, crossed the piazza,
opened the door without knocking, and entered
the house with the air of one thoroughly at home.

" Yes," said the young man to himself, " it 's
Rena, sure enough."

The house stood on a corner, around which the
cedar hedge turned, continuing along the side of

the garden until it reached the line of the front of
the house.   The piazza to a rear wing, at right
angles to the front of the house, was open to inspection from the side street, which, to judge from its
deserted look, seemed to be but little used.   Turning into this street and walking leisurely past the
back yard, which was only slightly screened from
the street by a china-tree, Warwick perceived the
young woman standing on the piazza, facing an
elderly woman, who sat in a large rocking-chair,
plying a pair of knitting-needles on a half-finished
stocking.   Warwick's walk led him within three
feet of the side gate, which he felt an almost irre-
sistible impulse to enter.   Every detail of the
house and garden was familiar; a thousand cords
of memory and affection drew him thither; but a
stronger counter-motive prevailed.   With a great
effort he restrained himself, and after a momentary
pause, walked slowly on past the house, with a
backward glance, which he turned away when he
saw that it was observed.

Warwick's attention had been so fully absorbed
by the house behind the cedars and the women
there, that he had scarcely noticed, on the other
side of the neglected by-street, two men working
by a large open window, in a low, rude building
with a clapboarded roof, directly opposite the back
piazza occupied by the two women.   Both the men
were busily engaged in shaping barrel-staves, each
wielding a sharp-edged drawing-knife on a piece of
seasoned oak clasped tightly in a wooden vise.

"I jes' wonder who dat man is, an' w'at he 's doin' on dis street," observed the younger of the two, with a suspicious air. He had noticed the gentleman's involuntary pause and his interest in the opposite house, and had stopped work for a moment to watch the stranger as he went on down the street.

"Nev' min' 'bout dat man," said the elder one. "You 'ten' ter yo' wuk an' finish dat bairl-stave. You spen's enti'ely too much er yo' time stretchin' yo' neck atter other people. An' you need n' 'sturb yo'se'f 'bout dem folks 'cross de street, fer dey ain't yo' kin', an' you 're wastin' yo' time both'in' yo' min' wid 'em, er wid folks w'at comes on de street on account of 'em.   Look sha'p now, boy, er you 'll git dat stave trim' too much."

The younger man resumed his work, but still found time to throw a slanting glance out of the window. The gentleman, he perceived, stood for a moment on the rotting bridge across the old canal, and then walked slowly ahead until he turned to the right into Back Street, a few rods farther on.

II

TOWARD evening of the same day, Warwick took his way down Front Street in the gathering dusk. By the time night had spread its mantle over the earth, he had reached the gate by which he had seen the girl of his morning walk enter the cedar-bordered garden. He stopped at the gate and glanced toward the house, which seemed dark and silent and deserted.

"It 's more than likely," he thought, " that they are in the kitchen. I reckon I 'd better try the back door."

But as he drew cautiously near the corner, he saw a man's figure outlined in the yellow light streaming from the open door of a small house between Front Street and the cooper shop. Wishing, for reasons of his own, to avoid observation, Warwick did not turn the corner, but walked on down Front Street until he reached a point from which he could see, at a long angle, a ray of light proceeding from the kitchen window of the house behind the cedars.

"They are there," he muttered with a sigh of relief, for he had feared they might be away. " I suspect I 'll have to go to the front door, after all. No one can see me through the trees."

He retraced his steps to the front gate, which
he essayed to open. There was apparently some
defect in the latch, for it refused to work. Warwick remembered the trick, and with a slight sense
of amusement, pushed his foot under the gate and
gave it a hitch to the left, after which it opened
readily enough. He walked softly up the sanded
path, tiptoed up the steps and across the piazza,
and rapped at the front door, not too loudly, lest
this too might attract the attention of the man
across the street. There was no response to his
rap. He put his ear to the door and heard voices
within, and the muffled sound of footsteps. After
a moment he rapped again, a little louder than
before.

There was an instant cessation of the sounds
within. He rapped a third time, to satisfy any
lingering doubt in the minds of those who he felt
sure were listening in some trepidation. A moment later a ray of light streamed through the
keyhole.

" Who's there ? " a woman's voice inquired
somewhat sharply.

" A gentleman," answered Warwick, not holding it yet time to reveal himself. " Does Mis'
Molly Walden live here ? "

" Yes," was the guarded answer. " I 'm Mis'
Walden. What 's yo'r business ? "

" I have a message to you from your son
John."

A key clicked in the lock. The door opened,

and the elder of the two women Warwick had
seen upon the piazza stood in the doorway, peering
curiously and with signs of great excitement into
the face of the stranger.

"You've got a message from my son, you say?"
she asked with tremulous agitation. "Is he sick,
or in trouble?"

"No. He's well and doing well, and sends
his love to you, and hopes you've not forgotten
him."

"Fergot him? No, God knows I ain't fergot
him! But come in, sir, an' tell me somethin'
mo' about him."

Warwick went in, and as the woman closed the
door after him, he threw a glance round the room.
On the wall, over the mantelpiece, hung a steel
engraving of General Jackson at the battle of
New Orleans, and, on the opposite wall, a framed
fashion-plate from "Godey's Lady's Book." In
the middle of the room an octagonal centre-table
with a single leg, terminating in three sprawling
feet, held a collection of curiously shaped sea-shells.
There was a great haircloth sofa, somewhat the
worse for wear, and a well-filled bookcase. The
screen standing before the fireplace was covered
with Confederate bank-notes of various denomi-
nations and designs, in which the heads of Jefferson Davis and other Confederate leaders were
conspicuous.

> "Imperious Cæsar, dead, and turned to clay,
> Might stop a hole to keep the wind away,"

murmured the young man, as his eye fell upon this specimen of decorative art.

The woman showed her visitor to a seat. She then sat down facing him and looked at him closely. " When did you last see my son ? " she asked.

" I 've never met your son," he replied.

Her face fell. " Then the message comes through you from somebody else ? "

" No, directly from your son."

She scanned his face with a puzzled look. This bearded young gentleman, who spoke so politely and was dressed so well, surely — no, it could not be ! and yet —

Warwick was smiling at her through a mist of tears. An electric spark of sympathy flashed between them. They rose as if moved by one impulse, and were clasped in each other's arms.

" John, my John ! It *is* John ! "

" Mother — my dear old mother ! "

" I did n't think," she sobbed, " that I 'd ever see you again."

He smoothed her hair and kissed her. " And are you glad to see me, mother ? "

" Am I glad to see you ? It 's like the dead comin' to life. I thought I 'd lost you forever, John, my son, my darlin' boy ! " she answered, hugging him strenuously.

" I could n't live without seeing you, mother," he said. He meant it, too, or thought he did, although he had not seen her for ten years.

" You 've grown so tall, John, and are such a

fine gentleman ! And you *are* a gentleman now, John, ain't you — sure enough ? Nobody knows the old story ? "

" Well, mother, I 've taken a man's chance in life, and have tried to make the most of it ; and I have n't felt under any obligation to spoil it by raking up old stories that are best forgotten. There are the dear old books : have they been read since I went away ? "

" No, honey, there 's be'n nobody to read 'em, excep' Rena, an' she don't take to books quite like you did. But I 've kep' 'em dusted clean, an' kep' the moths an' the bugs out ; for I hoped you 'd come back some day, an' knowed you 'd like to find 'em all in their places, jus' like you left 'em."

" That 's mighty nice of you, mother. You could have done no more if you had loved them for themselves. But where is Rena ? I saw her on the street to-day, but she did n't know me from Adam ; nor did I guess it was she until she opened the gate and came into the yard."

" I 've be'n so glad to see you that I 'd fergot about her," answered the mother. " Rena, oh, Rena ! "

The girl was not far away ; she had been standing in the next room, listening intently to every word of the conversation, and only kept from coming in by a certain constraint that made a brother whom she had not met for so many years seem almost as much a stranger as if he had not been connected with her by any tie.

" Yes, mamma," she answered, coming forward.

" Rena, child, here 's yo'r brother John, who 's come back to see us. Tell 'im howdy."

As she came forward, Warwick rose, put his arm around her waist, drew her toward him, and kissed her affectionately, to her evident embarrassment. She was a tall girl, but he towered above her in quite a protecting fashion; and she thought with a thrill how fine it would be to have such a brother as this in the town all the time. How proud she would be, if she could but walk up the street with such a brother by her side! She could then hold up her head before all the world, oblivious to the glance of pity or contempt. She felt a very pronounced respect for this tall gentleman who held her blushing face between his hands and looked steadily into her eyes.

" You 're the little sister I used to read stories to, and whom I promised to come and see some day. Do you remember how you cried when I went away? "

" It seems but yesterday," she answered. " I 've still got the dime you gave me."

He kissed her again, and then drew her down beside him on the sofa, where he sat enthroned between the two loving and excited women. No king could have received more sincere or delighted homage. He was a man, come into a household of women, — a man of whom they were proud, and to whom they looked up with fond reverence. For he was not only a son, — a brother — but he represented to them the world from which circum-

stances had shut them out, and to which distance
lent even more than its usual enchantment; and
they felt nearer to this far-off world because of the
glory which Warwick reflected from it.

"You're a very pretty girl," said Warwick,
regarding his sister thoughtfully. "I followed
you down Front Street this morning, and scarcely
took my eyes off you all the way; and yet I
did n't know you, and scarcely saw your face.
You improve on acquaintance; to-night, I find you
handsomer still."

"Now, John," said his mother, expostulating
mildly, "you'll spile her, if you don't min'."

The girl was beaming with gratified vanity.
What woman would not find such praise sweet
from almost any source, and how much more so
from this great man, who, from his exalted station
in the world, must surely know the things whereof
he spoke! She believed every word of it; she
knew it very well indeed, but wished to hear it
repeated and itemized and emphasized.

"No, he won't, mamma," she asserted, "for
he's flattering me. He talks as if I was some
rich young lady, who lives on the Hill," — the
Hill was the aristocratic portion of the town, —
"instead of a poor" —

"Instead of a poor young girl, who has the hill
to climb," replied her brother, smoothing her hair
with his hand. Her hair was long and smooth
and glossy, with a wave like the ripple of a summer breeze upon the surface of still water. It

was the girl's great pride, and had been sedulously cared for. " What lovely hair ! It has
just the wave that yours lacks, mother."

" Yes," was the regretful reply, " I 've never
be'n able to git that wave out. But her hair 's
be'n took good care of, an' there ain't nary gal in
town that 's got any finer."

" Don't worry about the wave, mother. It 's
just the fashionable ripple, and becomes her immensely. I think my little Albert favors his
Aunt Rena somewhat."

" Your little Albert ! " they cried. " You 've
got a child ? "

" Oh, yes," he replied calmly, " a very fine baby
boy."

They began to purr in proud contentment at
this information, and made minute inquiries about
the age and weight and eyes and nose and other
important details of this precious infant. They
inquired more coldly about the child's mother,
of whom they spoke with greater warmth when
they learned that she was dead. They hung
breathless on Warwick's words as he related
briefly the story of his life since he had left, years
before, the house behind the cedars — how with a
stout heart and an abounding hope he had gone
out into a seemingly hostile world, and made fortune stand and deliver. His story had for the
women the charm of an escape from captivity,
with all the thrill of a pirate's tale. With the
whole world before him, he had remained in the

South, the land of his fathers, where, he conceived, he had an inalienable birthright. By some
good chance he had escaped military service in
the Confederate army, and, in default of older
and more experienced men, had undertaken, during
the rebellion, the management of a large estate,
which had been left in the hands of women and
slaves. He had filled the place so acceptably, and
employed his leisure to such advantage, that at the
close of the war he found himself — he was modest enough to think, too, in default of a better
man — the husband of the orphan daughter of the
gentleman who had owned the plantation, and who
had lost his life upon the battlefield. Warwick's
wife was of good family, and in a more settled
condition of society it would not have been easy
for a young man of no visible antecedents to win
her hand. A year or two later, he had taken the
oath of allegiance, and had been admitted to the
South Carolina bar. Rich in his wife's right, he
had been able to practice his profession upon a
high plane, without the worry of sordid cares, and
with marked success for one of his age.

"I suppose," he concluded, "that I have got
along at the bar, as elsewhere, owing to the lack of
better men. Many of the good lawyers were killed
in the war, and most of the remainder were dis-
qualified; while I had the advantage of being alive,
and of never having been in arms against the government. People had to have lawyers, and they
gave me their business in preference to the carpet-

baggers. Fortune, you know, favors the available man."

His mother drank in with parted lips and glistening eyes the story of his adventures and the record of his successes. As Rena listened, the narrow walls that hemmed her in seemed to draw closer and closer, as though they must crush her. Her brother watched her keenly. He had been talking not only to inform the women, but with a deeper purpose, conceived since his morning walk, and deepened as he had followed, during his narrative, the changing expression of Rena's face and noted her intense interest in his story, her pride in his successes, and the occasional wistful look that indexed her self-pity so completely.

" An' I s'pose you 're happy, John ? " asked his mother.

" Well, mother, happiness is a relative term, and depends, I imagine, upon how nearly we think we get what we think we want. I have had my chance and have n't thrown it away, and I suppose I ought to be happy. But then, I have lost my wife, whom I loved very dearly, and who loved me just as much, and I 'm troubled about my child."

" Why ? " they demanded. " Is there anything the matter with him ? "

" No, not exactly. He 's well enough, as babies go, and has a good enough nurse, as nurses go. But the nurse is ignorant, and not always careful. A child needs some woman of its own blood to love it and look after it intelligently."

Mis' Molly's eyes were filled with tearful yearning.   She would have given all the world to warm
her son's child upon her bosom; but she knew
this could not be.

"Did your wife leave any kin?" she asked with
an effort.

"No near kin; she was an only child."

"You'll be gettin' married again," suggested
his mother.

"No," he replied; "I think not."

Warwick was still reading his sister's face, and
saw the spark of hope that gleamed in her expressive eye.

"If I had some relation of my own that I could
take into the house with me," he said reflectively,
"the child might be healthier and happier, and I
should be much more at ease about him."

The mother looked from son to daughter with a
dawning apprehension and a sudden pallor. When
she saw the yearning in Rena's eyes, she threw herself at her son's feet.

"Oh, John," she cried despairingly, "don't take
her away from me! Don't take her, John, darlin',
for it'd break my heart to lose her!"

Rena's arms were round her mother's neck, and
Rena's voice was sounding in her ears. "There,
there, mamma! Never mind! I won't leave you,
mamma — dear old mamma! Your Rena'll stay
with you always, and never, never leave you."

John smoothed his mother's hair with a com-
forting touch, patted her withered cheek sooth-

ingly, lifted her tenderly to her place by his side, and put his arm about her.

"You love your children, mother?"

"They 're all I 've got," she sobbed, "an' they cos' me all I had. When the las' one 's gone, I 'll want to go too, for I 'll be all alone in the world. Don't take Rena, John; for if you do, I 'll never see her again, an' I can't bear to think of it. How would you like to lose yo'r one child?"

"Well, well, mother, we 'll say no more about it. And now tell me all about yourself, and about the neighbors, and how you got through the war, and who 's dead and who 's married — and everything."

The change of subject restored in some degree Mis' Molly's equanimity, and with returning calmness came a sense of other responsibilities.

"Good gracious, Rena!" she exclaimed. "John 's be'n in the house an hour, and ain't had nothin' to eat yet! Go in the kitchen an' spread a clean tablecloth, an' git out that 'tater pone, an' a pitcher o' that las' kag o' persimmon beer, an' let John take a bite an' a sip."

Warwick smiled at the mention of these homely dainties. "I thought of your sweet-potato pone at the hotel to-day, when I was at dinner, and wondered if you 'd have some in the house. There was never any like yours; and I 've forgotten the taste of persimmon beer entirely."

Rena left the room to carry out her hospitable commission. Warwick, taking advantage of her

absence, returned after a while to the former
subject.

"Of course, mother," he said calmly, "I
would n't think of taking Rena away against your
wishes. A mother's claim upon her child is a high
and holy one. Of course she will have no chance
here, where our story is known. The war has
wrought great changes, has put the bottom rail on
top, and all that — but it has n't wiped *that* out.
Nothing but death can remove that stain, if it does
not follow us even beyond the grave. Here she
must forever be — nobody! With me she might
have got out into the world; with her beauty she
might have made a good marriage; and, if I mistake not, she has sense as well as beauty."

"Yes," sighed the mother, "she's got good
sense. She ain't as quick as you was, an' don't
read as many books, but she's keerful an' pains-
takin', an' always tries to do what's right. She's
be'n thinkin' about goin' away somewhere an'
tryin' to git a school to teach, er somethin', sence
the Yankees have started 'em everywhere for po'
white folks an' niggers too. But I don't like fer
her to go too fur."

"With such beauty and brains," continued
Warwick, "she could leave this town and make
a place for herself. The place is already made.
She has only to step into my carriage — after perhaps a little preparation — and ride up the hill
which I have had to climb so painfully. It would
be a great pleasure to me to see her at the top.

But of course it is impossible — a mere idle dream. *Your* claim comes first; her duty chains her here."

" It would be so lonely without her," murmured the mother weakly, " an' I love her so — my las' one ! "

" No doubt — no doubt," returned Warwick, with a sympathetic sigh; " of course you love her. It 's not to be thought of for a moment. It 's a pity that she could n't have a chance here — but how could she ? I had thought she might marry a gentleman ; but I dare say she 'll do as well as the rest of her friends — as well as Mary B., for instance, who married — Homer Pettifoot, did you say ? Or maybe Billy Oxendine might do for her. As long as she has never known any better, she 'll probably be as well satisfied as though she married a rich man, and lived in a fine house, and kept a carriage and servants, and moved with the best in the land."

The tortured mother could endure no more. The one thing she desired above all others was her daughter's happiness. Her own life had not been governed by the highest standards, but about her love for her beautiful daughter there was no taint of selfishness. The life her son had described had been to her always the ideal but unattainable life. Circumstances, some beyond her control, and others for which she was herself in a measure responsible, had put it forever and inconceivably beyond her reach. It had been conquered by her son. It beckoned to her daughter. The comparison of this free and noble life with the sordid existence of those around her broke down the last barrier of opposition.

"O Lord!" she moaned, "what shall I do without her? It 'll be lonely, John — so lonely!"

"You 'll have your home, mother," said Warwick tenderly, accepting the implied surrender. "You 'll have your friends and relatives, and the knowledge that your children are happy. I 'll let you hear from us often, and no doubt you can see Rena now and then. But you must let her go, mother, — it would be a sin against her to refuse."

"She may go," replied the mother brokenly. "I 'll not stand in her way — I 've got sins enough to answer for already."

Warwick watched her pityingly. He had stirred her feelings to unwonted depths, and his sympathy went out to her. If she had sinned, she had been more sinned against than sinning, and it was not his part to judge her. He had yielded to a sentimental weakness in deciding upon this trip to Patesville. A matter of business had brought him within a day's journey of the town, and an overmastering impulse had compelled him to seek the mother who had given him birth and the old town where he had spent the earlier years of his life. No one would have acknowledged sooner than he the folly of this visit. Men who have elected to govern their lives by principles of abstract right and reason, which happen, perhaps, to be at vari-

ance with what society considers equally right and
reasonable, should, for fear of complications, be
careful about descending from the lofty heights of
logic to the common level of impulse and affection.
Many years before, Warwick, when a lad of eighteen, had shaken the dust of the town from his feet,
and with it, he fondly thought, the blight of his
inheritance, and had achieved elsewhere a worthy
career. But during all these years of absence he
had cherished a tender feeling for his mother, and
now again found himself in her house, amid the
familiar surroundings of his childhood. His visit
had brought joy to his mother's heart, and was
now to bring its shrouded companion, sorrow. His
mother had lived her life, for good or ill. A wider
door was open to his sister — her mother must not
bar the entrance.

" She may go," the mother repeated sadly, dry-
ing her tears. " I 'll give her up for her good."

" The table 's ready, mamma," said Rena, coming
to the door.

The lunch was spread in the kitchen, a large un-
plastered room at the rear, with a wide fireplace at
one end. Only yesterday, it seemed to Warwick,
he had sprawled upon the hearth, turning sweet
potatoes before the fire, or roasting groundpeas in
the ashes ; or, more often, reading, by the light of
a blazing pine-knot or lump of resin, some volume
from the bookcase in the hall. From Bulwer's
novel, he had read the story of Warwick the
Kingmaker, and upon leaving home had chosen it

for his own.   He was a new man, but he had the
blood of an old race, and he would select for his
own one of its worthy names.   Overhead loomed
the same smoky beams, decorated with what might
have been, from all appearances, the same bunches
of dried herbs, the same strings of onions and red
peppers.   Over in the same corner stood the same
spinning-wheel, and through the open door of an
adjoining room he saw the old loom, where in
childhood he had more than once thrown the shut-
tle.   The kitchen was different from the stately
dining-room of the old colonial mansion where he
now lived ; but it was homelike, and it was familiar.
The sight of it moved his heart, and he felt for
the moment a sort of a blind anger against the
fate which made it necessary that he should visit
the home of his childhood, if at all, like a thief
in the night.   But he realized, after a moment,
that the thought was pure sentiment, and that one
who had gained so much ought not to complain if
he must give up a little.   He who would climb
the heights of life must leave even the pleasantest
valleys behind.

"Rena," asked her mother, "how 'd you like to
go an' pay yo'r brother John a visit ?   I guess I
might spare you for a little while."

The girl's eyes lighted up.   She would not have
gone if her mother had wished her to stay, but she
would always have regarded this as the lost opportunity of her life.

"Are you sure you don't care, mamma ? " she
asked, hoping and yet doubting.

" Oh, I 'll manage to git along somehow or other.
You can go an' stay till you git homesick, an' then
John 'll let you come back home."

But Mis' Molly believed that she would never
come back, except, like her brother, under cover of
the night.   She must lose her daughter as well as
her son, and this should be the penance for her sin.
That her children must expiate as well the sins of
their fathers, who had sinned so lightly, after the
manner of men, neither she nor they could foresee,
since they could not read the future.

The next boat by which Warwick could take his
sister away left early in the morning of the next
day but one.   He went back to his hotel with the
understanding that the morrow should be devoted
to getting Rena ready for her departure, and that
Warwick would visit the household again the following evening; for, as has been intimated, there
were several reasons why there should be no open
relations between the fine gentleman at the hotel
and the women in the house behind the cedars, who,
while superior in blood and breeding to the people
of the neighborhood in which they lived, were yet
under the shadow of some cloud which clearly shut
them out from the better society of the town.   Almost any resident could have given one or more of
these reasons, of which any one would have been
sufficient to most of them; and to some of them
Warwick's mere presence in the town would have
seemed a bold and daring thing.

III

On the morning following the visit to his mother, Warwick visited the old judge's office. The judge was not in, but the door stood open, and Warwick entered to await his return. There had been fewer changes in the office, where he had spent many, many hours, than in the town itself. The dust was a little thicker, the papers in the pigeon-holes of the walnut desk were a little yellower, the cobwebs in the corners a little more aggressive. The flies droned as drowsily and the murmur of the brook below was just as audible. Warwick stood at the rear window and looked out over a familiar view. Directly across the creek, on the low ground beyond, might be seen the dilapidated stone foundation of the house where once had lived Flora Macdonald, the Jacobite refugee, the most romantic character of North Carolina history. Old Judge Straight had had a tree cut away from the creek-side opposite his window, so that this historic ruin might be visible from his office; for the judge could trace the ties of blood that connected him collaterally with this famous personage. His pamphlet on Flora Macdonald,

printed for private circulation, was highly prized
by those of his friends who were fortunate enough
to obtain a copy. To the left of the window a
placid mill-pond spread its wide expanse, and to
the right the creek disappeared under a canopy of
overhanging trees.

A footstep sounded in the doorway, and Warwick, turning, faced the old judge. Time had left
greater marks upon the lawyer than upon his office.
His hair was whiter, his stoop more pronounced;
when he spoke to Warwick, his voice had some of
the shrillness of old age; and in his hand, upon
which the veins stood out prominently, a decided
tremor was perceptible.

"Good-morning, Judge Straight," said the
young man, removing his hat with the graceful
Southern deference of the young for the old.

"Good-morning, sir," replied the judge with
equal courtesy.

"You don't remember me, I imagine," suggested Warwick.

"Your face seems familiar," returned the judge
cautiously, "but I cannot for the moment recall
your name. I shall be glad to have you refresh
my memory."

"I was John Walden, sir, when you knew
me."

The judge's face still gave no answering light
of recognition.

"Your old office-boy," continued the younger
man.

" Ah, indeed, so you were ! " rejoined the judge warmly, extending his hand with great cordiality, and inspecting Warwick more closely through his spectacles. " Let me see — you went away a few years before the war, was n't it ? "

" Yes, sir, to South Carolina."

" Yes, yes, I remember now ! I had been thinking it was to the North. So many things have happened since then, that it taxes an old man's memory to keep track of them all. Well, well ! and how have you been getting along ? "

Warwick told his story in outline, much as he had given it to his mother and sister, and the judge seemed very much interested.

" And you married into a good family ? " he asked.

" Yes, sir."

" And have children ? "

" One."

" And you are visiting your mother ? "

" Not exactly. I have seen her, but I am stopping at a hotel."

" H'm ! Are you staying long ? "

" I leave to-morrow."

" It 's well enough. I would n't stay too long. The people of a small town are inquisitive about strangers, and some of them have long memories. I remember we went over the law, which was in your favor ; but custom is stronger than law — in these matters custom *is* law. It was a great pity that your father did not make a will. Well, my boy, I wish you continued good luck; I imagined you would make your way."

Warwick went away, and the old judge sat for a moment absorbed in reflection. " Right and wrong," he mused, " must be eternal verities, but our standards for measuring them vary with our latitude and our epoch. We make our customs lightly ; once made, like our sins, they grip us in bands of steel; we become the creatures of our creations. By one standard my old office-boy should never have been born. Yet he is a son of Adam, and came into existence in the way ordained by God from the beginning of the world. In equity he would seem to be entitled to his chance in life; it might have been wiser, though, for him to seek it farther afield than South Carolina. It was too near home, even though the laws were with him."

IV

NEITHER mother nor daughter slept a great deal during the night of Warwick's first visit. Mis' Molly anointed her sacrifice with tears and cried herself to sleep. Rena's emotions were more conflicting; she was sorry to leave her mother, but glad to go with her brother. The mere journey she was about to make was a great event for the two women to contemplate, to say nothing of the golden vision that lay beyond, for neither of them had ever been out of the town or its vicinity.

The next day was devoted to preparations for the journey. Rena's slender wardrobe was made ready and packed in a large valise. Towards sunset, Mis' Molly took off her apron, put on her slat-bonnet, — she was ever the pink of neatness, — picked her way across the street, which was muddy from a rain during the day, traversed the foot-bridge that spanned the ditch in front of the cooper shop, and spoke first to the elder of the two men working there.

" Good-evenin', Peter."

" Good-evenin', ma'm," responded the man briefly, and not relaxing at all the energy with which he was trimming a barrel-stave.

Mis' Molly then accosted the younger workman, a dark-brown young man, small in stature, but with a well-shaped head, an expressive forehead, and features indicative of kindness, intelligence, humor, and imagination. " Frank," she asked, " can I git you to do somethin' fer me soon in the mo'nin'? "

" Yas'm, I reckon so," replied the young man, resting his hatchet on the chopping-block. " W'at is it, Mis' Molly? "

" My daughter's goin' away on the boat, an' I 'lowed you would n' min' totin' her kyarpet-bag down to the w'arf, onless you'd ruther haul it down on yo'r kyart. It ain't very heavy. Of co'se I'll pay you fer yo'r trouble."

" Thank y', ma'm," he replied. He knew that she would not pay him, for the simple reason that he would not accept pay for such a service. " Is she gwine fur? " he asked, with a sorrowful look, which he could not entirely disguise.

" As fur as Wilmin'ton an' beyon'. She'll be visitin' her brother John, who lives in — another State, an' wants her to come an' see him."

" Yas'm, I'll come. I won' need de kyart — I'll tote de bag. 'Bout w'at time shill I come over? "

" Well, 'long 'bout seven o'clock or half pas'. She's goin' on the Old North State, an' it leaves at eight."

Frank stood looking after Mis' Molly as she picked her way across the street, until he was recalled to his duty by a sharp word from his father.

" 'Ten' ter yo' wuk, boy, 'ten' ter yo' wuk. You 're wastin' yo' time — wastin' yo' time!"

Yes, he was wasting his time. The beautiful young girl across the street could never be anything to him. But he had saved her life once, and had dreamed that he might render her again some signal service that might win her friendship, and convince her of his humble devotion. For Frank was not proud. A smile, which Peter would have regarded as condescending to a free man, who, since the war, was as good as anybody else ; a kind word, which Peter would have considered offensively patronizing ; a piece of Mis' Molly's famous potato pone from Rena's hands, — a bone to a dog, Peter called it once ; — were ample rewards for the thousand and one small services Frank had rendered the two women who lived in the house behind the cedars.

Frank went over in the morning a little ahead of the appointed time, and waited on the back piazza until his services were required.

" You ain't gwine ter be gone long, is you, Miss Rena ? " he inquired, when Rena came out dressed for the journey in her best frock, with broad white collar and cuffs.

Rena did not know. She had been asking herself the same question. All sorts of vague dreams had floated through her mind during the last few hours, as to what the future might bring forth. But she detected the anxious note in Frank's voice, and had no wish to give this faithful friend of the family unnecessary pain.

"Oh, no, Frank, I reckon not. I 'm supposed to be just going on a short visit. My brother has lost his wife, and wishes me to come and stay with him awhile, and look after his little boy."

"I 'm feared you 'll lack it better dere, Miss Rena," replied Frank sorrowfully, dropping his mask of unconcern, "an' den you won't come back, an' none er yo' frien's won't never see you no mo'."

"You don't think, Frank," asked Rena severely, "that I would leave my mother and my home and all my friends, and *never* come back again?"

"Why, no 'ndeed," interposed Mis' Molly wistfully, as she hovered around her daughter, giving her hair or her gown a touch here and there; "she 'll be so homesick in a month that she 'll be willin' to walk home."

"You would n' never hafter do dat, Miss Rena," returned Frank, with a disconsolate smile. "Ef you ever wanter come home, an' can't git back no other way, jes' let *me* know, an' I 'll take my mule an' my kyart an' fetch you back, ef it 's from de een' er de worl'."

"Thank you, Frank, I believe you would," said the girl kindly. "You 're a true friend, Frank, and I 'll not forget you while I 'm gone."

The idea of her beautiful daughter riding home

from the end of the world with Frank, in a cart,
behind a one-eyed mule, struck Mis' Molly as the
height of the ridiculous — she was in a state of
excitement where tears or laughter would have
come with equal ease — and she turned away to
hide her merriment.   Her daughter was going to
live in a fine house, and marry a rich man, and
ride in her carriage.   Of course a negro would
drive the carriage, but that was different from
riding with one in a cart.

When it was time to go, Mis' Molly and Rena
set out on foot for the river, which was only a
short distance away.   Frank followed with the
valise.   There was no gathering of friends to see
Rena off, as might have been the case under different circumstances.   Her departure had some of
the characteristics of a secret flight; it was as important that her destination should not be known, as
it had been that her brother should conceal his
presence in the town.

Mis' Molly and Rena remained on the bank until
the steamer announced, with a raucous whistle,
its readiness to depart.   Warwick was seen for a
moment on the upper deck, from which he greeted
them with a smile and a slight nod.   He had bid-
den his mother an affectionate farewell the evening before.   Rena gave her hand to Frank.

" Good-by, Frank," she said, with a kind smile ;
" I hope you and mamma will be good friends
while I 'm gone."

The whistle blew a second warning blast, and

the deck hands prepared to draw in the gang-plank. Rena flew into her mother's arms, and then, breaking away, hurried on board and retired to her state-room, from which she did not emerge during the journey. The window-blinds were closed, darkening the room, and the stewardess who came to ask if she should bring her some dinner could not see her face distinctly, but perceived enough to make her surmise that the young lady had been weeping.

" Po' chile," murmured the sympathetic colored woman, " I reckon some er her folks is dead, er her sweetheart 's gone back on her, er e'se she 's had some kin' er bad luck er 'nuther. W'ite folks has deir troubles jes' ez well ez black folks, an' sometimes feels 'em mo', 'cause dey ain't ez use' ter 'em."

Mis' Molly went back in sadness to the lonely house behind the cedars, henceforth to be peopled for her with only the memory of those she had loved. She had paid with her heart's blood another installment on the Shylock's bond exacted by society for her own happiness of the past and her children's prospects for the future.

The journey down the sluggish river to the seaboard in the flat-bottomed, stern-wheel steamer lasted all day and most of the night. During the first half-day, the boat grounded now and then upon a sand-bank, and the half-naked negro deckhands toiled with ropes and poles to release it. Several times before Rena fell asleep that night,

the steamer would tie up at a landing, and by the
light of huge pine torches she watched the boat
hands send the yellow turpentine barrels down the
steep bank in a long string, or pass cord-wood on
board from hand to hand.   The excited negroes,
their white teeth and eyeballs glistening in the
surrounding darkness to which their faces formed
no relief ; the white officers in brown linen, shout-
ing, swearing, and gesticulating; the yellow, flick-
ering torchlight over all, — made up a scene of
which the weird interest would have appealed to a
more *blasé* traveler than this girl upon her first
journey.

During the day, Warwick had taken his meals
in the dining-room, with the captain and the other
cabin passengers. It was learned that he was a
South Carolina lawyer, and not a carpet-bagger.
Such credentials were unimpeachable, and the
passengers found him a very agreeable traveling
companion.   Apparently sound on the subject of
negroes, Yankees, and the righteousness of the
lost cause, he yet discussed these themes in a lofty
and impersonal manner that gave his words greater
weight than if he had seemed warped by a personal grievance.   His attitude, in fact, piqued the
curiosity of one or two of the passengers.

" Did your people lose any niggers? " asked
one of them.

" My father owned a hundred," he replied
grandly.

Their respect for his views was doubled.   It is

easy to moralize about the misfortunes of others,
and to find good in the evil that they suffer ; —
only a true philosopher could speak thus lightly of
his own losses.

When the steamer tied up at the wharf at Wilmington, in the early morning, the young lawyer
and a veiled lady passenger drove in the same
carriage to a hotel. After they had breakfasted
in a private room, Warwick explained to his sister
the plan he had formed for her future. Henceforth she must be known as Miss Warwick, dropping the old name with the old life. He would
place her for a year in a boarding-school at
Charleston, after which she would take her place
as the mistress of his house. Having imparted
this information, he took his sister for a drive
through the town. There for the first time Rena
saw great ships, which, her brother told her, sailed
across the mighty ocean to distant lands, whose
flags he pointed out drooping lazily at the mast-
heads. The business portion of the town had " an
ancient and fishlike smell," and most of the trade
seemed to be in cotton and naval stores and pro-
ducts of the sea. The wharves were piled high
with cotton bales, and there were acres of barrels
of resin and pitch and tar and spirits of turpentine. The market, a long, low, wooden structure,
in the middle of the principal street, was filled
with a mass of people of all shades, from blue-
black to Saxon blonde, gabbling and gesticulating
over piles of oysters and clams and freshly caught

fish of varied hue. By ten o'clock the sun was
beating down so fiercely that the glitter of the
white, sandy streets dazzled and pained the eyes
unaccustomed to it, and Rena was glad to be
driven back to the hotel. The travelers left together on an early afternoon train.

Thus for the time being was severed the last tie
that bound Rena to her narrow past, and for some
time to come the places and the people who had
known her once were to know her no more.

Some few weeks later, Mis' Molly called upon
old Judge Straight with reference to the taxes on
her property.

"Your son came in to see me the other day,"
he remarked. "He seems to have got along."

"Oh, yes, judge, he 's done fine, John has ; an'
he 's took his sister away with him."

"Ah!" exclaimed the judge. Then after a
pause he added, "I hope she may do as well."

"Thank you, sir," she said, with a curtsy, as
she rose to go. "We 've always knowed that you
were our friend and wished us well."

The judge looked after her as she walked away.
Her bearing had a touch of timidity, a shade of
affectation, and yet a certain pathetic dignity.

"It is a pity," he murmured, with a sigh, "that
men cannot select their mothers. My young friend
John has builded, whether wisely or not, very
well; but he has come back into the old life and
carried away a part of it, and I fear that this
addition will weaken the structure."

V

THE TOURNAMENT

THE annual tournament of the Clarence Social Club was about to begin. The county fair-
ground, where all was in readiness, sparkled with
the youth and beauty of the town, standing here
and there under the trees in animated groups, or
moving toward the seats from which the pageant
might be witnessed. A quarter of a mile of the
race track, to right and left of the judges' stand,
had been laid off for the lists. Opposite the
grand stand, which occupied a considerable part
of this distance, a dozen uprights had been erected
at measured intervals. Projecting several feet
over the track from each of these uprights was an
iron crossbar, from which an iron hook depended.
Between the uprights stout posts were planted,
of such a height that their tops could be easily
reached by a swinging sword-cut from a mounted
rider passing upon the track. The influence of
Walter Scott was strong upon the old South.
The South before the war was essentially feudal,
and Scott's novels of chivalry appealed forcefully
to the feudal heart. During the month preceding
the Clarence tournament, the local bookseller had

closed out his entire stock of " Ivanhoe," consisting of five copies, and had taken orders for seven copies more. The tournament scene in this popular novel furnished the model after which these bloodless imitations of the ancient passages-at-arms were conducted, with such variations as were required to adapt them to a different age and civilization.

The best people gradually filled the grand stand, while the poorer white and colored folks found seats outside, upon what would now be known as the " bleachers," or stood alongside the lists. The knights, masquerading in fanciful costumes, in which bright-colored garments, gilt paper, and cardboard took the place of knightly harness, were mounted on spirited horses. Most of them were gathered at one end of the lists, while others practiced their steeds upon the unoccupied portion of the race track.

The judges entered the grand stand, and one of them, after looking at his watch, gave a signal. Immediately a herald, wearing a bright yellow sash, blew a loud blast upon a bugle, and, big with the importance of his office, galloped wildly down the lists. An attendant on horseback busied himself hanging upon each of the pendent hooks an iron ring, of some two inches in diameter, while another, on foot, placed on top of each of the shorter posts a wooden ball some four inches through.

" It 's my first tournament," observed a lady

near the front of the grand stand, leaning over
and addressing John Warwick, who was seated in
the second row, in company with a very handsome
girl. " It is somewhat different from Ashby-de-
la-Zouch."

" It is the renaissance of chivalry, Mrs. Newberry," replied the young lawyer, " and, like any
other renaissance, it must adapt itself to new times
and circumstances. For instance, when we build
a Greek portico, having no Pentelic marble near
at hand, we use a pine-tree, one of nature's columns, which Grecian art at its best could only
copy and idealize. Our knights are not weighted
down with heavy armor, but much more appro-
priately attired, for a day like this, in costumes
that recall the picturesqueness, without the discom-
fort, of the old knightly harness. For an iron-
headed lance we use a wooden substitute, with
which we transfix rings instead of hearts ; while
our trusty blades hew their way through wooden
blocks instead of through flesh and blood. It is
a South Carolina renaissance which has points of
advantage over the tournaments of the olden time."

" I 'm afraid, Mr. Warwick," said the lady,
" that you 're the least bit heretical about our chivalry — or else you 're a little too deep for me."

" The last would be impossible, Mrs. Newberry ;
and I 'm sure our chivalry has proved its valor on
many a hard-fought field. The spirit of a thing,
after all, is what counts ; and what is lacking
here ? We have the lists, the knights, the pran-

cing steeds, the trial of strength and skill. If our knights do not run the physical risks of Ashby-de-la-Zouch, they have all the mental stimulus. Wounded vanity will take the place of wounded limbs, and there will be broken hopes in lieu of broken heads. How many hearts in yonder group of gallant horsemen beat high with hope! How many possible Queens of Love and Beauty are in this group of fair faces that surround us!"

The lady was about to reply, when the bugle sounded again, and the herald dashed swiftly back upon his prancing steed to the waiting group of riders. The horsemen formed three abreast, and rode down the lists in orderly array. As they passed the grand stand, each was conscious of the battery of bright eyes turned upon him, and each gave by his bearing some idea of his ability to stand fire from such weapons. One horse pranced proudly, another caracoled with grace. One rider fidgeted nervously, another trembled and looked the other way. Each horseman carried in his hand a long wooden lance and wore at his side a cavalry sabre, of which there were plenty to be had since the war, at small expense. Several left the ranks and drew up momentarily beside the grand stand, where they took from fair hands a glove or a flower, which was pinned upon the rider's breast or fastened upon his hat — a ribbon or a veil, which was tied about the lance like a pennon, but far enough from the point not to interfere with the usefulness of the weapon.

As the troop passed the lower end of the grand stand, a horse, excited by the crowd, became somewhat unmanageable, and in the effort to curb him, the rider dropped his lance. The prancing animal reared, brought one of his hoofs down upon the fallen lance with considerable force, and sent a broken piece of it flying over the railing opposite the grand stand, into the middle of a group of spectators standing there. The flying fragment was dodged by those who saw it coming, but brought up with a resounding thwack against the head of a colored man in the second row, who stood watching the grand stand with an eager and curious gaze. He rubbed his head ruefully, and made a good-natured response to the chaffing of his neighbors, who, seeing no great harm done, made witty and original remarks about the advantage of being black upon occasions where one's skull was exposed to danger. Finding that the blow had drawn blood, the young man took out a red bandana handkerchief and tied it around his head, meantime letting his eye roam over the faces in the grand stand, as though in search of some one that he expected or hoped to find there.

The knights, having reached the end of the lists, now turned and rode back in open order, with such skillful horsemanship as to evoke a storm of applause from the spectators. The ladies in the grand stand waved their handkerchiefs vigorously, and the men clapped their hands. The beautiful girl seated by Warwick's side acciden-

tally let a little square of white lace-trimmed linen
slip from her hand. It fluttered lightly over the
railing, and, buoyed up by the air, settled slowly
toward the lists. A young rider in the approaching rear rank saw the handkerchief fall, and dart-
ing swiftly forward, caught it on the point of his
lance ere it touched the ground. He drew up his
horse and made a movement as though to extend
the handkerchief toward the lady, who was blushing profusely at the attention she had attracted by
her carelessness. The rider hesitated a moment,
glanced interrogatively at Warwick, and receiving
a smile in return, tied the handkerchief around
the middle of his lance and quickly rejoined his
comrades at the head of the lists.

The young man with the bandage round his
head, on the benches across the lists, had forced
his way to the front row and was leaning against
the railing. His restless eye was attracted by
the falling handkerchief, and his face, hitherto
anxious, suddenly lit up with animation.

"Yas, suh, yas, suh, it's her!" he muttered
softly. "It's Miss Rena, sho's you bawn. She
looked lack a' angel befo', but now, up dere
'mongs' all dem rich, fine folks, she looks lack a
whole flock er angels. Dey ain' one er dem ladies
w'at could hol' a candle ter her. I wonder w'at
dat man's gwine ter do wid her handkercher? I
s'pose he's her gent'eman now. I wonder ef
she'd know me er speak ter me ef she seed me?
I reckon she would, spite er her gittin' up so in

de worl' ; fer she wuz alluz good ter ev'ybody, an'
dat let even *me* in," he concluded with a sigh.

" Who is the lady, Tryon ? " asked one of the
young men, addressing the knight who had taken
the handkerchief.

" A Miss Warwick," replied the knight pleasantly, " Miss Rowena Warwick, the lawyer's
sister."

" I did n't know he had a sister," rejoined the
first speaker. " I envy you your lady. There
are six Rebeccas and eight Rowenas of my own
acquaintance in the grand stand, but she throws
them all into the shade. She has n't been here
long, surely ; I have n't seen her before."

" She has been away at school ; she came only
last night," returned the knight of the crimson
sash, briefly. He was already beginning to feel a
proprietary interest in the lady whose token he
wore, and did not care to discuss her with a casual
acquaintance.

The herald sounded the charge. A rider darted
out from the group and galloped over the course.
As he passed under each ring, he tried to catch it
on the point of his lance, — a feat which made
the management of the horse with the left hand
necessary, and required a true eye and a steady
arm. The rider captured three of the twelve
rings, knocked three others off the hooks, and
left six undisturbed. Turning at the end of the
lists, he took the lance with the reins in the left
hand and drew his sword with the right. He

then rode back over the course, cutting at the wooden balls upon the posts. Of these he clove one in twain, to use the parlance of chivalry, and knocked two others off their supports. His performance was greeted with a liberal measure of applause, for which he bowed in smiling acknowledgment as he took his place among the riders.

Again the herald's call sounded, and the tourney went forward. Rider after rider, with varying skill, essayed his fortune with lance and sword. Some took a liberal proportion of the rings; others merely knocked them over the boundaries, where they were collected by agile little negro boys and handed back to the attendants. A balking horse caused the spectators much amusement and his rider no little chagrin.

The lady who had dropped the handkerchief kept her eye upon the knight who had bound it round his lance. "Who is he, John?" she asked the gentleman beside her.

"That, my dear Rowena, is my good friend and client, George Tryon, of North Carolina. If he had been a stranger, I should have said that he took a liberty; but as things stand, we ought to regard it as a compliment. The incident is quite in accord with the customs of chivalry. If George were but masked and you were veiled, we should have a romantic situation, — you the mysterious damsel in distress, he the unknown champion. The parallel, my dear, might not be so hard to draw, even as things are. But look, it is his turn now; I'll wager that he makes a good run."

" I 'll take you up on that, Mr. Warwick," said Mrs. Newberry from behind, who seemed to have a very keen ear for whatever Warwick said.

Rena's eyes were fastened on her knight, so that she might lose no single one of his movements. As he rode down the lists, more than one woman found him pleasant to look upon. He was a tall, fair young man, with gray eyes, and a frank, open face. He wore a slight mustache, and when he smiled, showed a set of white and even teeth. He was mounted on a very handsome and spirited bay mare, was clad in a picturesque costume, of which velvet knee-breeches and a crimson scarf were the most conspicuous features, and displayed a marked skill in horsemanship. At the blast of the bugle his horse started forward, and, after the first few rods, settled into an even gallop. Tryon's lance, held truly and at the right angle, captured the first ring, then the second and third. His coolness and steadiness seemed not at all disturbed by the applause which followed, and one by one the remaining rings slipped over the point of his lance, until at the end he had taken every one of the twelve. Holding the lance with its booty of captured rings in his left hand, together with the bridle rein, he drew his sabre with the right and rode back over the course. His horse moved like clockwork, his eye was true and his hand steady. Three of the wooden balls fell from the posts, split fairly in the middle, while from the fourth he sliced off a goodly piece and left the remainder standing in its place.

This performance, by far the best up to this point, and barely escaping perfection, elicited a storm of applause. The rider was not so well known to the townspeople as some of the other participants, and his name passed from mouth to mouth in answer to numerous inquiries. The girl whose token he had worn also became an object of renewed interest, because of the result to her in case the knight should prove victor in the contest, of which there could now scarcely be a doubt; for but three riders remained, and it was very improbable that any one of them would excel the last. Wagers for the remainder of the tourney stood anywhere from five, and even from ten to one, in favor of the knight of the crimson sash, and when the last course had been run, his backers were jubilant. No one of those following him had displayed anything like equal skill.

The herald now blew his bugle and declared the tournament closed. The judges put their heads together for a moment. The bugle sounded again, and the herald announced in a loud voice that Sir George Tryon, having taken the greatest number of rings and split the largest number of balls, was proclaimed victor in the tournament and entitled to the flowery chaplet of victory.

Tryon, having bowed repeatedly in response to the liberal applause, advanced to the judges' stand and received the trophy from the hands of the chief judge, who exhorted him to wear the garland worthily, and to yield it only to a better man.

"It will be your privilege, Sir George," announced the judge, "as the chief reward of your valor, to select from the assembled beauty of Clarence the lady whom you wish to honor, to whom we will all do homage as the Queen of Love and Beauty."

Tryon took the wreath and bowed his thanks. Then placing the trophy on the point of his lance, he spoke earnestly for a moment to the herald, and rode past the grand stand, from which there was another outburst of applause. Returning upon his tracks, the knight of the crimson sash paused before the group where Warwick and his sister sat, and lowered the wreath thrice before the lady whose token he had won.

"Oyez! Oyez!" cried the herald; "Sir George Tryon, the victor in the tournament, has chosen Miss Rowena Warwick as the Queen of Love and Beauty, and she will be crowned at the feast to-night and receive the devoirs of all true knights."

The fair-ground was soon covered with scattered groups of the spectators of the tournament. In one group a vanquished knight explained in elaborate detail why it was that he had failed to win the wreath. More than one young woman wondered why some one of the home young men could not have taken the honors, or, if the stranger must win them, why he could not have selected some belle of the town as Queen of Love and Beauty instead of this upstart girl who had blown into the town over night, as one might say.

Warwick and his sister, standing under a spreading elm, held a little court of their own. A dozen gentlemen and several ladies had sought an introduction before Tryon came up.

" I suppose John would have a right to call me out, Miss Warwick," said Tryon, when he had been formally introduced and had shaken hands with Warwick's sister, " for taking liberties with the property and name of a lady to whom I had not had an introduction; but I know John so well that you seemed like an old acquaintance; and when I saw you, and recalled your name, which your brother had mentioned more than once, I felt instinctively that you ought to be the queen. I entered my name only yesterday, merely to swell the number and make the occasion more interesting. These fellows have been practicing for a month, and I had no hope of winning. I should have been satisfied, indeed, if I had n't made myself ridiculous; but when you dropped your handkerchief, I felt a sudden inspiration; and as soon as I had tied it upon my lance, victory perched upon my saddle-bow, guided my lance and sword, and rings and balls went down before me like chaff before the wind. Oh, it was a great inspiration, Miss Warwick ! "

Rena, for it was our Patesville acquaintance fresh from boarding-school, colored deeply at this frank and fervid flattery, and could only murmur an inarticulate reply. Her year of instruction, while distinctly improving her mind and manners, had scarcely prepared her for so sudden an elevation into a grade of society to which she had hitherto been a stranger. She was not without a certain courage, however, and her brother, who remained at her side, helped her over the most difficult situations.

" We 'll forgive you, George," replied Warwick, " if you 'll come home to luncheon with us."

" I 'm mighty sorry — awfully sorry," returned Tryon, with evident regret, " but I have another engagement, which I can scarcely break, even by the command of royalty. At what time shall I call for Miss Warwick this evening ? I believe that privilege is mine, along with the other honors and rewards of victory, — unless she is bound to some one else."

" She is entirely free," replied Warwick. " Come as early as you like, and I 'll talk to you until she 's ready."

Tryon bowed himself away, and after a number of gentlemen and a few ladies had paid their respects to the Queen of Love and Beauty, and received an introduction to her, Warwick signaled to the servant who had his carriage in charge, and was soon driving homeward with his sister. No one of the party noticed a young negro, with a handkerchief bound around his head, who followed them until the carriage turned into the gate and swept up the wide drive that led to Warwick's doorstep.

" Well, Rena," said Warwick, when they found themselves alone, " you have arrived. Your début into society is a little more spectacular than I should have wished, but we must rise to the occasion and make the most of it. You are winning the first fruits of your opportunity. You are the most envied woman in Clarence at this particular moment, and, unless I am mistaken, will be the most admired at the ball to-night."

VI

THE QUEEN OF LOVE AND BEAUTY

SHORTLY after luncheon, Rena had a visitor in
the person of Mrs. Newberry, a vivacious young
widow of the town, who proffered her services to
instruct Rena in the etiquette of the annual ball.

" Now, my dear," said Mrs. Newberry, " the
first thing to do is to get your coronation robe
ready.   It simply means a gown with a long train.
You have a lovely white waist.   Get right into my
buggy, and we 'll go down town to get the cloth,
take it over to Mrs. Marshall's, and have her run
you up a skirt this afternoon."

Rena placed herself unreservedly in the hands
of Mrs. Newberry, who introduced her to the best
dressmaker of the town, a woman of much experience in such affairs, who improvised during the
afternoon a gown suited to the occasion.   Mrs.
Marshall had made more than a dozen ball dresses
during the preceding month ; being a wise woman
and understanding her business thoroughly, she
had made each one of them so that with a few
additional touches it might serve for the Queen of
Love and Beauty.   This was her first direct order
for the specific garment.

Tryon escorted Rena to the ball, which was held in the principal public hall of the town, and attended by all the best people. The champion still wore the costume of the morning, in place of evening dress, save that long stockings and dancing-pumps had taken the place of riding-boots.

Rena went through the ordeal very creditably. Her shyness was palpable, but it was saved from awkwardness by her native grace and good sense. She made up in modesty what she lacked in aplomb. Her months in school had not eradicated a certain self-consciousness born of her secret. The brain-cells never lose the impressions of youth, and Rena's Patesville life was not far enough removed to have lost its distinctness of outline. Of the two, the present was more of a dream, the past was the more vivid reality. At school she had learned something from books and not a little from observation. She had been able to compare herself with other girls, and to see wherein she excelled or fell short of them. With a sincere desire for improvement, and a wish to please her brother and do him credit, she had sought to make the most of her opportunities. Building upon a foundation of innate taste and intelligence, she had acquired much of the self-possession which comes from a knowledge of correct standards of deportment. She had moreover learned without difficulty, for it suited her disposition, to keep silence when she could not speak to advantage. A certain necessary reticence about the past added strength to a natural reserve. Thus equipped, she held her own very well in the somewhat trying ordeal of the ball, at which the fiction of queenship and the attendant ceremonies, which were pretty and graceful, made her the most conspicuous figure. Few of those who watched her move with easy grace through the measures of the dance could have guessed how nearly her heart was in her mouth during much of the time.

"You 're doing splendidly, my dear," said Mrs. Newberry, who had constituted herself Rena's chaperone.

" I trust your Gracious Majesty is pleased with the homage of your devoted subjects," said Tryon, who spent much of his time by her side and kept up the character of knight in his speech and manner.

"Very much," replied the Queen of Love and Beauty, with a somewhat tired smile. It *was* pleasant, but she would be glad, she thought, when it was all over.

" Keep up your courage," whispered her brother. " You are not only queen, but the belle of the ball. I am proud of you. A dozen women here would give a year off the latter end of life to be in your shoes to-night."

Rena felt immensely relieved when the hour arrived at which she could take her departure, which was to be the signal for the breaking-up of the ball. She was driven home in Tryon's carriage, her brother accompanying them. The night was warm, and the drive homeward under the starlight, in the open carriage, had a soothing effect upon Rena's excited nerves. The calm restfulness of the night, the cool blue depths of the unclouded sky, the solemn croaking of the frogs in a distant swamp, were much more in harmony with her nature than the crowded brilliancy of the ball-room. She closed her eyes, and, leaning back in the carriage, thought of her mother, who she wished might have seen her daughter this night. A momentary pang of homesickness pierced her tender heart, and she furtively wiped away the tears that came into her eyes.

"Good-night, fair Queen!" exclaimed Tryon, breaking into her reverie as the carriage rolled up to the doorstep, "and let your loyal subject kiss your hand in token of his fealty. May your Majesty never abdicate her throne, and may she ever count me her humble servant and devoted knight."

"And now, sister," said Warwick, when Tryon had been driven away, "now that the masquerade is over, let us to sleep, and to-morrow take up the serious business of life. Your day has been a glorious success!"

He put his arm around her and gave her a kiss and a brotherly hug.

"It is a dream," she murmured sleepily, "only a dream. I am Cinderella before the clock has struck. Good-night, dear John."

"Good-night, Rowena."

VII

WARWICK'S residence was situated in the out-
skirts of the town. It was a fine old plantation
house, built in colonial times, with a stately colon-
nade, wide verandas, and long windows with Ve-
netian blinds. It was painted white, and stood
back several rods from the street, in a charming
setting of palmettoes, magnolias, and flowering
shrubs. Rena had always thought her mother's
house large, but now it seemed cramped and narrow, in comparison with this roomy mansion. The
furniture was old-fashioned and massive. The
great brass andirons on the wide hearth stood like
sentinels proclaiming and guarding the dignity of
the family. The spreading antlers on the wall tes-
tified to a mighty hunter in some past generation.
The portraits of Warwick's wife's ancestors —
high-featured, proud men and women, dressed in
the fashions of a bygone age — looked down from
tarnished gilt frames. It was all very novel to
her, and very impressive. When she ate off
china, with silver knives and forks that had come
down as heirlooms, escaping somehow the ravages
and exigencies of the war time, — Warwick told

her afterwards how he had buried them out of
reach of friend or foe, — she thought that her
brother must be wealthy, and she felt very proud
of him and of her opportunity.   The servants, of
whom there were several in the house, treated her
with a deference to which her eight months in
school had only partly accustomed her.   At school
she had been one of many to be served, and had
herself been held to obedience.   Here, for the first
time in her life, she was mistress, and tasted the
sweets of power.

The household consisted of her brother and
herself, a cook, a coachman, a nurse, and her
brother's little son Albert.   The child, with a fine
instinct, had put out his puny arms to Rena at first
sight, and she had clasped the little man to her
bosom with a motherly caress.   She had always
loved weak creatures.   Kittens and puppies had
ever found a welcome and a meal at Rena's hands,
only to be chased away by Mis' Molly, who had
had a wider experience.   No shiftless poor white,
no half-witted or hungry negro, had ever gone
unfed from Mis' Molly's kitchen door if Rena
were there to hear his plaint.   Little Albert was
pale and sickly when she came, but soon bloomed
again in the sunshine of her care, and was happy
only in her presence.   Warwick found pleasure in
their growing love for each other, and was glad
to perceive that the child formed a living link to
connect her with his home.

"Dat chile sutt'nly do lub Miss Rena, an'

dat 's a fac', sho 's you bawn," remarked 'Lissa the cook to Mimy the nurse one day. " You 'll get yo' nose put out er j'int, ef you don't min'."

" I ain't frettin', honey," laughed the nurse good-naturedly. She was not at all jealous. She had the same wages as before, and her labors were materially lightened by the aunt's attention to the child. This gave Mimy much more time to flirt with Tom the coachman.

It was a source of much gratification to Warwick that his sister seemed to adapt herself so easily to the new conditions. Her graceful movements, the quiet elegance with which she wore even the simplest gown, the easy authoritativeness with which she directed the servants, were to him proofs of superior quality, and he felt correspondingly proud of her. His feeling for her was something more than brotherly love, — he was quite conscious that there were degrees in brotherly love, and that if she had been homely or stupid, he would never have disturbed her in the stagnant life of the house behind the cedars. There had come to him from some source, down the stream of time, a rill of the Greek sense of proportion, of fitness, of beauty, which is indeed but proportion embodied, the perfect adaptation of means to ends. He had perceived, more clearly than she could have appreciated it at that time, the undeveloped elements of discord between Rena and her former life. He had imagined her lending grace and charm to his own household. Still another motive, a purely psychological one, had more or less consciously influenced him. He had no fear that the family secret would ever be discovered, — he had taken his precautions too thoroughly, he thought, for that; and yet he could not but feel, at times, that if peradventure — it was a conceivable hypothesis — it should become known, his fine social position would collapse like a house of cards. Because of this knowledge, which the world around him did not possess, he had felt now and then a certain sense of loneliness; and there was a measure of relief in having about him one who knew his past, and yet whose knowledge, because of their common interest, would not interfere with his present or jeopardize his future. For he had always been, in a figurative sense, a naturalized foreigner in the world of wide opportunity, and Rena was one of his old compatriots, whom he was glad to welcome into the populous loneliness of his adopted country.

VIII

THE COURTSHIP

In a few weeks the echoes of the tournament died away, and Rena's life settled down into a pleasant routine, which she found much more comfortable than her recent spectacular prominence. Her queenship, while not entirely forgiven by the ladies of the town, had gained for her a temporary social prominence. Among her own sex, Mrs. Newberry proved a warm and enthusiastic friend. Rumor whispered that the lively young widow would not be unwilling to console Warwick in the loneliness of the old colonial mansion, to which his sister was a most excellent medium of approach. Whether this was true or not it is unnecessary to inquire, for it is no part of this story, except as perhaps indicating why Mrs. Newberry played the part of the female friend, without whom no woman is ever launched successfully in a small and conservative society. Her brother's standing gave her the right of social entry; the tournament opened wide the door, and Mrs. Newberry performed the ceremony of introduction. Rena had many visitors during the month following the tournament, and

might have made her choice from among a dozen
suitors ; but among them all, her knight of the
handkerchief found most favor.

George Tryon had come to Clarence a few
months before upon business connected with the
settlement of his grandfather's estate. A rather
complicated litigation had grown up around the
affair, various phases of which had kept Tryon
almost constantly in the town. He had placed
matters in Warwick's hands, and had formed a
decided friendship for his attorney, for whom
he felt a frank admiration. Tryon was only
twenty-three, and his friend's additional five years,
supplemented by a certain professional gravity,
commanded a great deal of respect from the
younger man. When Tryon had known Warwick for a week, he had been ready to swear by
him. Indeed, Warwick was a man for whom
most people formed a liking at first sight. To
this power of attraction he owed most of his success — first with Judge Straight, of Patesville,
then with the lawyer whose office he had entered
at Clarence, with the woman who became his
wife, and with the clients for whom he transacted business. Tryon would have maintained
against all comers that Warwick was the finest
fellow in the world. When he met Warwick's
sister, the foundation for admiration had already been laid. If Rena had proved to be a
maiden lady of uncertain age and doubtful per-

sonal attractiveness, Tryon would probably have
found in her a most excellent lady, worthy of all
respect and esteem, and would have treated her
with profound deference and sedulous courtesy.
When she proved to be a young and handsome
woman, of the type that he admired most, he
was capable of any degree of infatuation. His
mother had for a long time wanted him to marry
the orphan daughter of an old friend, a vivacious
blonde, who worshiped him. He had felt friendly
towards her, but had shrunk from matrimony.
He did not want her badly enough to give up his
freedom. The war had interfered with his education, and though fairly well instructed, he had
never attended college. In his own opinion, he
ought to see something of the world, and have his
youthful fling. Later on, when he got ready to
settle down, if Blanche were still in the humor,
they might marry, and sink to the humdrum
level of other old married people. The fact that
Blanche Leary was visiting his mother during his
unexpectedly long absence had not operated at
all to hasten his return to North Carolina. He
had been having a very good time at Clarence,
and, at the distance of several hundred miles, was
safe for the time being from any immediate danger of marriage.

With Rena's advent, however, he had seen life
through different glasses. His heart had thrilled
at first sight of this tall girl, with the ivory complexion, the rippling brown hair, and the inscru-

table eyes. When he became better acquainted
with her, he liked to think that her thoughts cen-
tred mainly in himself ; and in this he was not
far wrong. He discovered that she had a short
upper lip, and what seemed to him an eminently
kissable mouth. After he had dined twice at
Warwick's, subsequently to the tournament, — his
lucky choice of Rena had put him at once upon
a household footing with the family, — his views
of marriage changed entirely. It now seemed to
him the duty, as well as the high and holy privilege of a young man, to marry and manfully to
pay his debt to society. When in Rena's presence, he could not imagine how he had ever contemplated the possibility of marriage with Blanche
Leary, — she was utterly, entirely, and hopelessly
unsuited to him. For a fair man of vivacious
temperament, this stately dark girl was the ideal
mate. Even his mother would admit this, if she
could only see Rena. To win this beautiful
girl for his wife would be a worthy task. He had
crowned her Queen of Love and Beauty ; since
then she had ascended the throne of his heart.
He would make her queen of his home and mistress of his life.

To Rena this brief month's courtship came as a
new education. Not only had this fair young man
crowned her queen, and honored her above all
the ladies in town ; but since then he had waited
assiduously upon her, had spoken softly to her, had
looked at her with shining eyes, and had sought to

be alone with her. The time soon came when to touch his hand in greeting sent a thrill through her frame, — a time when she listened for his footstep and was happy in his presence. He had been bold enough at the tournament; he had since become somewhat bashful and constrained. He must be in love, she thought, and wondered how soon he would speak. If it were so sweet to walk with him in the garden, or along the shaded streets, to sit with him, to feel the touch of his hand, what happiness would it not be to hear him say that he loved her — to bear his name, to live with him always. To be thus loved and honored by this handsome young man, — she could hardly believe it possible. He would never speak — he would discover her secret and withdraw. She turned pale at the thought, — ah, God! something would happen, — it was too good to be true. The Prince would never try on the glass slipper.

Tryon first told his love for Rena one summer evening on their way home from church. They were walking in the moonlight along the quiet street, which, but for their presence, seemed quite deserted.

" Miss Warwick — Rowena," he said, clasping with his right hand the hand that rested on his left arm, " I love you! Do you — love me?"

To Rena this simple avowal came with much greater force than a more formal declaration could have had. It appealed to her own simple nature. Indeed, few women at such a moment criticise the form in which the most fateful words of life — but one — are spoken. Words, while pleasant, are really superfluous. Her whispered "Yes" spoke volumes.

They walked on past the house, along the country road into which the street soon merged. When they returned, an hour later, they found Warwick seated on the piazza, in a rocking-chair, smoking a fragrant cigar.

"Well, children," he observed with mock severity, "you are late in getting home from church. The sermon must have been extremely long."

"We have been attending an after-meeting," replied Tryon joyfully, "and have been discussing an old text, 'Little children, love one another,' and its corollary, 'It is not good for man to live alone.' John, I am the happiest man alive. Your sister has promised to marry me. I should like to shake my brother's hand."

Never does one feel so strongly the universal brotherhood of man as when one loves some other fellow's sister. Warwick sprang from his chair and clasped Tryon's extended hand with real emotion. He knew of no man whom he would have preferred to Tryon as a husband for his sister.

"My dear George — my dear sister," he exclaimed, "I am very, very glad. I wish you every happiness. My sister is the most fortunate of women."

"And I am the luckiest of men," cried Tryon.

"I wish you every happiness," repeated Warwick; adding, with a touch of solemnity, as a certain thought, never far distant, occurred to him, " I hope that neither of you may ever regret your choice."

Thus placed upon the footing of an accepted lover, Tryon's visits to the house became more frequent. He wished to fix a time for the marriage, but at this point Rena developed a strange reluctance.

"Can we not love each other for a while?" she asked. "To be engaged is a pleasure that comes but once; it would be a pity to cut it too short."

"It is a pleasure that I would cheerfully dispense with," he replied, "for the certainty of possession. I want you all to myself, and all the time. Things might happen. If I should die, for instance, before I married you" —

"Oh, don't suppose such awful things," she cried, putting her hand over his mouth.

He held it there and kissed it until she pulled it away.

"I should consider," he resumed, completing the sentence, "that my life had been a failure."

"If I should die," she murmured, "I should die happy in the knowledge that you had loved me."

"In three weeks," he went on, "I shall have finished my business in Clarence, and there will be but one thing to keep me here. When shall it be? I must take you home with me."

"I will let you know," she replied, with a troubled sigh, "in a week from to-day."

"I'll call your attention to the subject every day

in the mean time," he asserted.   " I should n't like you to forget it."

Rena's shrinking from the irrevocable step of marriage was due to a simple and yet complex cause.   Stated baldly, it was the consciousness of her secret; the complexity arose out of the various ways in which it seemed to bear upon her future.   Our lives are so bound up with those of our fellow men that the slightest departure from the beaten path involves a multiplicity of small adjustments.   It had not been difficult for Rena to conform her speech, her manners, and in a measure her modes of thought, to those of the people around her; but when this readjustment went beyond mere externals and concerned the vital issues of life, the secret that oppressed her took on a more serious aspect, with tragic possibilities.   A discursive imagination was not one of her characteristics, or the danger of a marriage of which perfect frankness was not a condition might well have presented itself before her heart had become involved.   Under the influence of doubt and fear acting upon love, the invisible bar to happiness glowed with a lambent flame that threatened dire disaster.

" Would he have loved me at all," she asked herself, " if he had known the story of my past? Or, having loved me, could he blame me now for what I cannot help ? "

There were two shoals in the channel of her life, upon either of which her happiness might go

to shipwreck.   Since leaving the house behind the
cedars, where she had been brought into the
world without her own knowledge or consent, and
had first drawn the breath of life by the involuntary contraction of certain muscles, Rena had
learned, in a short time, many things ; but she
was yet to learn that the innocent suffer with the
guilty, and feel the punishment the more keenly
because unmerited.   She had yet to learn that the
old Mosaic formula, " The sins of the fathers
shall be visited upon the children," was graven
more indelibly upon the heart of the race than
upon the tables of Sinai.

But would her lover still love her, if he knew
all ?   She had read some of the novels in the
bookcase in her mother's hall, and others at boarding-school.   She had read that love was a con-
queror, that neither life nor death, nor creed nor
caste, could stay his triumphant course.   Her secret
was no legal bar to their union.   If Rena could
forget the secret, and Tryon should never know it,
it would be no obstacle to their happiness.   But
Rena felt, with a sinking of the heart, that happiness was not a matter of law or of fact, but lay
entirely within the domain of sentiment.   We are
happy when we think ourselves happy, and with a
strange perversity we often differ from others with
regard to what should constitute our happiness.
Rena's secret was the worm in the bud, the skele-
ton in the closet.

" He says that he loves me.   He *does* love me.

Would he love me, if he knew?" She stood before an oval mirror brought from France by one of Warwick's wife's ancestors, and regarded her image with a coldly critical eye. She was as little vain as any of her sex who are endowed with beauty. She tried to place herself, in thus passing upon her own claims to consideration, in the hostile attitude of society toward her hidden disability. There was no mark upon her brow to brand her as less pure, less innocent, less desirable, less worthy to be loved, than these proud women of the past who had admired themselves in this old mirror.

"I think a man might love me for myself," she murmured pathetically, "and if he loved me truly, that he would marry me. If he would not marry me, then it would be because he did n't love me. I 'll tell George my secret. If he leaves me, then he does not love me."

But this resolution vanished into thin air before it was fully formulated. The secret was not hers alone; it involved her brother's position, to whom she owed everything, and in less degree the future of her little nephew, whom she had learned to love so well. She had the choice of but two courses of action, to marry Tryon or to dismiss him. The thought that she might lose him made him seem only more dear; to think that he might leave her made her sick at heart. In one week she was bound to give him an answer; he was more likely to ask for it at their next meeting.

IX

DOUBTS AND FEARS

Rena's heart was too heavy with these misgivings for her to keep them to herself. On the morning after the conversation with Tryon in which she had promised him an answer within a week, she went into her brother's study, where he usually spent an hour after breakfast before going to his office. He looked up amiably from the book before him and read trouble in her face.

"Well, Rena, dear," he asked with a smile, "what's the matter? Is there anything you want — money, or what? I should like to have Aladdin's lamp — though I'd hardly need it — that you might have no wish unsatisfied."

He had found her very backward in asking for things that she needed. Generous with his means, he thought nothing too good for her. Her success had gratified his pride, and justified his course in taking her under his protection.

"Thank you, John. You give me already more than I need. It is something else, John. George wants me to say when I will marry him. I am afraid to marry him, without telling him. If he should find out afterwards, he might cast me off,

or cease to love me. If he did not know it, I
should be forever thinking of what he would do if
he *should* find it out; or, if I should die without
his having learned it, I should not rest easy in
my grave for thinking of what he would have
done if he *had* found it out."

Warwick's smile gave place to a grave expression
at this somewhat comprehensive statement. He
rose and closed the door carefully, lest some one
of the servants might overhear the conversation.
More liberally endowed than Rena with imagination, and not without a vein of sentiment, he had
nevertheless a practical side that outweighed them
both. With him, the problem that oppressed his
sister had been in the main a matter of argument,
of self-conviction. Once persuaded that he had
certain rights, or ought to have them, by virtue of
the laws of nature, in defiance of the customs of
mankind, he had promptly sought to enjoy them.
This he had been able to do by simply concealing
his antecedents and making the most of his opportunities, with no troublesome qualms of conscience
whatever. But he had already perceived, in their
brief intercourse, that Rena's emotions, while less
easily stirred, touched a deeper note than his, and
dwelt upon it with greater intensity than if they
had been spread over the larger field to which a
more ready sympathy would have supplied so many
points of access;— hers was a deep and silent current flowing between the narrow walls of a self-
contained life, his the spreading river that ran

through a pleasant landscape. Warwick's imagination, however, enabled him to put himself in touch
with her mood and recognize its bearings upon her
conduct. He would have preferred her taking the
practical point of view, to bring her round to which
he perceived would be a matter of diplomacy.

"How long have these weighty thoughts been
troubling your small head?" he asked with assumed
lightness.

"Since he asked me last night to name our
wedding day."

"My dear child," continued Warwick, "you take
too tragic a view of life. Marriage is a reciprocal
arrangement, by which the contracting parties give
love for love, care for keeping, faith for faith. It
is a matter of the future, not of the past. What
a poor soul it is that has not some secret chamber,
sacred to itself; where one can file away the things
others have no right to know, as well as things that
one himself would fain forget! We are under no
moral obligation to inflict upon others the history
of our past mistakes, our wayward thoughts, our
secret sins, our desperate hopes, or our heart-
breaking disappointments. Still less are we bound
to bring out from this secret chamber the dusty
record of our ancestry.

'Let the dead past bury its dead.'

George Tryon loves you for yourself alone; it is
not your ancestors that he seeks to marry."

"But would he marry me if he knew?" she
persisted.

Warwick paused for reflection.   He would have preferred to argue the question in a general way, but felt the necessity of satisfying her scruples, as far as might be.   He had liked Tryon from the very beginning of their acquaintance.   In all their intercourse, which had been very close for several months, he had been impressed by the young man's sunny temper, his straightforwardness, his intellectual honesty.   Tryon's deference to Warwick as the elder man had very naturally proved an attraction.   Whether this friendship would have stood the test of utter frankness about his own past was a merely academic speculation with which Warwick did not trouble himself.   With his sister the question had evidently become a matter of conscience, — a difficult subject with which to deal in a person of Rena's temperament.

"My dear sister," he replied, "why should he know ?   We have n't asked him for his pedigree ; we don't care to know it.   If he cares for ours, he should ask for it, and it would then be time enough to raise the question.   You love him, I imagine, and wish to make him happy ? "

It is the highest wish of the woman who loves.   The enamored man seeks his own happiness ; the loving woman finds no sacrifice too great for the loved one.   The fiction of chivalry made man serve woman ; the fact of human nature makes woman happiest when serving where she loves.

"Yes, oh, yes," Rena exclaimed with fervor, clasping her hands unconsciously.   "I 'm afraid he 'd be unhappy if he knew, and it would make me miserable to think him unhappy."

"Well, then," said Warwick, "suppose we should tell him our secret and put ourselves in his power, and that he should then conclude that he could n't marry you ?   Do you imagine he would be any happier than he is now, or than if he should never know ? "

Ah, no ! she could not think so.   One could not tear love out of one 's heart without pain and suffering.

There was a knock at the door.   Warwick opened it to the nurse, who stood with little Albert in her arms.

" Please, suh," said the girl, with a curtsy, " de baby 's be'n cryin' an' frettin' fer Miss Rena, an' I 'lowed she mought want me ter fetch 'im, ef it would n't 'sturb her."

" Give me the darling," exclaimed Rena, coming forward and taking the child from the nurse.   " It wants its auntie.   Come to its auntie, bless its little heart ! "

Little Albert crowed with pleasure and put up his pretty mouth for a kiss.   Warwick found the sight a pleasant one.   If he could but quiet his sister's troublesome scruples, he might erelong see her fondling beautiful children of her own.   Even if Rena were willing to risk her happiness, and he to endanger his position, by a quixotic frankness, the future of his child must not be compromised.

" You would n't want to make George unhappy,"

Warwick resumed when the nurse retired. " Very
well; would you not be willing, for his sake, to keep
a secret — your secret and mine, and that of the
innocent child in your arms ?   Would you involve
all of us in difficulties merely to secure your own
peace of mind ?   Does n't such a course seem just
the least bit selfish ?   Think the matter over from
that point of view, and we 'll speak of it later in the
day.   I shall be with George all the morning, and
I may be able, by a little management, to find out
his views on the subject of birth and family, and
all that.   Some men are very liberal, and love is a
great leveler.   I 'll sound him, at any rate."

He kissed the baby and left Rena to her own
reflections, to which his presentation of the case had
given a new turn.   It had never before occurred to
her to regard silence in the light of self-sacrifice.
It had seemed a sort of sin ; her brother's argument made of it a virtue.   It was not the first
time, nor the last, that right and wrong had been
a matter of view-point.

Tryon himself furnished the opening for Warwick 's proposed examination.   The younger man
could not long remain silent upon the subject uppermost in his mind.   " I am anxious, John," he said,
" to have Rowena name the happiest day of my
life — our wedding day.   When the trial in Edge-
combe County is finished, I shall have no further
business here, and shall be ready to leave for home.
I should like to take my bride with me, and surprise
my mother."

Mothers, thought Warwick, are likely to prove inquisitive about their sons' wives, especially when taken unawares in matters of such importance. This seemed a good time to test the liberality of Tryon's views, and to put forward a shield for his sister's protection.

" Are you sure, George, that your mother will find the surprise agreeable when you bring home a bride of whom you know so little and your mother nothing at all? "

Tryon had felt that it would be best to surprise his mother. She would need only to see Rena to approve of her, but she was so far prejudiced in favor of Blanche Leary that it would be wisest to present the argument after having announced the irrevocable conclusion. Rena herself would be a complete justification for the accomplished deed.

" I think you ought to know, George," continued Warwick, without waiting for a reply to his question, " that my sister and I are not of an old family, or a rich family, or a distinguished family; that she can bring you nothing but herself; that we have no connections of which you could boast, and no relatives to whom we should be glad to introduce you. You must take us for ourselves alone — we are new people."

" My dear John," replied the young man warmly, " there is a great deal of nonsense about families. If a man is noble and brave and strong, if a woman is beautiful and good and true, what matters it about his or her ancestry? If an

old family can give them these things, then it is
valuable ; if they possess them without it, then of
what use is it, except as a source of empty pride,
which they would be better without ? If all new
families were like yours, there would be no advantage in belonging to an old one. All I care to
know of Rowena's family is that she is your sister ;
and you 'll pardon me, old fellow, if I add that she
hardly needs even you, — she carries the stamp of
her descent upon her face and in her heart."

"It makes me glad to hear you speak in that
way," returned Warwick, delighted by the young
man's breadth and earnestness.

" Oh, I mean every word of it," replied Tryon.
" Ancestors, indeed, for Rowena ! I will tell you
a family secret, John, to prove how little I care for
ancestors. My maternal great-great-grandfather, a
hundred and fifty years ago, was hanged, drawn,
and quartered for stealing cattle across the Scottish border. How is that for a pedigree ? Behold
in me the lineal descendant of a felon ! "

Warwick felt much relieved at this avowal.
His own statement had not touched the vital point
involved ; it had been at the best but a half-truth ;
but Tryon's magnanimity would doubtless protect
Rena from any close inquiry concerning her past.
It even occurred to Warwick for a moment that
he might safely disclose the secret to Tryon ; but
an appreciation of certain facts of history and
certain traits of human nature constrained him
to put the momentary thought aside. It was a

great relief, however, to imagine that Tryon might think lightly of this thing that he need never know.

"Well, Rena," he said to his sister when he went home at noon : "I've sounded George."

"What did he say ?" she asked eagerly.

"I told him we were people of no family, and that we had no relatives that we were proud of. He said he loved you for yourself, and would never ask you about your ancestry."

"Oh, I am so glad !" exclaimed Rena joyfully. This report left her very happy for about three hours, or until she began to analyze carefully her brother's account of what had been said. Warwick's statement had not been specific, — he had not told Tryon *the* thing. George's reply, in turn, had been a mere generality. The concrete fact that oppressed her remained unrevealed, and her doubt was still unsatisfied.

Rena was occupied with this thought when her lover next came to see her. Tryon came up the sanded walk from the gate and spoke pleasantly to the nurse, a good-looking yellow girl who was seated on the front steps, playing with little Albert. He took the boy from her arms, and she went to call Miss Warwick.

Rena came out, followed by the nurse, who offered to take the child.

"Never mind, Mimy, leave him with me," said Tryon.

The nurse walked discreetly over into the garden, remaining within call, but beyond the hearing of conversation in an ordinary tone.

" Rena, darling," said her lover, " when shall it be ? Surely you won't ask me to wait a week. Why, that 's a lifetime ! "

Rena was struck by a brilliant idea. She would test her lover. Love was a very powerful force ; she had found it the greatest, grandest, sweetest thing in the world. Tryon had said that he loved her ; he had said scarcely anything else for several weeks, surely nothing else worth remembering. She would test his love by a hypothetical question.

" You say you love me," she said, glancing at him with a sad thoughtfulness in her large dark eyes. " How much do you love me ? "

" I love you all one can love. True love has no degrees ; it is all or nothing ! "

" Would you love me," she asked, with an air of coquetry that masked her concern, pointing toward the girl in the shrubbery, " if I were Albert's nurse yonder ? "

" If you were Albert's nurse," he replied, with a joyous laugh, " he would have to find another within a week, for within a week we should be married."

The answer seemed to fit the question, but in fact, Tryon's mind and Rena's did not meet. That two intelligent persons should each attach a different meaning to so simple a form of words as Rena's question was the best ground for her mis-giving with regard to the marriage. But love blinded her. She was anxious to be convinced. She interpreted the meaning of his speech by her own thought and by the ardor of his glance, and was satisfied with the answer.

"And now, darling," pleaded Tryon, "will you not fix the day that shall make me happy? I shall be ready to go away in three weeks. Will you go with me?"

"Yes," she answered, in a tumult of joy. She would never need to tell him her secret now. It would make no difference with him, so far as she was concerned; and she had no right to reveal her brother's secret. She was willing to bury the past in forgetfulness, now that she knew it would have no interest for her lover.

X

THE marriage was fixed for the thirtieth of the
month, immediately after which Tryon and his
bride were to set out for North Carolina. Warwick would have liked it much if Tryon had
lived in South Carolina; but the location of his
North Carolina home was at some distance from
Patesville, with which it had no connection by
steam or rail, and indeed lay altogether out of the
line of travel to Patesville. Rena had no acquaintance with people of social standing in North Carolina; and with the added maturity and charm
due to her improved opportunities, it was unlikely
that any former resident of Patesville who might
casually meet her would see in the elegant young
matron from South Carolina more than a passing
resemblance to a poor girl who had once lived in an
obscure part of the old town. It would of course
be necessary for Rena to keep away from Patesville; save for her mother's sake, she would hardly
be tempted to go back.

On the twentieth of the month, Warwick set
out with Tryon for the county seat of the adjoining county, to try one of the lawsuits which had

required Tryon's presence in South Carolina for
so long a time. Their destination was a day's
drive from Clarence, behind a good horse, and the
trial was expected to last a week.

" This week will seem like a year," said Tryon
ruefully, the evening before their departure, " but
I'll write every day, and shall expect a letter as
often."

" The mail goes only twice a week, George,"
replied Rena.

" Then I shall have three letters in each mail."

Warwick and Tryon were to set out in the cool
of the morning, after an early breakfast. Rena
was up at daybreak that she might preside at the
breakfast-table and bid the travelers good-by.

" John," said Rena to her brother in the morning, " I dreamed last night that mother was ill."

" Dreams, you know, Rena," answered Warwick lightly, " go by contraries. Yours undoubtedly signifies that our mother, God bless her
simple soul! is at the present moment enjoying
her usual perfect health. She was never sick in
her life."

For a few months after leaving Patesville with
her brother, Rena had suffered tortures of homesickness; those who have felt it know the pang.
The severance of old ties had been abrupt and
complete. At the school where her brother had
taken her, there had been nothing to relieve the
strangeness of her surroundings — no schoolmate
from her own town, no relative or friend of the

family near by.   Even the compensation of human
sympathy was in a measure denied her, for Rena
was too fresh from her prison-house to doubt that
sympathy would fail before the revelation of
the secret the consciousness of which oppressed
her at that time like a nightmare.   It was not
strange that Rena, thus isolated, should have been
prostrated by homesickness for several weeks
after leaving Patesville.   When the paroxysm
had passed, there followed a dull pain, which gradually subsided into a resignation as profound, in
its way, as had been her longing for home.   She
loved, she suffered, with a quiet intensity of which
her outward demeanor gave no adequate expression.   From some ancestral source she had derived
a strain of the passive fatalism by which alone
one can submit uncomplainingly to the inevitable.
By the same token, when once a thing had been
decided, it became with her a finality, which only
some extraordinary stress of emotion could disturb.   She had acquiesced in her brother's plan ;
for her there was no withdrawing ; her homesickness was an incidental thing which must be en-
dured, as patiently as might be, until time should
have brought a measure of relief.

Warwick had made provision for an occasional
letter from Patesville, by leaving with his mother a
number of envelopes directed to his address.   She
could have her letters written, inclose them in
these envelopes, and deposit them in the post-
office with her own hand.   Thus the place of War-

wick's residence would remain within her own
knowledge, and his secret would not be placed at
the mercy of any wandering Patesvillian who
might perchance go to that part of South Carolina.
By this simple means Rena had kept as closely in
touch with her mother as Warwick had considered
prudent; any closer intercourse was not consistent
with their present station in life.

The night after Warwick and Tryon had ridden away, Rena dreamed again that her mother
was ill. Better taught people than she, in regions
more enlightened than the South Carolina of that
epoch, are disturbed at times by dreams. Mis'
Molly had a profound faith in them. If God, in
ancient times, had spoken to men in visions of the
night, what easier way could there be for Him to
convey his meaning to people of all ages? Science,
which has shattered many an idol and destroyed
many a delusion, has made but slight inroads
upon the shadowy realm of dreams. For Mis'
Molly, to whom science would have meant nothing
and psychology would have been a meaningless
term, the land of dreams was carefully mapped
and bounded. Each dream had some special significance, or was at least susceptible of classification
under some significant head. Dreams, as a general
rule, went by contraries; but a dream three times
repeated was a certain portent of the thing de-
fined. Rena's few years of schooling at Patesville and her months at Charleston had scarcely disturbed these hoary superstitions which lurk in the

dim corners of the brain. No lady in Clarence, perhaps, would have remained undisturbed by a vivid dream, three times repeated, of some event bearing materially upon her own life.

The first repetition of a dream was decisive of nothing, for two dreams meant no more than one. The power of the second lay in the suspense, the uncertainty, to which it gave rise. Two doubled the chance of a third. The day following this second dream was an anxious one for Rena. She could not for an instant dismiss her mother from her thoughts, which were filled too with a certain self-reproach. She had left her mother alone; if her mother were really ill, there was no one at home to tend her with loving care. This feeling grew in force, until by nightfall Rena had become very unhappy, and went to bed with the most dismal forebodings. In this state of mind, it is not surprising that she now dreamed that her mother was lying at the point of death, and that she cried out with heart-rending pathos : —

" Rena, my darlin', why did you forsake yo'r pore old mother ? Come back to me, honey ; I 'll die ef I don't see you soon."

The stress of subcóhscious emotion engendered by the dream was powerful enough to wake Rena, and her mother's utterance seemed to come to her with the force of a fateful warning and a great reproach. Her mother was sick and needed her, and would die if she did not come. She felt that she must see her mother, — it would be almost like murder to remain away from her under such circumstances.

After breakfast she went into the business part of the town and inquired at what time a train would leave that would take her toward Patesville. Since she had come away from the town, a railroad had been opened by which the long river voyage might be avoided, and, making allowance for slow trains and irregular connections, the town of Patesville could be reached by an all-rail route in about twelve hours. Calling at the post-office for the family mail, she found there a letter from her mother, which she tore open in great excitement. It was written in an unpracticed hand and badly spelled, and was in effect as follows: —

MY DEAR DAUGHTER, — I take my pen in hand to let you know that I am not very well. I have had a kind of misery in my side for two weeks, with palpitations of the heart, and I have been in bed for three days. I'm feeling mighty poorly, but Dr. Green says that I'll get over it in a few days. Old Aunt Zilphy is staying with me, and looking after things tolerably well. I hope this will find you and John enjoying good health. Give my love to John, and I hope the Lord will bless him and you too. Cousin Billy Oxendine has had a rising on his neck, and has had to have it lanced. Mary B. has another young one, a boy this time. Old man Tom Johnson was killed last week while trying to whip black Jim Brown, who lived down

on the Wilmington Road. Jim has run away.
There has been a big freshet in the river, and it
looked at one time as if the new bridge would be
washed away.

Frank comes over every day or two and asks
about you. He says to tell you that he don't believe you are coming back any more, but you are
to remember him, and that foolishness he said
about bringing you back from the end of the
world with his mule and cart. He's very good to
me, and brings over shavings and kindling-wood,
and made me a new well-bucket for nothing. It's
a comfort to talk to him about you, though I
have n't told him where you are living.

I hope this will find you and John both well,
and doing well. I should like to see you, but if
it's the Lord's will that I should n't, I shall be
thankful anyway that you have done what was
the best for yourselves and your children, and that
I have given you up for your own good.

Your affectionate mother,
MARY WALDEN.

Rena shed tears over this simple letter, which,
to her excited imagination, merely confirmed the
warning of her dream. At the date of its writing
her mother had been sick in bed, with the symp-
toms of a serious illness. She had no nurse but a
purblind old woman. Three days of progressive
illness had evidently been quite sufficient to reduce
her parent to the condition indicated by the third

dream. The thought that her mother might die without the presence of any one who loved her pierced Rena's heart like a knife and lent wings to her feet. She wished for the enchanted horse of which her brother had read to her so many years before on the front piazza of the house behind the cedars, that she might fly through the air to her dying mother's side. She determined to go at once to Patesville.

Returning home, she wrote a letter to Warwick inclosing their mother's letter, and stating that she had dreamed an alarming dream for three nights in succession; that she had left the house in charge of the servants and gone to Patesville; and that she would return as soon as her mother was out of danger.

To her lover she wrote that she had been called away to visit a sick-bed, and would return very soon, perhaps by the time he got back to Clarence. These letters Rena posted on her way to the train, which she took at five o'clock in the afternoon. This would bring her to Patesville early in the morning of the following day.

XI

A LETTER AND A JOURNEY

WAR has been called the court of last resort. A lawsuit may with equal aptness be compared to a battle — the parallel might be drawn very closely all along the line. First we have the *casus belli*, the cause of action ; then the various protocols and proclamations and general orders, by way of pleas, demurrers, and motions ; then the preliminary skirmishes at the trial table ; and then the final struggle, in which might is quite as likely to prevail as right, victory most often resting with the strongest battalions, and truth and justice not seldom overborne by the weight of odds upon the other side.

The lawsuit which Warwick and Tryon had gone to try did not, however, reach this ultimate stage, but, after a three days' engagement, resulted in a treaty of peace. The case was compromised and settled, and Tryon and Warwick set out on their homeward drive. They stopped at a farmhouse at noon, and while at table saw the stagecoach from the town they had just left, bound for their own destination. In the mail-bag under the driver's seat were Rena's two letters ; they had been delivered at the town in the morning, and immediately remailed to Clarence, in accordance with orders left at the post-office the evening before. Tryon and Warwick drove leisurely homeward through the pines, all unconscious of the fateful squares of white paper moving along the road a few miles before them, which a mother's yearning and a daughter's love had thrown, like the apple of discord, into the narrow circle of their happiness.

They reached Clarence at four o'clock. Warwick got down from the buggy at his office. Tryon drove on to his hotel, to make a hasty toilet before visiting his sweetheart.

Warwick glanced at his mail, tore open the envelope addressed in his sister's handwriting, and read the contents with something like dismay. She had gone away on the eve of her wedding, her lover knew not where, to be gone no one knew how long, on a mission which could not be frankly disclosed. A dim foreboding of disaster flashed across his mind. He thrust the letter into his pocket, with others yet unopened, and started toward his home. Reaching the gate, he paused a moment and then walked on past the house. Tryon would probably be there in a few minutes, and he did not care to meet him without first having had the opportunity for some moments of reflection. He must fix upon some line of action in this emergency.

Meanwhile Tryon had reached his hotel and opened his mail. The letter from Rena was read

first, with profound disappointment. He had
really made concessions in the settlement of that
lawsuit — had yielded several hundred dollars of
his just dues, in order that he might get back to
Rena three days earlier. Now he must cool his
heels in idleness for at least three days before she
would return. It was annoying, to say the least.
He wished to know where she had gone, that he
might follow her and stay near her until she should
be ready to come back. He might ask Warwick —
no, she might have had some good reason for not
having mentioned her destination. She had probably gone tu visit some of the poor relations of
whom her brother had spoken so frankly, and she
would doubtless prefer that he should not see her
amid any surroundings but the best. Indeed, he
did not know that he would himself care to endanger, by suggestive comparisons, the fine aureole of
superiority that surrounded her. She represented
in her adorable person and her pure heart the
finest flower of the finest race that God had ever
made — the supreme effort of creative power, than
which there could be no finer. The flower would
soon be his ; why should he care to dig up the soil
in which it grew ?

Tryon went on opening his letters. There were
several bills and circulars, and then a letter from
his mother, of which he broke the seal : —

MY DEAREST GEORGE, — This leaves us well.
Blanche is still with me, and we are impatiently

awaiting your return.   In your absence she seems
almost like a daughter to me.   She joins me in
the hope that your lawsuits are progressing favor-
ably, and that you will be with us soon. . . .

On your way home, if it does not keep you
away from us too long, would it not be well for
you to come by way of Patesville, and find out
whether there is any prospect of our being able
to collect our claim against old Mr. Duncan Mc-
Swayne's estate?   You must have taken the papers
with you, along with the rest, for I do not find
them here.   Things ought to be settled enough now
for people to realize on some of their securities.
Your grandfather always believed the note was
good, and meant to try to collect it, but the war
interfered.   He said to me, before he died, that if
the note was ever collected, he would use the money
to buy a wedding present for your wife.   Poor
father ! he is dead and gone to heaven ; but I am
sure that even there he would be happier if he
knew the note was paid and the money used as he
intended.

If you go to Patesville, call on my cousin, Dr.
Ed. Green, and tell him who you are.   Give him
my love.   I have n't seen him for twenty years.
He used to be very fond of the ladies, a very gallant man.   He can direct you to a good lawyer,
no doubt.   Hoping to see you soon,

Your loving mother,

ELIZABETH TRYON.

P. S. Blanche joins me in love to you.

This affectionate and motherly letter did not give Tryon unalloyed satisfaction. He was glad to hear that his mother was well, but he had hoped that Blanche Leary might have finished her visit by this time. The reasonable inference from the letter was that Blanche meant to await his return. Her presence would spoil the fine romantic flavor of the surprise he had planned for his mother ; it would never do to expose his bride to an unannounced meeting with the woman whom he had tacitly rejected. There would be one advantage in such a meeting : the comparison of the two women would be so much in Rena's favor that his mother could not hesitate for a moment between them. The situation, however, would have elements of constraint, and he did not care to expose either Rena or Blanche to any disagreeable contingency. It would be better to take his wife on a wedding trip, and notify his mother, before he returned home, of his marriage. In the extremely improbable case that she should disapprove his choice after having seen his wife, the ice would at least have been broken before his arrival at home.

"By Jove!" he exclaimed suddenly, striking his knee with his hand, " why should n't I run up to Patesville while Rena 's gone ? I can leave here at five o'clock, and get there some time to-morrow morning. I can transact my business during the day, and get back the day after to-morrow ; for Rena might return ahead of time, just as we did, and

I shall want to be here when she comes; I'd rather
wait a year for a legal opinion on a doubtful old
note than to lose one day with my love. The
train goes in twenty minutes. My bag is already
packed. I'll just drop a line to George and tell
him where I've gone."

He put Rena's letter into his breast pocket, and
turning to his trunk, took from it a handful of
papers relating to the claim in reference to which
he was going to Patesville. These he thrust into
the same pocket with Rena's letter; he wished to
read both letter and papers while on the train. It
would be a pleasure merely to hold the letter before
his eyes and look at the lines traced by her hand.
The papers he wished to study, for the more practical purpose of examining into the merits of his
claim against the estate of Duncan McSwayne.

When Warwick reached home, he inquired if
Mr. Tryon had called.

"No, suh," answered the nurse, to whom he had
put the question; "he ain't be'n here yet, suh."

Warwick was surprised and much disturbed.

"De baby's be'n cryin' for Miss Rena," suggested the nurse, "an' I s'pec' he'd like to see you,
suh. Shall I fetch 'im?"

"Yes, bring him to me."

He took the child in his arms and went out upon
the piazza. Several porch pillows lay invitingly
near. He pushed them toward the steps with his
foot, sat down upon one, and placed little Albert
upon another. He was scarcely seated when a

messenger from the hotel came up the walk from
the gate and handed him a note. At the same
moment he heard the long shriek of the afternoon
train leaving the station on the opposite side of the
town.

He tore the envelope open anxiously, read the
note, smiled a sickly smile, and clenched the paper
in his hand unconsciously. There was nothing he
could do. The train had gone; there was no
telegraph to Patesville, and no letter could leave
Clarence for twenty-four hours. The best laid
schemes go wrong at times — the stanchest ships
are sometimes wrecked, or skirt the breakers
perilously. Life is a sea, full of strange currents
and uncharted reefs — whoever leaves the traveled
path must run the danger of destruction. Warwick was a lawyer, however, and accustomed to
balance probabilities.

"He may easily be in Patesville a day or two
without meeting her. She will spend most of her
time at mother's bedside, and he will be occupied
with his own affairs."

If Tryon should meet her — well, he was very
much in love, and he had spoken very nobly of
birth and blood. Warwick would have preferred,
nevertheless, that Tryon's theories should not be
put to this particular test. Rena's scruples had so
far been successfully combated; the question would
be opened again, and the situation unnecessarily
complicated, if Tryon should meet Rena in Patesville.

" Will he or will he not ? " he asked himself.
He took a coin from his pocket and spun it upon
the floor. " Heads, he sees her; tails, he does
not."

The coin spun swiftly and steadily, leaving upon
the eye the impression of a revolving sphere.   Little
Albert, left for a moment to his own devices, had
crept behind his father and was watching the whirl-
ing disk with great pleasure.   He felt that he would
like to possess this interesting object.   The coin
began to move more slowly, and was wabbling to its
fall, when the child stretched forth his chubby fist
and caught it ere it touched the floor.

XII

TRYON GOES TO PATESVILLE

TRYON arrived in the early morning and put up at the Patesville Hotel, a very comfortable inn. After a bath, breakfast, and a visit to the barbershop, he inquired of the hotel clerk the way to the office of Dr. Green, his mother's cousin.

" On the corner, sir," answered the clerk, " by the market-house, just over the drugstore. The doctor drove past here only hal" an hour ago. You 'll probably catch him in his office."

Tryon found the office without difficulty. He climbed the stair, but found no one in except a young colored man seated in the outer office, who rose promptly as Tryon entered.

" No, suh," replied the man to Tryon's question, " he ain't hyuh now. He 's gone out to see a patient, suh, but he 'll be back soon. Won't you set down in de private office an' wait fer 'im, suh ? "

Tryon had not slept well during his journey, and felt somewhat fatigued. Through the open door of the next room he saw an inviting armchair, with a window at one side, and upon the other a table strewn with papers and magazines.

" Yes," he answered, " I 'll wait."

He entered the private office, sank into the arm-chair, and looked out of the window upon the square below. The view was mildly interesting. The old brick market-house with the tower was quite pictur-esque. On a wagon-scale at one end the public weighmaster was weighing a load of hay. In the booths under the wide arches several old negro women were frying fish on little charcoal stoves — the odor would have been appetizing to one who had not breakfasted. On the shady side stood half a dozen two-wheeled carts, loaded with lightwood and drawn by diminutive steers, or superannuated army mules branded on the flank with the cabalis-tic letters "C. S. A.," which represented a vanished dream, or "U. S. A.," which, as any negro about the market-house would have borne witness, signified a very concrete fact. Now and then a lady or gen-tleman passed with leisurely step — no one ever hur-ried in Patesville — or some poor white sandhiller slouched listlessly along toward store or bar-room.

Tryon mechanically counted the slabs of ginger-bread on the nearest market-stall, and calculated the cubical contents of several of the meagre loads of wood. Having exhausted the view, he turned to the table at his elbow and picked up a medical journal, in which he read first an account of a marvelous surgical operation. Turning the leaves idly, he came upon an article by a Southern writer, upon the perennial race problem that has vexed the country for a century. The writer maintained that owing to a special tendency of the negro blood, however diluted, to revert to the African type, any future amalgamation of the white and black races, which foolish and wicked Northern negrophiles predicted as the ultimate result of the new conditions confronting the South, would therefore be an ethnological impossibility ; for the smallest trace of negro blood would inevitably drag down the superior race to the level of the inferior, and reduce the fair Southland, already devastated by the hand of the invader, to the frightful level of Hayti, the awful example of negro incapacity. To forefend their beloved land, now doubly sanctified by the blood of her devoted sons who had fallen in the struggle to maintain her liberties and preserve her property, it behooved every true Southron to stand firm against the abhorrent tide of radicalism, to maintain the supremacy and purity of his all-pervading, all-conquering race, and to resist by every available means the threatened domination of an inferior and degraded people, who were set to rule hereditary freemen ere they had themselves scarce ceased to be slaves.

When Tryon had finished the article, which seemed to him a well-considered argument, albeit a trifle bombastic, he threw the book upon the table. Finding the armchair wonderfully comfortable, and feeling the fatigue of his journey, he yielded to a drowsy impulse, leaned his head on the cushioned back of the chair, and fell asleep. According to the habit of youth, he dreamed, and pursuant to his own individual habit, he dreamed of Rena. They were walking in the moonlight, along the quiet road in front of her brother's house. The air was redolent with the perfume of flowers. His arm was around her waist. He had asked her if she loved him, and was awaiting her answer in tremulous but confident expectation. She opened her lips to speak. The sound that came from them seemed to be : —

" Is Dr. Green in? No? Ask him, when he comes back, please, to call at our house as soon as he can."

Tryon was in that state of somnolence in which one may dream and yet be aware that one is dreaming, — the state where one, during a dream, dreams that one pinches one's self to be sure that one is not dreaming. He was therefore aware of a ringing quality about the words he had just heard that did not comport with the shadowy converse of a dream — an incongruity in the remark, too, which marred the harmony of the vision. The shock was sufficient to disturb Tryon's slumber, and he struggled slowly back to consciousness. When fully awake, he thought he heard a light footfall descending the stairs.

" Was there some one here? " he inquired of the attendant in the outer office, who was visible through the open door.

" Yas, suh," replied the boy, " a young cullud 'oman wuz in jes' now, axin' fer de doctuh."

Tryon felt a momentary touch of annoyance that a negro woman should have intruded herself into his dream at its most interesting point. Neverthe-

less, the voice had been so real, his imagination had
reproduced with such exactness the dulcet tones so
dear to him, that he turned his head involuntarily
and looked out of the window. He could just see
the flutter of a woman's skirt disappearing around
the corner.

A moment later the doctor came bustling in, —
a plump, rosy man of fifty or more, with a frank,
open countenance and an air of genial good nature.
Such a doctor, Tryon fancied, ought to enjoy a
wide popularity. His mere presence would suggest
life and hope and healthfulness.

" My dear boy," exclaimed the doctor cordially,
after Tryon had introduced himself, " I 'm delighted to meet you — or any one of the old blood.
Your mother and I were sweethearts, long ago,
when we both wore pinafores, and went to see our
grandfather at Christmas; and I met her more
than once, and paid her more than one compliment,
after she had grown to be a fine young woman.
You 're like her, too, but not quite so handsome —
you 've more of what I suppose to be the Tryon
favor, though I never met your father. So one of
old Duncan McSwayne's notes went so far as that?
Well, well, I don't know where you won't find
them. One of them turned up here the other day
from New York.

" The man you want to see," he added later in
the conversation, " is old Judge Straight. He 's
getting somewhat stiff in the joints, but he knows
more law, and more about the McSwayne estate,

than any other two lawyers in town. If anybody can collect your claim, Judge Straight can. I 'll send my boy Dave over to his office. Dave," he called to his attendant, " run over to Judge Straight's office and see if he 's there.

" There was a freshet here a few weeks ago," he went on, when the colored man had departed, " and they had to open the flood-gates and let the water out of the mill pond, for if the dam had broken, as it did twenty years ago, it would have washed the pillars from under the judge's office and let it down in the creek, and " —

" Jedge Straight ain't in de office jes' now, suh," reported the doctor's man Dave, from the head of the stairs.

" Did you ask when he 'd be back ? "

" No, suh, you did n't tell me ter, suh."

" Well, now, go back and inquire.

" The niggers," he explained to Tryon, " are getting mighty trifling since they 've been freed. Before the war, that boy would have been around there and back before you could say Jack Robinson ; now, the lazy rascal takes his time just like a white man.'

Dave returned more promptly than from his first trip. " Jedge Straight 's dere now, suh," he said. " He 's done come in."

" I 'll take you right around and introduce you," said the doctor, running on pleasantly, like a babbling brook. " I don't know whether the judge ever met your mother or not, but he knows a gentleman when he sees one, and will be glad to meet you and look after your affair. See to the patients, Dave, and say I 'll be back shortly, and don't forget any messages left for me. Look sharp, now! You know your failing! "

They found Judge Straight in his office. He was seated by the rear window, and had fallen into a gentle doze — the air of Patesville was conducive to slumber. A visitor from some bustling city might have rubbed his eyes, on any but a market-day, and imagined the whole town asleep — that the people were somnambulists and did not know it. The judge, an old hand, roused himself so skillfully, at the sound of approaching footsteps, that his visitors could not guess but that he had been wide awake. He shook hands with the doctor, and acknowledged the introduction to Tryon with a rare old-fashioned courtesy, which the young man thought a very charming survival of the manners of a past and happier age.

" No," replied the judge, in answer to a question by Dr. Green, " I never met his mother ; I was a generation ahead of her. I was at school with her father, however, fifty years ago — fifty years ago! No doubt that seems to you a long time, young gentleman ? "

" It is a long time, sir," replied Tryon. " I must live more than twice as long as I have in order to cover it."

" A long time, and a troubled time," sighed the judge. " I could wish that I might see this unhappy land at peace with itself before I die. Things are in a sad tangle; I can't see the way out. But the worst enemy has been slain, in spite of us. We are well rid of slavery."

"But the negro we still have with us," remarked the doctor, "for here comes my man Dave. What is it, Dave?" he asked sharply, as the negro stuck his head in at the door.

"Doctuh Green," he said, "I fuhgot ter tell you, suh, dat dat young 'oman wuz at de office agin jes' befo' you come in, an' said fer you to go right down an' see her mammy ez soon ez you could."

"Ah, yes, and you've just remembered it! I'm afraid you're entirely too forgetful for a doctor's office. You forgot about old Mrs. Latimer, the other day, and when I got there she had almost choked to death. Now get back to the office, and remember, the next time you forget anything, I'll hire another boy; remember that! That boy's head," he remarked to his companions, after Dave had gone, "reminds me of nothing so much as a dried gourd, with a handful of cowpeas rattling around it, in lieu of gray matter. An old woman out in Redbank got a fishbone in her throat, the other day, and nearly choked to death before I got there. A white woman, sir, came very near losing her life because of a lazy, trifling negro!"

"I should think you would discharge him, sir," suggested Tryon.

"What would be the use?" rejoined the doctor.

" All negroes are alike, except that now and then there's a pretty woman along the border-line. Take this patient of mine, for instance, — I 'll call on her after dinner, her case is not serious, — thirty years ago she would have made any man turn his head to look at her. You know who I mean, don't you, judge ? "

" Yes. I think so," said the judge promptly. " I 've transacted a little business for her now and then."

" I don't know whether you 've seen the daughter or not — I 'm sure you have n't for the past year or so, for she 's been away. But she 's in town now, and, by Jove, the girl is really beautiful. And I 'm a judge of beauty. Do you remember my wife thirty years ago, judge ? "

" She was a very handsome woman, Ed," replied the other judicially. " If I had been twenty years younger, I should have cut you out."

" You mean you would have tried. But as I was saying, this girl is a beauty ; I reckon we might guess where she got some of it, eh, Judge? Human nature is human nature, but it 's a d—d shame that a man should beget a child like that and leave it to live the life open for a negro. If she had been born white, the young fellows would be tumbling over one another to get her. Her mother would have to look after her pretty closely as things are, if she stayed here ; but she disappeared mysteriously a year or two ago, and has been at the North, I 'm told, passing for white.

She 'll probably marry a Yankee; he won't know
any better, and it will serve him right — she 's
only too white for them.   She has a very striking
figure, something on the Greek order, stately and
slow-moving.   She has the manners of a lady, too
— a beautiful woman, if she is a nigger !"

" I quite agree with you, Ed," remarked the
judge dryly, " that the mother had better look
closely after the daughter."

"Ah, no, judge," replied the other, with a flattered smile, " my admiration for beauty is purely
abstract.   Twenty-five years ago, when I was
younger " —

" When you were young," corrected the judge.

" When you and I were younger," continued
the doctor ingeniously, — " twenty-five years ago, I
could not have answered for myself.   But I would
advise the girl to stay at the North, if she can.
She 's certainly out of place around here."

Tryon found the subject a little tiresome, and
the doctor's enthusiasm not at all contagious.   He
could not possibly have been interested in a colored girl, under any circumstances, and he was
engaged to be married to the most beautiful white
woman on earth.   To mention a negro woman in
the same room where he was thinking of Rena
seemed little short of profanation.   His friend the
doctor was a jovial fellow, but it was surely doubtful taste to refer to his wife in such a conversation.
He was very glad when the doctor dropped the
subject and permitted him to go more into detail

about the matter which formed his business in
Patesville. He took out of his pocket the papers
concerning the McSwayne claim and laid them on
the judge's desk.

" You 'll find everything there, sir,— the note,
the contract, and some correspondence that will
give you the hang of the thing. Will you be able
to look over them to-day? I should like," he added
a little nervously, " to go back to-morrow."

" What! " exclaimed Dr. Green vivaciously,
" insult our town by staying only one day? It
won't be long enough to get acquainted with our
young ladies. Patesville girls are famous for their
beauty. But perhaps there 's a loadstone in South
Carolina to draw you back? Ah, you change color!
To my mind there's nothing finer than the ingenu-
ous blush of youth. But we 'll spare you if you 'll
answer one question — is it serious? "

" I 'm to be married in two weeks, sir," answered
Tryon. The statement sounded very pleasant, in
spite of the slight embarrassment caused by the
inquiry.

" Good boy! " rejoined the doctor, taking his
arm familiarly — they were both standing now.
" You ought to have married a Patesville girl, but
you people down towards the eastern counties seldom come this way, and we are evidently too late
to catch you."

" I 'll look your papers over this morning," said
the judge, " and when I come from dinner will
stop at the court house and examine the records

and see whether there's anything we can get hold of. If you'll drop in around three or four o'clock, I may be able to give you an opinion."

"Now, George," exclaimed the. doctor, "we'll go back to the office for a spell, and then I'll take you home with me to luncheon."

Tryon hesitated.

"Oh, you must come! Mrs. Green would never forgive me if I didn't bring you. Strangers are rare birds in our society, and when they come we make them welcome. Our enemies may overturn our institutions, and try to put the bottom rail on top, but they cannot destroy our Southern hospitality. There are so many carpet-baggers and other social vermin creeping into the South, with the Yankees trying to force the niggers on us, that it's a genuine pleasure to get acquainted with another real Southern gentleman, whom one can invite into one's house without fear of contamination, and before whom one can express his feelings freely and be sure of perfect sympathy."

XIII

WHEN Judge Straight's visitors had departed, he took up the papers which had been laid loosely on the table as they were taken out of Tryon's breast-pocket, and commenced their perusal. There was a note for five hundred dollars, many years over-due, but not yet outlawed by lapse of time; a contract covering the transaction out of which the note had grown ; and several letters and copies of letters modifying the terms of the contract. The judge had glanced over most of the papers, and was getting well into the merits of the case, when he unfolded a letter which read as follows : —

MY DEAREST GEORGE, — I am going away for about a week, to visit the bedside of an old friend, who is very ill, and may not live. Do not be alarmed about me, for I shall very likely be back by the time you are.

Yours lovingly,
ROWENA WARWICK.

The judge was unable to connect this letter with the transaction which formed the subject of his examination. Age had dimmed his perceptions somewhat, and it was not until he had finished the letter, and read it over again, and noted the signature at the bottom a second time, that he perceived that the writing was in a woman's hand, that the ink was comparatively fresh, and that the letter was dated only a couple of days before. While he still held the sheet in his hand, it dawned upon him slowly that he held also one of the links in a chain of possible tragedy which he himself, he became uncomfortably aware, had had a hand in forging.

" It is the Walden woman's daughter, as sure as fate ! Her name is Rena. Her brother goes by the name of Warwick. She has come to visit her sick mother. My young client, Green's relation, is her lover — is engaged to marry her — is in town, and is likely to meet her ! "

The judge was so absorbed in the situation thus suggested that he laid the papers down and pondered for a moment the curious problem involved. He was quite aware that two races had not dwelt together, side by side, for nearly three hundred years, without mingling their blood in greater or less degree ; he was old enough, and had seen curious things enough, to know that in this mingling the current had not always flowed in one direction. Certain old decisions with which he was familiar ; old scandals that had crept along obscure channels ; old facts that had come to the knowledge of an old practitioner, who held in the hollow of his hand the honor of more than one family, made him know that there was dark blood among the white people — not a great deal, and that very much diluted, and, so long as it was sedulously concealed or vigorously denied, or lost in the mists of tradition, or ascribed to a foreign or an aboriginal strain, having no perceptible effect upon the racial type.

Such people were, for the most part, merely on the ragged edge of the white world, seldom rising above the level of overseers, or slave-catchers, or sheriff's officers, who could usually be relied upon to resent the drop of black blood that tainted them, and with the zeal of the proselyte to visit their hatred of it upon the unfortunate blacks that fell into their hands.   One curse of negro slavery was, and one part of its baleful heritage is, that it poisoned the fountains of human sympathy. Under a system where men might sell their own children without social reprobation or loss of prestige, it was not surprising that some of them should hate their distant cousins.   There were not in Patesville half a dozen persons capable of thinking Judge Straight's thoughts upon the question before him, and perhaps not another who would have adopted the course he now pursued toward this anomalous family in the house behind the cedars.

" Well, here we are again, as the clown in the circus remarks," murmured the judge. "Ten years ago, in a moment of sentimental weakness and of

quixotic loyalty to the memory of an old friend, —
who, by the way, had not cared enough for his own
children to take them away from the South, as he
might have done, or to provide for them handsomely,
as he perhaps meant to do, — I violated the traditions of my class and stepped from the beaten path
to help the misbegotten son of my old friend out of
the slough of despond, in which he had learned, in
some strange way, that he was floundering. Ten
years later, the ghost of my good deed returns to
haunt me, and makes me doubt whether I have
wrought more evil than good. I wonder," he mused,
" if he will find her out ? "

The judge was a man of imagination ; he had
read many books and had personally outlived some
prejudices. He let his mind run on the various
phases of the situation.

" If he found her out, would he by any possibility marry her ? "

" It is not likely," he answered himself. " If he
made the discovery here, the facts would probably
leak out in the town. It is something that a man
might do in secret, but only a hero or a fool would
do openly."

The judge sighed as he contemplated another
possibility. He had lived for seventy years under
the old régime. The young man was a gentleman
— so had been the girl's father. Conditions were
changed, but human nature was the same. Would
the young man's love turn to disgust and repulsion,
or would it merely sink from the level of worship

to that of desire? Would the girl, denied marriage, accept anything less? Her mother had, — but conditions were changed. Yes, conditions were changed, so far as the girl was concerned; there was a possible future for her under the new order of things; but white people had not changed their opinion of the negroes, except for the worse. The general belief was that they were just as inferior as before, and had, moreover, been spoiled by a disgusting assumption of equality, driven into their thick skulls by Yankee malignity bent upon humiliating a proud though vanquished foe.

If the judge had had sons and daughters of his own, he might not have done what he now proceeded to do. But the old man's attitude toward society was chiefly that of an observer, and the narrow stream of sentiment left in his heart chose to flow toward the weaker party in this unequal conflict, — a young woman fighting for love and opportunity against the ranked forces of society, against immemorial tradition, against pride of family and of race.

" It may be the unwisest thing I ever did," he said to himself, turning to his desk and taking up a quill pen, " and may result in more harm than good ; but I was always from childhood in sympathy with the under dog. There is certainly as much reason in my helping the girl as the boy, for being a woman, she is less able to help herself."

He dipped his pen into the ink and wrote the following lines : —

MADAM, — If you value your daughter's happiness, keep her at home for the next day or two.

This note he dried by sprinkling it with sand from a box near at hand, signed with his own name, and, with a fine courtesy, addressed to "Mrs. Molly Walden." Having first carefully sealed it in an envelope, he stepped to the open door, and spied, playing marbles on the street near by, a group of negro boys, one of whom the judge called by name.

"Here, Billy," he said, handing the boy the note, "take this to Mis' Molly Walden. Do you know where she lives — down on Front Street, in the house behind the cedars?"

"Yas, suh, I knows de place."

"Make haste, now. When you come back and tell me what she says, I'll give you ten cents. On second thoughts, I shall be gone to lunch, so here's your money," he added, handing the lad the bit of soiled paper by which the United States government acknowledged its indebtedness to the bearer in the sum of ten cents.

Just here, however, the judge made his mistake. Very few mortals can spare the spring of hope, the motive force of expectation. The boy kept the note in his hand, winked at his companions, who had gathered as near as their awe of the judge would permit, and started down the street. As soon as the judge had disappeared, Billy beckoned to his friends, who speedily overtook him. When the party turned the corner of Front Street and were safely out of sight of Judge Straight's office, the capitalist entered the grocery store and invested his unearned increment in gingerbread. When the ensuing saturnalia was over, Billy finished the game of marbles which the judge had interrupted, and then set out to execute his commission. He had nearly reached his objective point when he met upon the street a young white lady, whom he did not know, and for whom, the path being narrow at that point, he stepped out into the gutter. He reached the house behind the cedars, went round to the back door, and handed the envelope to Mis' Molly, who was seated on the rear piazza, propped up by pillows in a comfortable rocking-chair.

"Laws-a-massy!" she exclaimed weakly, "what is it?"

"It's a lettuh, ma'm," answered the boy, whose expanding nostrils had caught a pleasant odor from the kitchen, and who was therefore in no hurry to go away.

"Who's it fur?" she asked.

"It's fuh you, ma'm," replied the lad.

"An' who's it from?" she inquired, turning the envelope over and over, and examining it with the impotent curiosity of one who cannot read.

"F'm ole Jedge Straight, ma'm. He tole me ter fetch it ter you. Is you got a roasted 'tater you could gimme, ma'm?"

"Shorely, chile. I'll have Aunt Zilphy fetch

you a piece of 'tater pone, if you 'll hol' on a minute."

She called to Aunt Zilphy, who soon came hobbling out of the kitchen with a large square of the delicacy, — a flat cake made of mashed sweet potatoes, mixed with beaten eggs, sweetened and flavored to suit the taste, and baked in a Dutch oven upon the open hearth.

The boy took the gratuity, thanked her, and turned to go. Mis' Molly was still scanning the superscription of the letter. " I wonder," she murmured, " what old Judge Straight can be writin' to me about. Oh, boy ! "

" Yas 'm," answered the messenger, looking back.

" Can you read writin' ? "

" No 'm."

" All right. Never mind."

She laid the letter carefully on the chimney-piece of the kitchen. " I reckon it 's somethin' mo' 'bout the taxes," she thought, " or maybe somebody wants to buy one er my lots. Rena 'll be back terreckly, an' she kin read it an' find out. I 'm glad my child'en have be'n to school. They never could have got where they are now if they had n't."

XIV

A LOYAL FRIEND

MENTION has been made of certain addressed envelopes which John Warwick, on the occasion of his visit to Patesville, had left with his illiterate mother, by the use of which she might communicate with her children from time to time. On one occasion, Mis' Molly, having had a letter written, took one of these envelopes from the chest where she kept her most valued possessions, and was about to inclose the letter when some one knocked at the back door. She laid the envelope and letter on a table in her bedroom, and went to answer the knock. The wind, blowing across the room through the open windows, picked up the envelope and bore it into the street. Mis' Molly, on her return, missed it, looked for it, and being unable to find it, took another envelope. An hour or two later another gust of wind lifted the bit of paper from the ground and carried it into the open door of the cooper shop. Frank picked it up, and observing that it was clean and unused, read the superscription. In his conversations with Mis' Molly, which were often about Rena, — the subject uppermost in both their minds, — he had noted the mystery maintained by Mis' Molly about her daughter's whereabouts, and had often wondered where she might be. Frank was an intelligent fellow, and could put this and that together. The envelope was addressed to a place in South Carolina. He was aware, from some casual remark of Mis' Molly's, that Rena had gone to live in South Carolina. Her son's name was John — that he had changed his last name was more than likely. Frank was not long in reaching the conclusion that Rena was to be found near the town named on the envelope, which he carefully preserved for future reference.

For a whole year Frank had yearned for a smile or a kind word from the only woman in the world. Peter, his father, had rallied him somewhat upon his moodiness after Rena's departure.

"Now 's de time, boy, fer you ter be lookin' roun' fer some nice gal er yo' own color, w'at 'll 'preciate you, an' won't be 'shamed er you. You 're wastin' time, boy, wastin' time, shootin' at a mark outer yo' range."

But Frank said nothing in reply, and afterwards the old man, who was not without discernment, respected his son's mood and was silent in turn ; while Frank fed his memory with his imagination, and by their joint aid kept hope alive.

Later an opportunity to see her presented itself. Business in the cooper shop was dull. A barrel factory had been opened in the town, and had well-nigh paralyzed the cooper's trade. The best mechanic could hardly compete with a machine. One man could now easily do the work of Peter's shop.   An agent appeared in town seeking laborers for one of the railroads which the newly organized carpet-bag governments were promoting. Upon inquiry Frank learned that their destination was near the town of Clarence, South Carolina. He promptly engaged himself for the service, and was soon at work in the neighborhood of Warwick's home.   There he was employed steadily until a certain holiday, upon which a grand tournament was advertised to take place in a neighboring town.   Work was suspended, and foremen and laborers attended the festivities.

Frank had surmised that Rena would be present on such an occasion.   He had more than guessed, too, that she must be looked for among the white people rather than among the black.   Hence the interest with which he had scanned the grand stand. The result has already been recounted.   He had recognized her sweet face; he had seen her enthroned among the proudest and best.   He had witnessed and gloried in her triumph.   He had seen her cheek flushed with pleasure, her eyes lit up with smiles.   He had followed her carriage, had made the acquaintance of Mimy the nurse, and had learned all about the family.   When finally he left the neighborhood to return to Patesville, he had learned of Tryon's attentions, and had heard the servants' gossip with reference to the marriage, of which they knew the details long before the

principals had approached the main fact. Frank
went away without having received one smile or
heard one word from Rena; but he had seen her:
she was happy; he was content in the knowledge of
her happiness. She was doubtless secure in the belief that her secret was unknown. Why should he,
by revealing his presence, sow the seeds of doubt
or distrust in the garden of her happiness? He
sacrificed the deepest longing of a faithful heart,
and went back to the cooper shop lest perchance she
might accidentally come upon him some day and
suffer the shock which he had sedulously spared her.

"I would n' want ter skeer her," he mused, " er
make her feel bad, an' dat's w'at I 'd mos' lackly do
ef she seed me. She 'll be better off wid me out'n
de road. She 'll marry dat rich w'ite gent'eman, —
he won't never know de diffe'nce, — an' be a w'ite
lady, ez she would 'a' be'n, ef some ole witch had n'
changed her in her cradle. But maybe some time
she 'll 'member de little nigger w'at use' ter nuss
her w'en she wuz a chile, an' fished her out'n de ole
canal, an' would 'a' died fer her ef it would 'a' done
any good."

Very generously too, and with a fine delicacy,
he said nothing to Mis' Molly of his having seen
her daughter, lest she might be disquieted by the
knowledge that he shared the family secret, — no
great mystery now, this pitiful secret, but more far-
reaching in its consequences than any blood-curdling
crime. The taint of black blood was the unpardonable sin, from the unmerited penalty of which there

was no escape except by concealment. If there be
a dainty reader of this tale who scorns a lie, and
who writes the story of his life upon his sleeve for
all the world to read, let him uncurl his scornful
lip and come down from the pedestal of superior
morality, to which assured position and wide opportunity have lifted him, and put himself in the
place of Rena and her brother, upon whom God had
lavished his best gifts, and from whom society would
have withheld all that made these gifts valuable.
To undertake what they tried to do required great
courage. Had they possessed the sneaking, cringing, treacherous character traditionally ascribed
to people of mixed blood — the character which the
blessed institutions of a free slave-holding republic
had been well adapted to foster among them ; had
they been selfish enough to sacrifice to their ambition the mother who gave them birth, society would
have been placated or humbugged, and the voyage
of their life might have been one of unbroken
smoothness.

When Rena came back unexpectedly at the
behest of her dream, Frank heard again the music
of her voice, felt the joy of her presence and the
benison of her smile. There was, however, a subtle
difference in her bearing. Her words were not less
kind, but they seemed to come from a remoter
source. She was kind, as the sun is warm or the
rain refreshing ; she was especially kind to Frank,
because he had been good to her mother. If Frank
felt the difference in her attitude, he ascribed it to

the fact that she had been white, and had taken on something of the white attitude toward the negro; and Frank, with an equal unconsciousness, clothed her with the attributes of the superior race. Only her drop of black blood, he conceived, gave him the right to feel toward her as he would never have felt without it; and if Rena guessed her faithful devotee's secret, the same reason saved his worship from presumption. A smile and a kind word were little enough to pay for a life's devotion.

On the third day of Rena's presence in Patesville, Frank was driving up Front Street in the early afternoon, when he nearly fell off his cart in astonishment as he saw seated in Dr. Green's buggy, which was standing in front of the Patesville Hotel, the young gentleman who had won the prize at the tournament, and who, as he had learned, was to marry Rena. Frank was quite certain that she did not know of Tryon's presence in the town. Frank had been over to Mis' Molly's in the morning, and had offered his services to the sick woman, who had rapidly become convalescent upon her daughter's return. Mis' Molly had spoken of some camphor that she needed. Frank had volunteered to get it. Rena had thanked him, and had spoken of going to the drugstore during the afternoon. It was her intention to leave Patesville on the following day.

"Ef dat man sees her in dis town," said Frank to himself, "dere 'll be trouble. She don't know *he's* here, an' I 'll bet he don't know *she's* here."

Then Frank was assailed by a very strong temptation. If, as he surmised, the joint presence of the two lovers in Patesville was a mere coincidence, a meeting between them would probably result in the discovery of Rena's secret.

" If she 's found out," argued the tempter, " she 'll come back to her mother, and you can see her every day."

But Frank's love was not of the selfish kind. He put temptation aside, and applied the whip to the back of his mule with a vigor that astonished the animal and moved him to unwonted activity. In an unusually short space of time he drew up before Mis' Molly's back gate, sprang from the cart, and ran up to Mis' Molly on the porch.

" Is Miss Rena here? " he demanded breathlessly.

" No, Frank; she went up town 'bout an hour ago to see the doctor an' git me some camphor gum."

Frank uttered a groan, rushed from the house, sprang into the cart, and goaded the terrified mule into a gallop that carried him back.to the market-house in half the time it had taken him to reach Mis' Molly's.

" I wonder what in the worl' 's the matter with Frank," mused Mis' Molly, in vague alarm. " Ef he had n't be'n in such a hurry, I 'd 'a' axed him to read Judge Straight's letter. But Rena 'll be home soon."

When Frank reached the doctor's office, he saw Tryon seated in the doctor's buggy, which was standing by the window of the drugstore. Frank ran upstairs and asked the doctor's man if Miss Walden had been there.

"Yas," replied Dave, " she wuz here a little w'ile ago, an' said she wuz gwine downstairs ter de drugsto'. I would n' be s'prise' ef you 'd fin' her dere now."

XV

THE drive by which Dr. Green took Tryon to
his own house led up Front Street about a mile, to
the most aristocratic portion of the town, situated
on the hill known as Haymount, or, more briefly,
" The Hill." The Hill had lost some of its former
glory, however, for the blight of a four years' war
was everywhere. After reaching the top of this
wooded eminence, the road skirted for some little
distance the brow of the hill. Below them lay the
picturesque old town, a mass of vivid green, dotted
here and there with gray roofs that rose above the
tree-tops. Two long ribbons of streets stretched
away from the Hill to the faint red line that marked
the high bluff beyond the river at the farther side
of the town. The market-house tower and the
slender spires of half a dozen churches were sharply
outlined against the green background. The face
of the clock was visible, but the hours could have
been read only by eyes of phenomenal sharpness.
Around them stretched ruined walls, dismantled
towers, and crumbling earthworks — footprints of
the god of war, one of whose temples had crowned
this height. For many years before the rebellion a

Federal arsenal had been located at Patesville.
Seized by the state troops upon the secession of
North Carolina, it had been held by the Confed-
erates until the approach of Sherman's victorious
army, whereupon it was evacuated and partially
destroyed. The work of destruction begun by the
retreating garrison was completed by the conquer-
ors, and now only ruined walls and broken cannon
remained of what had once been the chief ornament
and pride of Patesville.

The front of Dr. Green's spacious brick house,
which occupied an ideally picturesque site, was
overgrown by a network of clinging vines, contrasting most agreeably with the mellow red background. A low brick wall, also overrun with
creepers, separated the premises from the street
and shut in a well-kept flower garden, in which
Tryon, who knew something of plants, noticed
many rare and beautiful specimens.

Mrs. Green greeted Tryon cordially. He did
not have the doctor's memory with which to fill out
the lady's cheeks or restore the lustre of her hair
or the sparkle of her eyes, and thereby justify her
husband's claim to be a judge of beauty ; but her
kind-hearted hospitality was obvious, and might
have made even a plain woman seem handsome.
She and her two fair daughters, to whom Tryon
was duly presented, looked with much favor upon
their handsome young kinsman ; for among the
people of Patesville, perhaps by virtue of the pre-
valence of Scottish blood, the ties of blood were

cherished as things of value, and never forgotten
except in case of the unworthy — an exception, by
the way, which one need hardly go so far to seek.

The Patesville people were not exceptional in
the weaknesses and meannesses which are common
to all mankind, but for some of the finer social
qualities they were conspicuously above the average. Kindness, hospitality, loyalty, a chivalrous
deference to women, — all these things might be
found in large measure by those who saw Patesville
with the eyes of its best citizens, and accepted
their standards of politics, religion, manners, and
morals.

The doctor, after the introductions, excused
himself for a moment. Mrs. Green soon left
Tryon with the young ladies and went to look
after luncheon. Her first errand, however, was
to find the doctor.

" Is he well off, Ed ? " she asked her husband.

" Lots of land, and plenty of money, if he is
ever able to collect it. He has inherited two
estates."

" He 's a good-looking fellow," she mused.   " Is
he married ? "

" There you go again," replied her husband,
shaking his forefinger at her in mock reproach.
" To a woman with marriageable daughters all
roads lead to matrimony, the centre of a woman's
universe.   All men must be sized up by their
matrimonial availability.   No, he is n't married."

" That 's nice," she rejoined reflectively.   " I

think we ought to ask him to stay with us while he is in town, don't you?"

"He's not married," rejoined the doctor slyly, "but the next best thing — he's engaged."

"Come to think of it," said the lady, "I'm afraid we would n't have the room to spare, and the girls would hardly have time to entertain him. But we'll have him up several times. I like his looks. I wish you had sent me word he was coming; I'd have had a better luncheon."

"Make him a salad," rejoined the doctor, "and get out a bottle of the best claret. Thank God, the Yankees did n't get into my wine cellar! The young man must be treated with genuine Southern hospitality, — even if he were a Mormon and married ten times over."

"Indeed, he would not, Ed, — the idea! I'm ashamed of you. Hurry back to the parlor and talk to him. The girls may want to primp a little before luncheon; we don't have a young man every day."

"Beauty unadorned," replied the doctor, "is adorned the most. My profession qualifies me to speak upon the subject. They are the two handsomest young women in Patesville, and the daughters of the most beautiful" —

"Don't you dare to say the word," interrupted Mrs. Green, with placid good nature. "I shall never grow old while I am living with a big boy like you. But I must go and make the salad."

At dinner the conversation ran on the family

connections and their varying fortunes in the late war.   Some had died upon the battlefield, and slept in unknown graves ; some had been financially ruined by their faith in the " lost cause," having invested their all in the securities of the Confederate Government.   Few had anything left but land, and land without slaves to work it was a drug in the market.

" I was offered a thousand acres, the other day, at twenty-five cents an acre," remarked the doctor.   " The owner is so land-poor that he can't pay the taxes.   They have taken our negroes and our liberties.   It may be better for our grand-children that the negroes are free, but it's confoundedly hard on us to take them without paying for them.   They may exalt our slaves over us temporarily, but they have not broken our spirit, and cannot take away our superiority of blood and breeding.   In time we shall regain control.   The negro is an inferior creature ; God has marked him with the badge of servitude, and has adjusted his intellect to a servile condition.   We will not long submit to his domination.   I give you a toast, sir : The Anglo-Saxon race : may it remain forever, as now, the head and front of creation, never yielding its rights, and ready always to die, if need be, in defense of its liberties ! "

" With all my heart, sir," replied Tryon, who felt in this company a thrill of that pleasure which accompanies conscious superiority, — " with all my heart, sir, if the ladies will permit me,"

" We will join you," they replied. The toast
was drunk with great enthusiasm.

" And now, my dear George," exclaimed the
doctor, " to change one good subject for another,
tell us who is the favored lady ? "

" A Miss Rowena Warwick, sir," replied Tryon,
vividly conscious of four pairs of eyes fixed upon
him, but, apart from the momentary embarrassment, welcoming the subject as the one he would
most like to speak upon.

" A good, strong old English name," observed
the doctor.

" The heroine of ' Ivanhoe ' ! " exclaimed Miss
Harriet.

" Warwick the Kingmaker ! " said Miss Mary.
" Is she tall and fair, and dignified and stately ? "

" She is tall, dark rather than fair, and full of
tender grace and sweet humility."

" She should have been named Rebecca instead
of Rowena," rejoined Miss Mary, who was well up
in her Scott.

" Tell us something about her people," asked
Mrs. Green, — to which inquiry the young ladies
looked assent.

In this meeting of the elect of his own class and
kin Warwick felt a certain strong illumination
upon the value of birth and blood.   Finding Rena
among people of the best social standing, the sub-
sequent intimation that she was a girl of no family
had seemed a small matter to one so much in love.
Nevertheless, in his present company he felt a

decided satisfaction in being able to present for his future wife a clean bill of social health.

"Her brother is the most prominent lawyer of Clarence. They live in a fine old family mansion, and are among the best people of the town."

"Quite right, my boy," assented the doctor. "None but the best are good enough for the best. You must bring her to Patesville some day. But bless my life!" he exclaimed, looking at his watch, "I must be going. Will you stay with the ladies awhile, or go back down town with me?"

"I think I had better go with you, sir. I shall have to see Judge Straight."

"Very well. But you must come back to supper, and we'll have a few friends in to meet you. You must see some of the best people."

The doctor's buggy was waiting at the gate. As they were passing the hotel on their drive down town, the clerk came out to the curbstone and called to the doctor.

"There's a man here, doctor, who's been taken suddenly ill. Can you come in a minute?"

"I suppose I'll have to. Will you wait for me here, George, or will you drive down to the office? I can walk the rest of the way."

"I think I'll wait here, doctor," answered Tryon. "I'll step up to my room a moment. I'll be back by the time you're ready."

It was while they were standing before the hotel, before alighting from the buggy, that Frank Fowler, passing on his cart, saw Tryon and set out as fast as he could to warn Mis' Molly and her daughter of his presence in the town.

Tryon went up to his room, returned after a while, and resumed his seat in the buggy, where he waited fifteen minutes longer before the doctor was ready. When they drew up in front of the office, the doctor's man Dave was standing in the doorway, looking up the street with an anxious expression, as though struggling hard to keep something upon his mind.

" Anything wanted, Dave ? " asked the doctor.

" Dat young 'oman 's be'n heah ag'in, suh, an' wants ter see you bad. She 's in de drugstore dere now, suh. Bless Gawd ! " he added to himself fervently, " I 'membered dat. Dis yer recommemb'ance er mine is gwine ter git me inter trouble ef I don' look out, an' dat 's a fac', sho'."

The doctor sprang from the buggy with an agility remarkable in a man of sixty. " Just keep your seat, George," he said to Tryon, " until I have spoken to the young woman, and then we 'll go across to Straight's. Or, if you 'll drive along a little farther, you can see the girl through the window. She 's worth the trouble, if you like a pretty face."

Tryon liked one pretty face; moreover, tinted beauty had never appealed to him. More to show a proper regard for what interested the doctor than from any curiosity of his own, he drove forward a few feet, until the side of the buggy was opposite the drugstore window, and then looked in.

Between the colored glass bottles in the window he could see a young woman, a tall and slender girl, like a lily on its stem. She stood talking with the doctor, who held his hat in his hand with as much deference as though she were the proudest dame in town. Her face was partly turned away from the window, but as Tryon's eye fell upon her, he gave a great start. Surely, no two women could be so much alike. The height, the graceful droop of the shoulders, the swan-like poise of the head, the well-turned little ear, — surely, no two women could have them all identical! But, pshaw! the notion was absurd, it was merely the reflex influence of his morning's dream.

She moved slightly; it was Rena's movement. Surely he knew the gown, and the style of hair-dressing! She rested her hand lightly on the back of a chair. The ring that glittered on her finger could be none other than his own.

The doctor bowed. The girl nodded in response, and, turning, left the store. Tryon leaned forward from the buggy-seat and kept his eye fixed on the figure that moved across the floor of the drugstore. As she came out, she turned her face casually toward the buggy, and there could no longer be any doubt as to her identity.

When Rena's eyes fell upon the young man in the buggy, she saw a face as pale as death, with starting eyes, in which love, which once had reigned there, had now given place to astonishment and horror. She stood a moment as if turned to

stone.   One appealing glance she gave, — a look
that might have softened adamant.   When she
saw that it brought no answering sign of love or
sorrow or regret, the color faded from her cheek,
the light from her eye, and she fell fainting to the
ground.

XVI

THE BOTTOM FALLS OUT

THE first effect of Tryon's discovery was, figuratively speaking, to knock the bottom out of things for him. It was much as if a boat on which he had been floating smoothly down the stream of pleasure had sunk suddenly and left him struggling in deep waters. The full realization of the truth, which followed speedily, had for the moment reversed his mental attitude toward her, and love and yearning had given place to anger and disgust. His agitation could hardly have escaped notice had not the doctor's attention, and that of the crowd that quickly gathered, been absorbed by the young woman who had fallen. During the time occupied in carrying her into the drugstore, restoring her to consciousness, and sending her home in a carriage, Tryon had time to recover in some degree his self-possession. When Rena had been taken home, he slipped away for a long walk, after which he called at Judge Straight's office and received the judge's report upon the matter presented. Judge Straight had found the claim, in his opinion, a good one; he had discovered property from which, in case the claim were allowed, the amount might be realized. The judge, who had already been informed of the incident at the drugstore, observed Tryon's preoccupation and guessed shrewdly at its cause, but gave no sign. Tryon left the matter of the note unreservedly in the lawyer's hands, with instructions to communicate to him any further developments.

Returning to the doctor's office, Tryon listened to that genial gentleman's comments on the accident, his own concern in which he, by a great effort, was able to conceal. The doctor insisted upon his returning to the Hill for supper. Tryon pleaded illness. The doctor was solicitous, felt his pulse, examined his tongue, pronounced him feverish, and prescribed a sedative. Tryon sought refuge in his room at the hotel, from which he did not emerge again until morning.

His emotions were varied and stormy. At first he could see nothing but the fraud of which he had been made the victim. A negro girl had been foisted upon him for a white woman, and he had almost committed the unpardonable sin against his race of marrying her. Such a step, he felt, would have been criminal at any time; it would have been the most odious treachery at this epoch, when his people had been subjugated and humiliated by the Northern invaders, who had preached negro equality and abolished the wholesome laws decreeing the separation of the races. But no Southerner who loved his poor, downtrodden country, or his race, the proud Anglo-Saxon race which traced

the clear stream of its blood to the cavaliers of
England, could tolerate the idea that even in distant generations that unsullied current could be
polluted by the blood of slaves. The very thought
was an insult to the white people of the South.
For Tryon's liberality, of which he had spoken so
nobly and so sincerely, had been confined unconsciously, and as a matter of course, within the boundaries of his own race. The Southern mind, in
discussing abstract questions relative to humanity,
makes always, consciously or unconsciously, the
mental reservation that the conclusions reached do
not apply to the negro, unless they can be made to
harmonize with the customs of the country.

But reasoning thus was not without effect upon
a mind by nature reasonable above the average.
Tryon's race impulse and social prejudice had
carried him too far, and the swing of the mental
pendulum brought his thoughts rapidly back in
the opposite direction. Tossing uneasily on the
bed, where he had thrown himself down without
undressing, the air of the room oppressed him, and
he threw open the window. The cool night air
calmed his throbbing pulses. The moonlight,
streaming through the window, flooded the room
with a soft light, in which he seemed to see Rena
standing before him, as she had appeared that
afternoon, gazing at him with eyes that implored
charity and forgiveness. He burst into tears, —
bitter tears, that strained his heartstrings. He
was only a youth. She was his first love, and he

had lost her forever. She was worse than dead
to him; for if he had seen her lying in her shroud
before him, he could at least have cherished her
memory; now, even this consolation was denied
him.

The town clock — which so long as it was wound
up regularly recked nothing of love or hate, joy or
sorrow — solemnly tolled out the hour of midnight
and sounded the knell of his lost love. Lost she
was, as though she had never been, as she had
indeed had no right to be. He resolutely determined to banish her image from his mind. See
her again he could not; it would be painful to
them both; it could be productive of no good to
either. He had felt the power and charm of love,
and no ordinary shock could have loosened its
hold; but this catastrophe, which had so rudely
swept away the groundwork of his passion, had
stirred into new life all the slumbering pride of
race and ancestry which characterized his caste.
How much of this sensitive superiority was essen-
tial and how much accidental; how much of it
was due to the ever-suggested comparison with a
servile race; how much of it was ignorance and
self-conceit; to what extent the boasted purity of
his race would have been contaminated by the fair
woman whose image filled his memory, — of these
things he never thought. He was not influenced
by sordid considerations; he would have denied
that his course was controlled by any narrow prudence. If Rena had been white, pure white (for

in his creed there was no compromise), he would have braved any danger for her sake. Had she been merely of illegitimate birth, he would have overlooked the bar sinister. Had her people been simply poor and of low estate, he would have brushed aside mere worldly considerations, and would have bravely sacrificed convention for love ; for his liberality was not a mere form of words. But the one objection which he could not overlook was, unhappily, the one that applied to the only woman who had as yet moved his heart. He tried to be angry with her, but after the first hour he found it impossible. He was a man of too much imagination not to be able to put himself, in some measure at least, in her place, — to perceive that for her the step which had placed her in Tryon's world was the working out of nature's great law of self-preservation, for which he could not blame her. But for the sheerest accident, — no, rather, but for a providential interference, — he would have married her, and might have gone to the grave unconscious that she was other than she seemed.

The clock struck the hour of two. With a shiver he closed the window, undressed by the moonlight, drew down the shade, and went to bed. He fell into an unquiet slumber, and dreamed again of Rena. He must learn to control his waking thoughts ; his dreams could not be curbed. In that realm Rena's image was for many a day to remain supreme. He dreamed of her sweet smile, her soft touch, her gentle voice. In all her

fair young beauty she stood before him, and then
by some hellish magic she was slowly transformed
into a hideous black hag.   With agonized eyes he
watched her beautiful tresses become mere wisps
of coarse wool, wrapped round with dingy cotton
strings; he saw her clear eyes grow bloodshot,
her ivory teeth turn to unwholesome fangs.   With
a shudder he awoke, to find the cold gray dawn
of a rainy day stealing through the window.

He rose, dressed himself, went down to breakfast, then entered the writing-room and penned a
letter which, after reading it over, he tore into
small pieces and threw into the waste-basket.   A
second shared the same fate.   Giving up the task,
he left the hotel and walked down to Dr. Green's
office.

"Is the doctor in?" he asked of the colored
attendant.

"No, suh," replied the man; "he's gone ter see
de young cullud gal w'at fainted w'en de doctuh
was wid you yistiddy."

Tryon sat down at the doctor's desk and hastily
scrawled a note, stating that business compelled
his immediate departure.   He thanked the doctor
for courtesies extended, and left his regards for
the ladies.   Returning. to the hotel, he paid his
bill and took a hack for the wharf, from which a
boat was due to leave at nine o'clock.

As the hack drove down Front Street, Tryon
noted idly the houses that lined the street.   When
he reached the sordid district in the lower part of

the town, there was nothing to attract his attention until the carriage came abreast of a row of cedar-trees, beyond which could be seen the upper part of a large house with dormer windows. Before the gate stood a horse and buggy, which Tryon thought he recognized as Dr. Green's. He leaned forward and addressed the driver.

"Can you tell me who lives there?" Tryon asked, pointing to the house.

"A cullud 'oman, suh," the man replied, touching his hat. "Mis' Molly Walden an' her daughter Rena."

The vivid impression he received of this house, and the spectre that rose before him of a pale, broken-hearted girl within its gray walls, weeping for a lost lover and a vanished dream of happiness, did not argue well for Tryon's future peace of mind. Rena's image was not to be easily expelled from his heart; for the laws of nature are higher and more potent than merely human institutions, and upon anything like a fair field are likely to win in the long run.

XVII

WARWICK awaited events with some calmness and some philosophy, — he could hardly have had the one without the other; and it required much philosophy to make him wait a week in patience for information upon a subject in which he was so vitally interested. The delay pointed to disaster. Bad news being expected, delay at least put off the evil day. At the end of the week he received two letters, — one addressed in his own handwriting and postmarked Patesville, N. C.; the other in the handwriting of George Tryon. He opened the Patesville letter, which ran as follows: —

MY DEAR SON, — Frank is writing this letter for me. I am not well, but, thank the Lord, I am better than I was.

Rena has had a heap of trouble on account of me and my sickness. If I could of dreamt that I was going to do so much harm, I would of died and gone to meet my God without writing one word to spoil my girl's chances in life; but I did n't know what was going to happen, and I hope the Lord will forgive me.

Frank knows all about it, and so I am having him write this letter for me, as Rena is not well enough yet. Frank has been very good to me and to Rena. He was down to your place and saw Rena there, and never said a word about it to nobody, not even to me, because he did n't want to do Rena no harm. Frank is the best friend I have got in town, because he does so much for me and don't want nothing in return. (He tells me not to put this in about him, but I want you to know it.)

And now about Rena. She come to see me, and I got better right away, for it was longing for her as much as anything else that made me sick, and I was mighty mizzable. When she had been here three days and was going back next day, she went up town to see the doctor for me, and while she was up there she fainted and fell down in the street, and Dr. Green sent her home in his buggy and come down to see her. He could n't tell what was the matter with her, but she has been sick ever since and out of her head some of the time, and keeps on calling on somebody by the name of George, which was the young white man she told me she was going to marry. It seems he was in town the day Rena was took sick, for Frank saw him up street and run all the way down here to tell me, so that she could keep out of his way, while she was still up town waiting for the doctor and getting me some camphor gum for my camphor bottle. Old Judge Straight must have knowed something about

it, for he sent me a note to keep Rena in the house,
but the little boy he sent it by did n't bring it till
Rena was already gone up town, and, as I could n't
read, of course I did n't know what it said. Dr.
Green heard Rena running on while she was out of
her head, and I reckon he must have suspicioned
something, for he looked kind of queer and went
away without saying nothing. Frank says she met
this man on the street, and when he found out she
was n't white, he said or done something that broke
her heart and she fainted and fell down.

I am writing you this letter because I know you
will be worrying about Rena not coming back. If
it was n't for Frank, I hardly know how I could
write to you. Frank is not going to say nothing
about Rena's passing for white and meeting this
man, and neither am I ; and I don't suppose Judge
Straight will say nothing, because he is our good
friend ; and Dr. Green won't say nothing about it,
because Frank says Dr. Green's cook Nancy says
this young man named George stopped with him
and was some cousin or relation to the family, and
they would n't want people to know that any of their
kin was thinking about marrying a colored girl,
and the white folks have all been mad since J. B.
Thompson married his black housekeeper when she
got religion and would n't live with him no more.

All the rest of the connection are well. I have
just been in to see how Rena is. She is feeling
some better, I think, and says give you her love
and she will write you a letter in a few days, as

soon as she is well enough.   She bust out crying
while she was talking, but I reckon that is better
than being out of her head.   I hope this may find
you well, and that this man of Rena's won't say
nor do nothing down there to hurt you.   He has
not wrote to Rena nor sent her no word.   I reckon
he is very mad.

Your affectionate mother,
MARY WALDEN.

This letter, while confirming Warwick's fears,
relieved his suspense.   He at least knew the worst,
unless there should be something still more disturb-
ing in Tryon's letter, which he now proceeded to
open, and which ran as follows : —

JOHN WARWICK, ESQ.

Dear Sir, — When I inform you, as you are
doubtless informed ere the receipt of this, that I
saw your sister in Patesville last week and learned
the nature of those antecedents of yours and hers
at which you hinted so obscurely in a recent conversation, you will not be surprised to learn that
I take this opportunity of renouncing any pretensions to Miss Warwick's hand, and request you to
convey this message to her, since it was through
you that I formed her acquaintance.   I think perhaps that few white men would deem it necessary
to make an explanation under the circumstances,
and I do not know that I need say more than
that no one, considering where and how I met your

sister, would have dreamed of even the possibility of what I have learned. I might with justice reproach you for trifling with the most sacred feelings of a man's heart; but I realize the hardship of your position and hers, and can make allowances. I would never have sought to know this thing; I would doubtless have been happier had I gone through life without finding it out; but having the knowledge, I cannot ignore it, as you must understand perfectly well. I regret that she should be distressed or disappointed, — she has not suffered alone.

I need scarcely assure you that I shall say nothing about this affair, and that I shall keep your secret as though it were my own. Personally, I shall never be able to think of you as other than a white man, as you may gather from the tone of this letter; and while I cannot marry your sister, I wish her every happiness, and remain,

Yours very truly,

GEORGE TRYON.

Warwick could not know that this formal epistle was the last of a dozen that Tryon had written and destroyed during the week since the meeting in Patesville, — hot, blistering letters, cold, cutting letters, scornful, crushing letters. Though none of them was sent, except this last, they had furnished a safety-valve for his emotions, and had left him in a state of mind that permitted him to write the foregoing.

And now, while Rena is recovering from her illness, and Tryon from his love, and while Fate is shuffling the cards for another deal, a few words may be said about the past life of the people who lived in the rear of the flower garden, in the quaint old house beyond the cedars, and how their lives were mingled with those of the men and women around them and others that were gone. For connected with our kind we must be; if not by our virtues, then by our vices, — if not by our services, at least by our needs.

XVIII

UNDER THE OLD REGIME

For many years before the civil war there had
lived, in the old house behind the cedars, a free
colored woman who went by the name of Molly
Walden — her rightful name, for her parents
were free-born and legally married. She was a tall
woman, straight as an arrow. Her complexion in
youth was of an old ivory tint, which at the period
of this story, time had darkened measurably. Her
black eyes, now faded, had once sparkled with the
fire of youth. High cheek-bones, straight black
hair, and a certain dignified reposefulness of manner pointed to an aboriginal descent. Tradition
gave her to the negro race. Doubtless she had a
strain of each, with white blood very visibly pre-
dominating over both. In Louisiana or the West
Indies she would have been called a quadroon, or
more loosely, a creole; in North Carolina, where
fine distinctions were not the rule in matters
of color, she was sufficiently differentiated when
described as a bright mulatto.

Molly's free birth carried with it certain advantages, even in the South before the war. Though
degraded from its high estate, and shorn of its

choicest attributes, the word " freedom " had
nevertheless a cheerful sound, and described a condition that left even to colored people who could
claim it some liberty of movement and some control of their own persons.   They were not citizens,
yet they were not slaves.   No negro, save in books,
ever refused freedom ; many of them ran frightful
risks to achieve it.   Molly's parents were of the
class, more numerous in North Carolina than elsewhere, known as " old issue free negroes," which
took its rise in the misty colonial period, when race
lines were not so closely drawn, and the population
of North Carolina comprised many Indians, run-
away negroes, and indentured white servants from
the seaboard plantations, who mingled their blood
with great freedom and small formality.   Free
colored people in North Carolina exercised the
right of suffrage as late as 1835, and some of them,
in spite of galling restrictions, attained to a considerable degree of prosperity, and dreamed of a
still brighter future, when the growing tyranny of
the slave power crushed their hopes and crowded
the free people back upon the black mass just
beneath them.   Mis' Molly's father had been at
one time a man of some means.   In an evil hour,
with an overweening confidence in his fellow men,
he indorsed a note for a white man who, in a
moment of financial hardship, clapped his colored
neighbor on the back and called him brother.   Not
poverty, but wealth, is the most potent leveler.
In due time the indorser was called upon to meet

the maturing obligation. This was the beginning
of a series of financial difficulties which speedily
involved him in ruin. He died prematurely, a disappointed and disheartened man, leaving his family
in dire poverty.

His widow and surviving children lived on for
a little while at the house he had owned, just outside of the town, on one of the main traveled roads.
By the wayside, near the house, there was a famous
deep well. The slim, barefoot girl, with sparkling
eyes and voluminous hair, who played about the
yard and sometimes handed water in a gourd to
travelers, did not long escape critical observation.
A gentleman drove by one day, stopped at the
well, smiled upon the girl, and said kind words. He
came again, more than once, and soon, while
scarcely more than a child in years, Molly was
living in her own house, hers by deed of gift, for
her protector was rich and liberal. Her mother
nevermore knew want. Her poor relations could
always find a meal in Molly's kitchen. She did
not flaunt her prosperity in the world's face; she
hid it discreetly behind the cedar screen. Those
who wished could know of it, for there were few
secrets in Patesville; those who chose could as
easily ignore it. There were few to trouble themselves about the secluded life of an obscure woman
of a class which had no recognized place in the
social economy. She worshiped the ground upon
which her lord walked, was humbly grateful for
his protection, and quite as faithful as the forbidden

marriage vow could possibly have made her.   She
led her life in material peace and comfort, and
with a certain amount of dignity.   Of her false
relation to society she was not without some
vague conception ; but the moral point involved
was so confused with other questions growing out
of slavery and caste as to cause her, as a rule, but
little uneasiness ; and only now and then, in the
moments of deeper feeling that come sometimes to
all who live and love, did there break through the
mists of ignorance and prejudice surrounding her
a flash of light by which she saw, so far as she
was capable of seeing, her true position, which in
the clear light of truth no special pleading could
entirely justify.   For she was free, she had not
the slave's excuse.   With every inducement to do
evil and few incentives to do well, and hence
entitled to charitable judgment, she yet had freedom of choice, and therefore could not wholly escape blame.   Let it be said, in further extenuation,
that no other woman lived in neglect or sorrow
because of her.   She robbed no one else.   For
what life gave her she returned an equivalent ; and
what she did not pay, her children settled to the
last farthing.

Several years before the war, when Mis' Molly's
daughter Rena was a few years old, death had
suddenly removed the source of their prosperity.

The household was not left entirely destitute.
Mis' Molly owned her home, and had a store of
gold pieces in the chest beneath her bed.   A small

WHAT HAS SHE BEEN ROBBED OF ?
HISTORY, NAME, PATRIMONY

piece of real estate stood in the name of each of
the children, the income from which contributed to
their maintenance.   Larger expectations were de-
pendent upon the discovery of a promised will,
which never came to light.   Mis' Molly wore black
for several years after this bereavement, until the
teacher and the preacher, following close upon the
heels of military occupation, suggested to the colored people new standards of life and character, in
the light of which Mis' Molly laid her mourning
sadly and shamefacedly aside.   She had eaten of
the fruit of the Tree of Knowledge.   After the war
she formed the, habit of church-going, and might
have been seen now and then, with her daughter, in
a retired corner of the gallery of the white Episco-
pal church.   Upon the ground floor was a certain
pew which could be seen from her seat, where once
had sat a gentleman whose pleasures had not interfered with the practice of his religion.   She might
have had a better seat in a church where a Northern
missionary would have preached a sermon better
suited to her comprehension and her moral needs,
but she preferred the other.   She was not white,
alas ! she was shut out from this seeming paradise ;
but she liked to see the distant glow of the celestial
city, and to recall the days when she had basked in
its radiance.   She did not sympathize greatly with
the new era opened up for the emancipated slaves ;
she had no ideal love of liberty ; she was no broader
and no more altruistic than the white people around
her, to whom she had always looked up ; and she

sighed for the old days, because to her they had been the good days. Now, not only was her king dead, but the shield of his memory protected her no longer.

Molly had lost one child, and his grave was visible from the kitchen window, under a small clump of cedars in the rear of the two-acre lot. For even in the towns many a household had its private cemetery in those old days when the living were close to the dead, and ghosts were not the mere chimeras of a sick imagination, but real though unsubstantial entities, of which it was almost disgraceful not to have seen one or two. Had not the Witch of Endor called up the shade of Samuel the prophet? Had not the spirit of Mis' Molly's dead son appeared to her, as well as the ghostly presence of another she had loved?

In 1855, Mis' Molly's remaining son had grown into a tall, slender lad of fifteen, with his father's patrician features and his mother's Indian hair, and no external sign to mark him off from the white boys on the street. He soon came to know, however, that there was a difference. He was informed one day that he was black. He denied the proposition and thrashed the child who made it. The scene was repeated the next day, with a variation, — he was himself thrashed by a larger boy. When he had been beaten five or six times, he ceased to argue the point, though to himself he never admitted the charge. His playmates might call him black ; the mirror proved that God, the

Father of all, had made him white ; and God, he had been taught, made no mistakes, — having made him white, He must have meant him to be white.

In the " hall " or parlor of his mother's house stood a quaintly carved black walnut bookcase, containing a small but remarkable collection of books, which had at one time been used, in his hours of retreat and relaxation from business and politics, by the distinguished gentleman who did not give his name to Mis' Molly's children, — to whom it would have been a valuable heritage, could they have had the right to bear it. Among the books were a volume of Fielding's complete works, in fine print, set in double columns ; a set of Bulwer's novels ; a collection of everything that Walter Scott — the literary idol of the South — had ever written ; Beaumont and Fletcher's plays, cheek by jowl with the history of the virtuous Clarissa Harlowe ; the Spectator and Tristram Shandy, Robinson Crusoe and the Arabian Nights. On these secluded shelves Roderick Random, Don Quixote, and Gil Blas for a long time ceased their wanderings, the Pilgrim's Progress was suspended, Milton's mighty harmonies were dumb, and Shakespeare reigned over a silent kingdom. An illustrated Bible, with a wonderful Apocrypha, was flanked on one side by Volney's Ruins of Empire and on the other by Paine's Age of Reason, for the collector of the books had been a man of catholic taste as well as of inquiring mind, and no one who could have criticised his reading ever penetrated behind the cedar hedge. A history of the French Revolution consorted amiably with a homespun chronicle of North Carolina, rich in biographical notices of distinguished citizens and inscriptions from their tombstones, upon reading which one might well wonder why North Carolina had not long ago eclipsed the rest of the world in wealth, wisdom, glory, and renown. On almost every page of this monumental work could be found the most ardent panegyrics of liberty, side by side with the slavery statistics of the State, — an incongruity of which the learned author was deliciously unconscious.

When John Walden was yet a small boy, he had learned all that could be taught by the faded mulatto teacher in the long, shiny black frock coat, whom local public opinion permitted to teach a handful of free colored children for a pittance barely enough to keep soul and body together. When the boy had learned to read, he discovered the library, which for several years had been without a reader, and found in it the portal of a new world, peopled with strange and marvelous beings. Lying prone upon the floor of the shaded front piazza, behind the fragrant garden, he followed the fortunes of Tom Jones and Sophia; he wept over the fate of Eugene Aram; he penetrated with Richard the Lion-heart into Saladin's tent, with Gil Blas into the robbers' cave; he flew through the air on the magic carpet or the enchanted horse, or tied with Sindbad to the roc's leg. Sometimes

he read or repeated the simpler stories to his little
sister, sitting wide-eyed by his side.   When he had
read all the books, — indeed, long before he had
read them all, — he too had tasted of the fruit of
the Tree of Knowledge : contentment took its flight,
and happiness lay far beyond the sphere where
he was born.   The blood of his white fathers, the
heirs of the ages, cried out for its own, and after
the manner of that blood set about getting the
object of its desire.

Near the corner of Mackenzie Street, just one
block north of the Patesville market-house, there
had stood for many years before the war, on the
verge of the steep bank of Beaver Creek, a small
frame office building, the front of which was level
with the street, while the rear rested on long brick
pillars founded on the solid rock at the edge of the
brawling stream below.   Here, for nearly half a
century, Archibald Straight had transacted legal
business for the best people of Northumberland
County.   Full many a lawsuit had he won, lost, or
settled ; many a spendthrift had he saved from
ruin, and not a few families from disgrace.   Several times honored by election to the bench, he
had so dispensed justice tempered with mercy as
to win the hearts of all good citizens, and especially those of the poor, the oppressed, and the
socially disinherited.   The rights of the humblest
negro, few as they might be, were as sacred to
him as those of the proudest aristocrat, and he
had sentenced a man to be hanged for the murder

of his own slave. An old-fashioned man, tall and
spare of figure and bowed somewhat with age, he
was always correctly clad in a long frock coat of
broadcloth, with a high collar and a black stock.
Courtly in address to his social equals (superiors
he had none), he was kind and considerate to
those beneath him. He owned a few domestic
servants, no one of whom had ever felt the weight
of his hand, and for whose ultimate freedom he
had provided in his will. In the long-drawn-out
slavery agitation he had taken a keen interest,
rather as observer than as participant. As the heat
of controversy increased, his lack of zeal for the
peculiar institution led to his defeat for the bench
by a more active partisan. His was too just a
mind not to perceive the arguments on both sides ;
but, on the whole, he had stood by the ancient
landmarks, content to let events drift to a conclusion he did not expect to see ; the institutions of
his fathers would probably last his lifetime.

One day Judge Straight was sitting in his
office reading a recently published pamphlet, — pre-
senting an elaborate pro-slavery argument, based
upon the hopeless intellectual inferiority of the
negro, and the physical and moral degeneration
of mulattoes, who combined the worst qualities of
their two ancestral races, — when a barefooted boy
walked into the office, straw hat in hand, came
boldly up to the desk at which the old judge was
sitting, and said as the judge looked up through
his gold-rimmed glasses, —

"Sir, I want to be a lawyer!"

"God bless me!" exclaimed the judge. "It is a singular desire, from a singular source, and expressed in a singular way. Who the devil are you, sir, that wish so strange a thing as to become a lawyer — everybody's servant?"

"And everybody's master, sir," replied the lad stoutly.

"That is a matter of opinion, and open to argument," rejoined the judge, amused and secretly flattered by this tribute to his profession, "though there may be a grain of truth in what you say. But what is your name, Mr. Would-be-lawyer?"

"John Walden, sir," answered the lad.

"John Walden? — Walden?" mused the judge. "What Walden can that be? Do you belong in town?"

"Yes, sir."

"Humph! I can't imagine who you are. It's plain that you are a lad of good blood, and yet I don't know whose son you can be. What is your father's name?"

The lad hesitated, and flushed crimson.

The old gentleman noted his hesitation. "It is a wise son," he thought, "that knows his own father. He is a bright lad, and will have this question put to him more than once. I'll see how he will answer it."

The boy maintained an awkward silence, while the old judge eyed him keenly.

"My father's dead," he said at length, in a low

voice. " I 'm Mis' Molly Walden's son." He
had expected, of course, to tell who he was, if
asked, but had not foreseen just the form of the
inquiry; and while he had thought more of his
race than of his illegitimate birth, he realized at
this moment as never before that this question too
would be always with him. As put now by Judge
Straight, it made him wince. He had not read his
father's books for nothing.

" God bless my soul ! " exclaimed the judge in
genuine surprise at this answer ; " and you want
to be a lawyer ! "   The situation was so much
worse than he had suspected that even an old
practitioner, case-hardened by years of life at the
trial table and on the bench, was startled for a
moment into a comical sort of consternation, so
apparent that a lad less stout-hearted would have
weakened and fled at the sight of it.

" Yes, sir. Why not ? " responded the boy,
trembling a little at the knees, but stoutly holding
his ground.

" He wants to be a lawyer, and he asks me why
not ! " muttered the judge, speaking apparently to
himself. He rose from his chair, walked across
the room, and threw open a window. The cool
morning air brought with it the babbling of the
stream below and the murmur of the mill near by.
He glanced across the creek to the ruined foundation of an old house on the low ground beyond the
creek. Turning from the window, he looked back
at the boy, who had remained standing between

him and the door.   At that moment another lad
came along the street and stopped opposite the
open doorway.   The presence of the two boys in
connection with the book he had been reading
suggested a comparison.   The judge knew the lad
outside as the son of a leading merchant of the
town.   The merchant and his wife were both of
old families which had lived in the community
for several generations, and whose blood was
presumably of the purest strain; yet the boy
was sallow, with amorphous features, thin shanks,
and stooping shoulders.   The youth standing in
the judge's office, on the contrary, was straight,
shapely, and well-grown.   His eye was clear, and
he kept it fixed on the old gentleman with a look
in which there was nothing of cringing.   He was
no darker than many a white boy bronzed by the
Southern sun; his hair and eyes were black, and
his features of the high-bred, clean-cut order that
marks the patrician type the world over.   What
struck the judge most forcibly, however, was the
lad's resemblance to an old friend and companion
and client.   He recalled a certain conversation
with this old friend, who had said to him one day:

"Archie, I'm coming in to have you draw my
will.   There are some children for whom I would
like to make ample provision.   I can't give them
anything else, but money will make them free of
the world."

The judge's friend had died suddenly before
carrying out this good intention.   The judge had

— REVERSAL;
COINCIDENCE

HIS PATRIMONY — CAN'T GAVE THEM NAME, STANDING, STATUS

taken occasion to suggest the existence of these
children, and their father's intentions concerning
them, to the distant relatives who had inherited
his friend's large estate.   They had chosen to take
offense at the suggestion.   One had thought it in
shocking bad taste ; another considered any mention of such a subject an insult to his cousin's
memory.   A third had said, with flashing eyes, that
the woman and her children had already robbed
the estate of enough ; that it was a pity the little
niggers were not slaves — that they would have
added measurably to the value of the property.
Judge Straight's manner indicated some disapproval
of their attitude, and the settlement of the estate
was placed in other hands than his.   Now, this son,
with his father's face and his father's voice, stood
before his father's friend, demanding entrance to
the golden gate of opportunity, which society barred
to all who bore the blood of the despised race.

As he kept on looking at the boy, who began at
length to grow somewhat embarrassed under this
keen scrutiny, the judge's mind reverted to certain
laws and judicial decisions that he had looked up
once or twice in his lifetime.   Even the law, the
instrument by which tyranny riveted the chains
upon its victims, had revolted now and then against
the senseless and unnatural prejudice by which a
race ascribing its superiority to right of blood
permitted a mere suspicion of servile blood to out-
weigh a vast preponderance of its own.

" Why, indeed, should he not be a lawyer, or

anything else that a man might be, if it be in him?"
asked the judge, speaking rather to himself than
to the boy. "Sit down," he ordered, pointing to
a chair on the other side of the room. That he
should ask a colored lad to be seated in his presence
was of itself enough to stamp the judge as eccentric.
"You want to be a lawyer," he went on, adjusting
his spectacles. "You are aware, of course, that
you are a negro?"

"I am white," replied the lad, turning back his
sleeve and holding out his arm, "and I am free, as
all my people were before me."

The old lawyer shook his head, and fixed his eyes
upon the lad with a slightly quizzical smile. "You
are black," he said, "and you are not free. You
cannot travel without your papers; you cannot
secure accommodations at an inn; you could not
vote, if you were of age; you cannot be out after
nine o'clock without a permit. If a white man
struck you, you could not return the blow, and you
could not testify against him in a court of justice.
You are black, my lad, and you are not free. Did
you ever hear of the Dred Scott decision, delivered
by the great, wise, and learned Judge Taney?"

"No, sir," answered the boy.

"It is too long to read," rejoined the judge,
taking up the pamphlet he had laid down upon the
lad's entrance, "but it says in substance, as quoted
by this author, that negroes are beings 'of an
inferior order, and altogether unfit to associate
with the white race, either in social or political

relations; in fact, so inferior that they have no rights which the white man is bound to respect, and that the negro may justly and lawfully be reduced to slavery for his benefit.' That is the law of this nation, and that is the reason why you cannot be a lawyer."

"It may all be true," replied the boy, "but it don't apply to me. It says ' the negro.' A negro is black; I am white, and not black."

"Black as ink, my lad," returned the lawyer, shaking his head. " ' One touch of nature makes the whole world kin,' says the poet. Somewhere, sometime, you had a black ancestor. One drop of black blood makes the whole man black."

" Why should n't it be the other way, if the white blood is so much superior?" inquired the lad.

"Because it is more convenient as it is — and more profitable."

"It is not right," maintained the lad.

"God bless me!" exclaimed the old gentleman, "he is invading the field of ethics! He will be questioning the righteousness of slavery next! I 'm afraid you would n't make a good lawyer, in any event. Lawyers go by the laws — they abide by the accomplished fact; to them, whatever is, is right. The laws do not permit men of color to practice law, and public sentiment would not allow one of them to study it."

"I had thought," said the lad, "that I might pass for white. There are white people darker than I am."

" Ah, well, that is another matter ; but "—

The judge stopped for a moment, struck by the absurdity of his arguing such a question with a mulatto boy. He really must be falling into premature dotage. The proper thing would be to rebuke the lad for his presumption and advise him to learn to take care of horses, or make boots, or lay bricks. But again he saw his old friend in the lad's face, and again he looked in vain for any sign of negro blood. The least earmark would have turned the scale, but he could not find it.

" That is another matter," he repeated. " Here you have started as black, and must remain so. But if you wish to move away, and sink your past into oblivion, the case might be different. Let us see what the law is ; you might not need it if you went far enough, but it is well enough to be within it — liberty is sweeter when founded securely on the law."

He took down a volume bound in legal calf and glanced through it. " The color line is drawn in North Carolina at four generations removed from the negro ; there have been judicial decisions to that effect. I imagine that would cover your case. But let us see what South Carolina may say about it," he continued, taking another book. " I think the law is even more liberal there. Ah, this is the place : —

" ' The term mulatto,' " he read, " ' is not invariably applicable to every admixture of African blood with the European, nor is one having all the features

of a white to be ranked with the degraded class
designated by the laws of this State as persons of
color, because of some remote taint of the negro
race. Juries would probably be justified in holding a person to be white in whom the admixture
of African blood did not exceed one eighth. And
even where color or feature are doubtful, it is a
question for the jury to decide by reputation, by
reception into society, and by their exercise of the
privileges of the white man, as well as by admixture
of blood.' "

"Then I need not be black?" the boy cried,
with sparkling eyes.

"No," replied the lawyer, "you need not be
black, away from Patesville. You have the somewhat unusual privilege, it seems, of choosing
between two races, and if you are a lad of spirit,
as I think you are, it will not take you long to make
your choice. As you have all the features of a
white man, you would, at least in South Carolina,
have simply to assume the place and exercise the
privileges of a white man. You might, of course,
do the same thing anywhere, as long as no one knew
your origin. But the matter has been adjudicated
there in several cases, and on the whole I think
South Carolina is the place for you. They're more
liberal there, perhaps because they have many
more blacks than whites, and would like to lessen
the disproportion."

"From this time on," said the boy, "I am white."

"Softly, softly, my Caucasian fellow citizen,"

returned the judge, chuckling with quiet amusement. " You are white in the abstract, before the
law. You may cherish the fact in secret, but I
would not advise you to proclaim it openly just
yet. You must wait until you go away — to South
Carolina."

" And can I learn to be a lawyer, sir ? " asked
the lad.

" It seems to me that you ought to be reason-
ably content for one day with what you have
learned already. You cannot be a lawyer until
you are white, in position as well as in theory, nor
until you are twenty-one years old. I need an
office boy. If you are willing to come into my
office, sweep it, keep my books dusted, and stay
here when I am out, I do not care. To the rest
of the town you will be my servant, and still a
negro. If you choose to read my books when no
one is about and be white in your own private
opinion, I have no objection. When you have
made up your mind to go away, perhaps what you
have read may help you. But mum's the word !
If I hear a whisper of this from any other source,
out you go, neck and crop ! I am willing to help
you make a man of yourself, but it can only be
done under the rose."

For two years John Walden openly swept the
office and surreptitiously read the law books of old
Judge Straight. When he was eighteen, he asked
his mother for a sum of money, kissed her good-
by, and went out into the world. When his sis-

WHAT DOES IT MEAN TO BE WHITE?
    (1) POWER
    (2) PRESTIGE
    (3) PRIVELEDGE

ter, then a pretty child of seven, cried because her big brother was going away, he took her up in his arms, gave her a silver dime with a hole in it for a keepsake, hugged her close, and kissed her.

"Nev' min', sis," he said soothingly. "Be a good little gal, an' some o' these days I'll come back to see you and bring you somethin' fine."

In after years, when Mis' Molly was asked what had become of her son, she would reply with sad complacency, —

"He's gone over on the other side."

As we have seen, he came back ten years later.

Many years before, when Mis' Molly, then a very young woman, had taken up her residence in the house behind the cedars, the gentleman heretofore referred to had built a cabin on the opposite corner, in which he had installed a trusted slave by the name of Peter Fowler and his wife Nancy. Peter was a good mechanic, and hired his time from his master with the provision that Peter and his wife should do certain work for Mis' Molly and serve as a sort of protection for her. In course of time Peter, who was industrious and thrifty, saved enough money to purchase his freedom and that of his wife and their one child, and to buy the little house across the street, with the cooper shop behind it. After they had acquired their freedom, Peter and Nancy did no work for Mis' Molly save as they were paid for it, and as a rule preferred not to work at all for the woman who had been practically their mistress; it made them seem less free. Nevertheless, the two households had remained upon good terms, even after the death of the man whose will had brought them together, and who had remained Peter's patron after he had ceased to be his master. There was no intimate association between the two families. Mis' Molly felt herself infinitely superior to Peter and his wife, — scarcely less superior than her poor white neighbors felt themselves to Mis' Molly. Mis' Molly always meant to be kind, and treated Peter and Nancy with a certain good-natured condescension. They resented this, never openly or offensively, but always in a subconscious sort of way, even when they did not speak of it among themselves — much as they had resented her mistress-ship in the old days. For after all, they argued, in spite of her airs and graces, her white face and her fine clothes, was she not a negro, even as themselves? and since the slaves had been freed, was not one negro as good as another?

Peter's son Frank had grown up with little Rena. He was several years older than she, and when Rena was a small child Mis' Molly had often confided her to his care, and he had watched over her and kept her from harm. When Frank became old enough to go to work in the cooper shop, Rena, then six or seven, had often gone across to play among the clean white shavings. Once Frank, while learning the trade, had let slip a sharp steel tool, which flying toward Rena had grazed

her arm and sent the red blood coursing along the
white flesh and soaking the muslin sleeve. He
had rolled up the sleeve and stanched the blood
and dried her tears. For a long time thereafter
her mother kept her away from the shop and was
very cold to Frank. One day the little girl wandered down to the bank of the old canal. It had
been raining for several days, and the water was
quite deep in the channel. The child slipped and
fell into the stream. From the open window of
the cooper shop Frank heard a scream. He ran
down to the canal and pulled her out, and carried
her all wet and dripping to the house. From that
time he had been restored to favor. He had
watched the girl grow up to womanhood in the
years following the war, and had been sorry when
she became too old to play about the shop.

He never spoke to her of love, — indeed, he
never thought of his passion in such a light.
There would have been no legal barrier to their
union ; there would have been no frightful menace
to white supremacy in the marriage of the negro
and the octoroon : the drop of dark blood bridged
the chasm. But Frank knew that she did not
love him, and had not hoped that she might. His
was one of those rare souls that can give with
small hope of return. When he had made the
scar upon her arm, by the same token she had
branded him her slave forever ; when he had saved
her from a watery grave, he had given his life to
her. There are depths of fidelity and devotion in

the negro heart that have never been fathomed or
fully appreciated.   Now and then in the kindlier
phases of slavery these qualities were brightly conspicuous, and in them, if wisely appealed to, lies
the strongest hope of amity between the two races
whose destiny seems bound up together in the
Western world.   Even a dumb brute can be won
by kindness.   Surely it were worth while to try
some other weapon than scorn and contumely and
hard words upon people of our common race, —
the human race, which is bigger and broader than
Celt or Saxon, barbarian or Greek, Jew or Gen-
tile, black or white; for we are all children of a
common Father, forget it as we may, and each one
of us is in some measure his brother's keeper.

XIX

GOD MADE US ALL

RENA was convalescent from a two-weeks' illness when her brother came to see her. He arrived
at Patesville by an early morning train before the
town was awake, and walked unnoticed from the
station to his mother's house. His meeting with
his sister was not without emotion: he embraced
her tenderly, and Rena became for a few minutes
a very Niobe of grief.

"Oh, it was cruel, cruel!" she sobbed. "I
shall never get over it."

"I know it, my dear," replied Warwick soothingly, — "I know it, and I'm to blame for it. If
I had never taken you away from here, you would
have escaped this painful experience. But do not
despair; all is not lost. Tryon will not marry
you, as I hoped he might, while I feared the contrary; but he is a gentleman, and will be silent.
Come back and try again."

"No, John. I couldn't go through it a second
time. I managed very well before, when I thought
our secret was unknown; but now I could never
be sure. It would be borne on every wind, for
aught I knew, and every rustling leaf might
whisper it. The law, you said, made us white;

but not the law, nor even love, can conquer prejudice. *He* spoke of my beauty, my grace, my
sweetness! I looked into his eyes and believed
him. And yet he left me without a word! What
would I do in Clarence now? I came away engaged to be married, with even the day set; I
should go back forsaken and discredited; even the
servants would pity me."

"Little Albert is pining for you," suggested
Warwick. "We could make some explanation
that would spare your feelings."

"Ah, do not tempt me, John! I love the child,
and am grieved to leave him. I'm grateful, too,
John, for what you have done for me. I am not
sorry that I tried it. It opened my eyes, and I
would rather die of knowledge than live in ignorance. But I could not go through it again, John;
I am not strong enough. I could do you no good;
I have made you trouble enough already. Get a
mother for Albert — Mrs. Newberry would marry
you, secret and all, and would be good to the child.
Forget me, John, and take care of yourself. Your
friend has found you out through me — he may
have told a dozen people. You think he will be
silent; — I thought he loved me, and he left me
without a word, and with a look that told me how
he hated and despised me. I would not have
believed it — even of a white man."

"You do him an injustice," said her brother,
producing Tryon's letter. "He did not get off
unscathed. He sent you a message."

She turned her face away, but listened while he read the letter. " He did not love me," she cried angrily, when he had finished, " or he would not have cast me off — he would not have looked at me so. The law would have let him marry me. I seemed as white as he did. He might have gone anywhere with me, and no one would have stared at us curiously; no one need have known. The world is wide — there must be some place where a man could live happily with the woman he loved."

" Yes, Rena, there is ; and the world is wide enough for you to get along without Tryon."

" For a day or two," she went on, " I hoped he might come back. But his expression in that awful moment grew upon me, haunted me day and night, until I shuddered at the thought that I might ever see him again. He looked at me as though I were not even a human being. I do not love him any longer, John ; I would not marry him if I were white, or he were as I am. He did not love me — or he would have acted differently. He might have loved me and have left me — he could not have loved me and have looked at me so ! "

She was weeping hysterically. There was little he could say to comfort her. Presently she dried her tears. Warwick was reluctant to leave her in Patesville. Her childish happiness had been that of ignorance ; she could never be happy there again. She had flowered in the sunlight ; she must not pine away in the shade.

" If you won't come back with me, Rena, I 'll

send you to some school at the North, where you
can acquire a liberal education, and prepare yourself for some career of usefulness. You may
marry a better man than even Tryon."

" No," she replied firmly, " I shall never marry
any man, and I 'll not leave mother again. God
is against it ; I 'll stay with my own people."

" God has nothing to do with it," retorted Warwick. " God is too often a convenient stalking-
horse for human selfishness. If there is anything
to be done, so unjust, so despicable, so wicked that
human reason revolts at it, there is always some
smug hypocrite to exclaim, ' It is the will of God.' "

" God made us all," continued Rena dreamily,
" and for some good purpose, though we may not
always see it. He made some people white, and
strong, and masterful, and — heartless. He made
others black and homely, and poor and weak "—

" And a lot of others ' poor white ' and shiftless,"
smiled Warwick.

" He made us, too," continued Rena, intent upon
her own thought, " and He must have had a reason
for it. Perhaps He meant us to bring the others
together in his own good time. A man may make
a new place for himself — a woman is born and
bound to hers. God must have meant me to stay
here, or He would not have sent me back. I shall
accept things as they are. Why should I seek the
society of people whose friendship — and love —
one little word can turn to scorn ? I was right,
John ; I ought to have told him. Suppose he had
married me and then had found it out? "

To Rena's argument of divine foreordination Warwick attached no weight whatever. He had seen God's heel planted for four long years upon the land which had nourished slavery. Had God ordained the crime that the punishment might follow? It would have been easier for Omnipotence to prevent the crime. The experience of his sister had stirred up a certain bitterness against white people — a feeling which he had put aside years ago, with his dark blood, but which sprang anew into life when the fact of his own origin was brought home to him so forcibly through his sister's misfortune. His sworn friend and promised brother-in-law had thrown him over promptly, upon the discovery of the hidden drop of dark blood. How many others of his friends would do the same, if they but knew of it? He had begun to feel a little of the spiritual estrangement from his associates that he had noticed in Rena during her life at Clarence. The fact that several persons knew his secret had spoiled the fine flavor of perfect security hitherto marking his position. George Tryon was a man of honor among white men, and had deigned to extend the protection of his honor to Warwick as a man, though no longer as a friend; to Rena as a woman, but not as a wife. Tryon, however, was only human, and who could tell when their paths in life might cross again, or what future temptation Tryon might feel to use a damaging secret to their disadvantage? Warwick had cherished certain ambitions, but these he must now put behind him. In the obscurity of

private life, his past would be of little moment ; in
the glare of a political career, one's antecedents are
public property, and too great a reserve in regard
to one's past is regarded as a confession of something discreditable. Frank, too, knew the secret
— a good, faithful fellow, even where there was no
obligation of fidelity; he ought to do something for
Frank to show their appreciation of his conduct.
But what assurance was there that Frank would
always be discreet about the affairs of others?
Judge Straight knew the whole story, and old men
are sometimes garrulous. Dr. Green suspected the
secret ; he had a wife and daughters. If old Judge
Straight could have known Warwick's thoughts, he
would have realized the fulfillment of his prophecy.
Warwick, who had builded so well for himself, had
weakened the structure of his own life by trying to
share his good fortune with his sister.

"Listen, Rena," he said, with a sudden impulse,
"we'll go to the North or West — I'll go with
you — far away from the South and the Southern
people, and start life over again. It will be easier
for you, it will not be hard for me — I am young,
and have means. There are no strong ties to bind
me to the South. I would have a larger outlook
elsewhere."

"And what about our mother?" asked Rena.

It would be necessary to leave her behind, they
both perceived clearly enough, unless they were
prepared to surrender the advantage of their white-
ness and drop back to the lower rank. The mother

bore the mark of the Ethiopian — not pronouncedly, but distinctly; neither would Mis' Molly, in all probability, care to leave home and friends and the graves of her loved ones. She had no mental resources to supply the place of these; she was, moreover, too old to be transplanted; she would not fit into Warwick's scheme for a new life.

"I left her once," said Rena, "and it brought pain and sorrow to all three of us. She is not strong, and I will not leave her here to die alone. This shall be my home while she lives, and if I leave it again, it shall be for only a short time, to go where I can write to her freely, and hear from her often. Don't worry about me, John, — I shall do very well."

Warwick sighed. He was sincerely sorry to leave his sister, and yet he saw that for the time being her resolution was not to be shaken. He must bide his time. Perhaps, in a few months, she would tire of the old life. His door would be always open to her, and he would charge himself with her future.

"Well, then," he said, concluding the argument, "we'll say no more about it for the present. I'll write to you later. I was afraid that you might not care to go back just now, and so I brought your trunk along with me."

He gave his mother the baggage-check. She took it across to Frank, who, during the day, brought the trunk from the depot. Mis' Molly offered to pay him for the service, but he would accept nothing.

" Lawd, no, Mis' Molly ; I did n' hafter go out'n
my way ter git dat trunk. I had a load er sperrit-
bairls ter haul ter de still, an' de depot wuz right
on my way back. It 'd be robbin' you ter take
pay fer a little thing lack dat."

" My son John 's here," said Mis' Molly " an'
he wants to see you. Come into the settin'-room.
We don't want folks to know he 's in town ; but
you know all our secrets, an' we can trust you like
one er the family."

" I 'm glad to see you again, Frank," said Warwick, extending his hand and clasping Frank's
warmly. " You 've grown up since I saw you last,
but it seems you are still our good friend."

" Our very good friend," interjected Rena.

Frank threw her a grateful glance. " Yas, suh,"
he said, looking Warwick over with a friendly eye,
" an' you is growed some, too. I seed you, you
know, down dere where you live ; but I did n' let
on, fer you an' Mis' Rena wuz w'ite as anybody ;
an' eve'ybody said you wuz good ter cullud folks,
an' he'ped 'em in deir lawsuits an' one way er
'nuther, an' I wuz jes' plum' glad ter see you gettin' 'long so fine, dat I wuz, certain sho', an' no
mistake about it."

" Thank you, Frank, and I want you to understand how much I appreciate " —

" How much we all appreciate," corrected Rena.

" Yes, how much we all appreciate, and how
grateful we all are for your kindness to mother for
so many years. I know from her and from my
sister how good you 've been to them."

"Lawd, suh!" returned Frank deprecatingly, "you 're makin' a mountain out'n a molehill. I ain't done nuthin' ter speak of — not half ez much ez I would 'a' done. I wuz glad ter do w'at little I could, fer frien'ship's sake."

"We value your friendship, Frank, and we 'll not forget it."

"No, Frank," added Rena, "we will never forget it, and you shall always be our good friend."

Frank left the room and crossed the street with swelling heart. He would have given his life for Rena. A kind word was doubly sweet from her lips; no service would be too great to pay for her friendship.

When Frank went out to the stable next morning to feed his mule, his eyes opened wide with astonishment. In place of the decrepit, one-eyed army mule he had put up the night before, a fat, sleek specimen of vigorous mulehood greeted his arrival with the sonorous hehaw of lusty youth. Hanging on a peg near by was a set of fine new harness, and standing under the adjoining shed, as he perceived, a handsome new cart.

"Well, well!" exclaimed Frank; "ef I did n' mos' know whar dis mule, an' dis kyart, an' dis harness come from, I 'd 'low dere 'd be'n witchcraf' er cunjin' wukkin' here. But, oh my, dat is a fine mule! — I mos' wush I could keep 'im."

He crossed the road to the house behind the cedars, and found Mis' Molly in the kitchen.

" Mis' Molly," he protested, " I ain't done nuthin'
ter deserve dat mule. W'at little I done fer you
wa'n't done fer pay. I 'd ruther not keep dem
things."

" Fer goodness' sake, Frank ! " exclaimed his
neighbor, with a well-simulated air of mystification,
" what are you talkin' about ? "

" You knows w'at I 'm talkin' about, Mis'
Molly ; you knows well ernuff I 'm talkin' about
dat fine mule an' kyart an' harness over dere in
my stable."

" How should I know anything about 'em ? "
she asked.

" Now, Mis' Molly ! You folks is jes' tryin' ter
fool me, an' make me take somethin' fer nuthin'.
I lef' my ole mule an' kyart an' harness in de
stable las' night, an' dis mawnin' dey 're gone, an'
new ones in deir place. Co'se you knows whar
dey come from ! "

" Well, now, Frank, sence you mention it, I did
see a witch flyin' roun' here las' night on a broom-
stick, an' it 'peared ter me she lit on yo'r barn, an'
I s'pose she turned yo'r old things into new ones.
I would n't bother my mind about it if I was you,
for she may turn 'em back any night, you know ;
an' you might as well have the use of 'em in the
mean while."

" Dat 's all foolishness, Mis' Molly, an' I 'm
gwine ter fetch dat mule right over here an' tell
yo' son ter gimme my ole one back."

" My son 's gone," she replied, " an' I don't

know nothin' about yo'r old mule. And what would I do with a mule, anyhow ? I ain't got no barn to put him in."

"I suspect you don't care much for us after all, Frank," said Rena reproachfully — she had come in while they were talking. " You meet with a piece of good luck, and you 're afraid of it, lest it might have come from us."

"Now, Miss Rena, you ought n't ter say dat," expostulated Frank, his reluctance yielding immediately. " I 'll keep de mule an' de kyart an' de harness — fac', I 'll have ter keep 'em, 'cause I ain't got no others. But dey 're gwine ter be yo'n ez much ez mine. W'enever you wants anything hauled, er wants yo' lot ploughed, er anything — dat 's yo' mule, an' I 'm yo' man an' yo' mammy's."

So Frank went back to the stable, where he feasted his eyes on his new possessions, fed and watered the mule, and curried and brushed his coat until it shone like a looking-glass.

" Now dat," remarked Peter, at the breakfast-table, when informed of the transaction, " is somethin' lack rale w'ite folks."

No real white person had ever given Peter a mule or a cart. He had rendered one of them unpaid service for half a lifetime, and had paid for the other half ; and some of them owed him substantial sums for work performed. But " to him that hath shall be given " — Warwick paid for the mule, and the real white folks got most of the credit.

XX

DIGGING UP ROOTS

WHEN the first great shock of his discovery wore off, the fact of Rena's origin lost to Tryon some of its initial repugnance — indeed, the repugnance was not to the woman at all, as their past relations were evidence, but merely to the thought of her as a wife. It could hardly have failed to occur to so reasonable a man as Tryon that Rena's case could scarcely be unique. Surely in the past centuries of free manners and easy morals that had prevailed in remote parts of the South, there must have been many white persons whose origin would not have borne too microscopic an investigation. Family trees not seldom have a crooked branch; or, to use a more apposite figure, many a flock has its black sheep. Being a man of lively imagination, Tryon soon found himself putting all sorts of hypothetical questions about a matter which he had already definitely determined. If he had married Rena in ignorance of her secret, and had learned it afterwards, would he have put her aside? If, knowing her history, he had nevertheless married her, and she had subsequently displayed some trait of character that would suggest the negro, could he have

forgotten or forgiven the taint? Could he still
have held her in love and honor? If not, could
he have given her the outward seeming of affection,
or could he have been more than coldly tolerant?
He was glad that he had been spared this ordeal.
With an effort he put the whole matter definitely
and conclusively aside, as he had done a hundred
times already.

Returning to his home, after an absence of several months in South Carolina, it was quite apparent to his mother's watchful eye that he was in
serious trouble. He was absent-minded, monosyl-
labic, sighed deeply and often, and could not always
conceal the traces of secret tears. For Tryon was
young, and possessed of a sensitive soul — a source
of happiness or misery, as the Fates decree. To
those thus dowered, the heights of rapture are
accessible, the abysses of despair yawn threaten-
ingly; only the dull monotony of contentment is
denied.

Mrs. Tryon vainly sought by every gentle art
a woman knows to win her son's confidence.
" What is the matter, George, dear? " she would
ask, stroking his hot brow with her small, cool
hand as he sat moodily nursing his grief. " Tell
your mother, George. Who else could comfort
you so well as she? "

" Oh, it 's nothing, mother, — nothing at all,"
he would reply, with a forced attempt at lightness.
" It 's only your fond imagination, you best of
mothers."

It was Mrs. Tryon's turn to sigh and shed
a clandestine tear. Until her son had gone away
on this trip to South Carolina, he had kept no
secrets from her : his heart had been an open
book, of which she knew every page ; now, some
painful story was inscribed therein which he meant
she should not read. If she could have abdicated
her empire to Blanche Leary or have shared it
with her, she would have yielded gracefully ; but
very palpably some other influence than Blanche's
had driven joy from her son's countenance and
lightness from his heart.

Miss Blanche Leary, whom Tryon found in the
house upon his return, was a demure, pretty little
blonde, with an amiable disposition, a talent for
society, and a pronounced fondness for George
Tryon. A poor girl, of an excellent family im-
poverished by the war, she was distantly related
to Mrs. Tryon, had for a long time enjoyed that
lady's favor, and was her choice for George's wife
when he should be old enough to marry. A woman
less interested than Miss Leary would have perceived that there was something wrong with Tryon.
Miss Leary had no doubt that there was a woman
at the bottom of it, — for about what else should
youth worry but love ? or if one's love affairs run
smoothly, why should one worry about anything
at all ? Miss Leary, in the nineteen years of her
mundane existence, had not been without mild experiences of the heart, and had hovered for some

time on the verge of disappointment with respect
to Tryon himself. A sensitive pride would have
driven more than one woman away at the sight of
the man of her preference sighing like a furnace
for some absent fair one. But Mrs. Tryon was
so cordial, and insisted so strenuously upon her
remaining, that Blanche's love, which was strong,
conquered her pride, which was no more than a reasonable young woman ought to have who sets success above mere sentiment. She remained in the
house and bided her opportunity. If George practically ignored her for a time, she did not throw
herself at all in his way. She went on a visit to
some girls in the neighborhood and remained away
a week, hoping that she might be missed. Tryon
expressed no regret at her departure and no particular satisfaction upon her return. If the house
was duller in her absence, he was but dimly conscious of the difference. He was still fighting a
battle in which a susceptible heart and a reasonable mind had locked horns in a well-nigh hopeless
conflict. Reason, common-sense, the instinctive
ready-made judgments of his training and environment, — the deep-seated prejudices of race and
caste, — commanded him to dismiss Rena from
his thoughts. His stubborn heart simply would
not let go.

XXI

ALTHOUGH the whole fabric of Rena's new life
toppled and fell with her lover's defection, her sym-
pathies, broadened by culture and still more by
her recent emotional experience, did not shrink, as
would have been the case with a more selfish soul,
to the mere limits of her personal sorrow, great as
this seemed at the moment. She had learned to
love, and when the love of one man failed her, she
turned to humanity, as a stream obstructed in its
course overflows the adjacent country. Her early
training had not directed her thoughts to the darker
people with whose fate her own was bound up so
closely, but rather away from them. She had been
taught to despise them because they were not so
white as she was, and had been slaves while she was
free. Her life in her brother's home, by removing
her from immediate contact with them, had given
her a different point of view, — one which emphasized their shortcomings, and thereby made vastly
clearer to her the gulf that separated them from
the new world in which she lived ; so that when
misfortune threw her back upon them, the reaction
brought her nearer than before. Where once she
had seemed able to escape from them, they were

now, it appeared, her inalienable race. Thus doubly
equipped, she was able to view them at once with
the mental eye of an outsider and the sympathy
of a sister: she could see their faults, and judge
them charitably; she knew and appreciated their
good qualities. With her quickened intelligence
she could perceive how great was their need and
how small their opportunity; and with this illumination came the desire to contribute to their help.
She had not the breadth or culture to see in all its
ramifications the great problem which still puzzles
statesmen and philosophers; but she was conscious
of the wish, and of the power, in a small way, to do
something for the advancement of those who had
just set their feet upon the ladder of progress.

This new-born desire to be of service to her re-
discovered people was not long without an opportunity for expression. Yet the Fates willed that
her future should be but another link in a connected chain: she was to be as powerless to put
aside her recent past as she had been to escape
from the influence of her earlier life. There are
sordid souls that eat and drink and breed and die,
and imagine they have lived. But Rena's life
since her great awakening had been that of the
emotions, and her temperament made of it a con-
tinuous life. Her successive states of consciousness were not detachable, but united to form a
single if not an entirely harmonious whole. To
her sensitive spirit to-day was born of yesterday,
to-morrow would be but the offspring of to-day.

One day, along toward noon, her mother received a visit from Mary B. Pettifoot, a second
cousin, who lived on Back Street, only a short
distance from the house behind the cedars. Rena
had gone out, so that the visitor found Mis' Molly
alone.

"I heared you say, Cousin Molly," said Mary
B. (no one ever knew what the B. in Mary's name
stood for, — it was a mere ornamental flourish),
"that Rena was talkin' 'bout teachin' school. I 've
got a good chance fer her, ef she keers ter take
it. My cousin Jeff Wain 'rived in town this
mo'nin', f'm 'way down in Sampson County, ter
git a teacher fer the nigger school in his deestric'.
I s'pose he mought 'a' got one f'm 'roun' Newbern,
er Goldsboro, er some er them places eas', but he
'lowed he 'd like to visit some er his kin an' ole
frien's, an' so kill two birds with one stone."

"I seed a strange mulatter man, with a bay hoss
an' a new buggy, drivin' by here this mo'nin' early,
from down to'ds the river," rejoined Mis' Molly.
"I wonder if that wuz him?"

"Did he have on a linen duster?" asked Mary B.

"Yas, an' 'peared to be a very well sot up man,"
replied Mis' Molly, "'bout thirty-five years old, I
should reckon."

"That wuz him," assented Mary B. "He 's got
a fine hoss an' buggy, an' a gol' watch an' chain,
an' a big plantation, an' lots er hosses an' mules
an' cows an' hawgs. He raise' fifty bales er cotton
las' year, an' he 's be'n ter the legislatur'."

"My gracious!" exclaimed Mis' Molly, struck
with awe at this catalogue of the stranger's possessions — he was evidently worth more than a great
many "rich" white people, — all white people in
North Carolina in those days were either "rich" or
"poor," the distinction being one of caste rather
than of wealth. "Is he married?" she inquired
with interest?

"No, — single. You mought 'low it was quare
that he should n' be married at his age; but he
was crossed in love oncet,"— Mary B. heaved a
self-conscious sigh, — "an' has stayed single ever
sence. That wuz ten years ago, but as some
husban's is long-lived, an' there ain' no mo' chance
fer 'im now than there wuz then, I reckon some
nice gal mought stan' a good show er ketchin' 'im,
ef she 'd play her kyards right."

To Mis' Molly this was news of considerable
importance. She had not thought a great deal of
Rena's plan to teach; she considered it lowering
for Rena, after having been white, to go among
the negroes any more than was unavoidable. This
opportunity, however, meant more than mere employment for her daughter. She had felt Rena's
disappointment keenly, from the practical point of
view, and, blaming herself for it, held herself all
the more bound to retrieve the misfortune in any
possible way. If she had not been sick, Rena
would not have dreamed the fateful dream that
had brought her to Patesville; for the connection
between the vision and the reality was even closer in

Mis' Molly's eyes than in Rena's. If the mother had not sent the letter announcing her illness and confirming the dream, Rena would not have ruined her promising future by coming to Patesville. But the harm had been done, and she was responsible, ignorantly of course, but none the less truly, and it only remained for her to make amends, as far as possible. Her highest ambition, since Rena had grown up, had been to see her married and comfortably settled in life. She had no hope that Tryon would come back. Rena had declared that she would make no further effort to get away from her people; and, furthermore, that she would never marry. To this latter statement Mis' Molly secretly attached but little importance. That a woman should go single from the cradle to the grave did not accord with her experience in life of the customs of North Carolina. She respected a grief she could not entirely fathom, yet did not for a moment believe that Rena would remain unmarried.

"You'd better fetch him roun' to see me, Ma'y B.," she said, "an' let's see what he looks like. I'm pertic'lar 'bout my gal. She says she ain't goin' to marry nobody; but of co'se we know that's all foolishness."

"I'll fetch him roun' this evenin' 'bout three o'clock," said the visitor, rising. "I mus' hurry back now an' keep him comp'ny. Tell Rena ter put on her bes' bib an' tucker; for Mr. Wain is pertic'lar too, an' I've already be'n braggin' 'bout her looks."

When Mary B., at the appointed hour, knocked at Mis' Molly's front door, — the visit being one of ceremony, she had taken her cousin round to the Front Street entrance and through the flower garden, — Mis' Molly was prepared to receive them. After a decent interval, long enough to suggest that she had not been watching their approach and was not over-eager about the visit, she answered the knock and admitted them into the parlor. Mr. Wain was formally introduced, and seated himself on the ancient haircloth sofa, under the framed fashion-plate, while Mary B. sat by the open door and fanned herself with a palm-leaf fan.

Mis' Molly's impression of Wain was favorable. His complexion was of a light brown — not quite so fair as Mis' Molly would have preferred; but any deficiency in this regard, or in the matter of the stranger's features, which, while not unpleasing, leaned toward the broad mulatto type, was more than compensated in her eyes by very straight black hair, and, as soon appeared, a great facility of complimentary speech. On his introduction Mr. Wain bowed low, assumed an air of great admiration, and expressed his extreme delight in making the acquaintance of so distinguished-looking a lady.

"You're flatt'rin' me, Mr. Wain," returned Mis' Molly, with a gratified smile. "But you want to meet my daughter befo' you commence th'owin' bokays. Excuse my leavin' you — I'll go an' fetch her."

She returned in a moment, followed by Rena.
" Mr. Wain, 'low me to int'oduce you to my daughter Rena. Rena, this is Ma'y B.'s cousin on her
pappy's side, who's come up from Sampson to git
a school-teacher."

Rena bowed gracefully. Wain stared a moment
in genuine astonishment, and then bent himself
nearly double, keeping his eyes fixed meanwhile
upon Rena's face. He had expected to see a pretty
yellow girl, but had been prepared for no such
radiant vision of beauty as this which now con-
fronted him.

" Does — does you mean ter say, Mis' Walden,
dat — dat dis young lady is yo' own daughter ? "
he stammered, rallying his forces for action.

" Why not, Mr. Wain ? " asked Mis' Molly,
bridling with mock resentment. " Do you mean
ter 'low that she wuz changed in her cradle, er is
she too good-lookin' to be my daughter ? "

" My deah Mis' Walden ! it 'ud be wastin' wo'ds
fer me ter say dat dey ain' no young lady too good-
lookin' ter be yo' daughter ; but you 're lookin'
so young yo'sef dat I 'd ruther take her fer yo'
sister."

" Yas," rejoined Mis' Molly, with animation,
" they ain't many years between us. I wuz ruther
young myself when she wuz bo'n."

" An', mo'over," Wain went on, " it takes me
a minute er so ter git my min' use' ter thinkin' er
Mis' Rena as a cullud young lady. I mought 'a'
seed her a hund'ed times, an' I 'd 'a' never dreamt

but w'at she wuz a w'ite young lady, f'm one er de bes' families."

" Yas, Mr. Wain," replied Mis' Molly complacently, " all three er my child'en wuz white, an' one of 'em has be'n on the other side fer many long years. Rena has be'n to school, an' has traveled, an' has had chances — better chances than anybody roun' here knows."

" She 's jes' de lady I 'm lookin' fer, ter teach ou' school," rejoined Wain, with emphasis. " Wid her schoolin' an' my riccommen', she kin git a fus'-class ce'tifikit an' draw fo'ty dollars a month ; an' a lady er her color kin keep a lot er little niggers straighter 'n a darker lady could. We jus' got ter have her ter teach ou' school — ef we kin git her."

Rena's interest in the prospect of employment at her chosen work was so great that she paid little attention to Wain's compliments. Mis' Molly led Mary B. away to the kitchen on some pretext, and left Rena to entertain the gentleman. She questioned him eagerly about the school, and he gave the most glowing accounts of the elegant school-house, the bright pupils, and the congenial society of the neighborhood. He spoke almost entirely in superlatives, and, after making due allowance for what Rena perceived to be a temperamental tendency to exaggeration, she concluded that she would find in the school a worthy field of usefulness, and in this polite and good-natured though somewhat wordy man a coadjutor upon whom she could rely in her first efforts; for she was not over-confident of her powers, which seemed to grow less as the way opened for their exercise.

" Do you think I 'm competent to teach the school ? " she asked of the visitor, after stating some of her qualifications.

" Oh, dere 's no doubt about it, Miss Rena," replied Wain, who had listened with an air of great wisdom, though secretly aware that he was too ignorant of letters to form a judgment ; " you kin teach de school all right, an' could ef you did n't know half ez much. You won't have no trouble managin' de child'en, nuther. Ef any of 'em gits onruly, jes' call on me fer he'p, an' I 'll make 'em walk Spanish. I 'm chuhman er de school committee, an' I 'll lam de hide off'n any scholar dat don' behave. You kin trus' me fer dat, sho' ez I 'm a-settin' here."

" Then," said Rena, " I 'll undertake it, and do my best. I 'm sure you 'll not be too exacting."

" Yo' bes', Miss Rena, 'll be de bes' dey is. Don' you worry ner fret. Dem niggers won't have no other teacher after dey 've once laid eyes on you : I 'll guarantee dat. Dere won't be no trouble, not a bit."

" Well, Cousin Molly," said Mary B. to Mis' Molly in the kitchen, " how does the plan strike you ? "

" Ef Rena 's satisfied, I am," replied Mis' Molly. " But you 'd better say nothin' about ketchin' a beau, or any such foolishness, er else she 'd be just as likely not to go nigh Sampson County."

" Befo' Cousin Jeff goes back," confided Mary
B., " I 'd like ter give 'im a party, but my house
is too small. I wuz wonderin'," she added tenta-
tively, " ef I could n' borry yo' house."

" Shorely, Ma'y B. I 'm int'rested in Mr.
Wain on Rena's account, an' it 's as little as I kin
do to let you use my house an' help you git things
ready."

The date of the party was set for Thursday
night, as Wain was to leave Patesville on Friday
morning, taking with him the new teacher. The
party would serve the double purpose of a compliment to the guest and a farewell to Rena, and it
might prove the precursor, the mother secretly
hoped, of other festivities to follow at some later
date.

XXII

IMPERATIVE BUSINESS

ONE Wednesday morning, about six weeks after
his return home, Tryon received a letter from
Judge Straight with reference to the note left
with him at Patesville for collection. This communication properly required an answer, which
might have been made in writing within the com-
pass of ten lines. No sooner, however, had Tryon
read the letter than he began to perceive reasons
why it should be answered in person. He had
left Patesville under extremely painful circumstances, vowing that he would never return ; and
yet now the barest pretext, by which no one could
have been deceived except willingly, was sufficient
to turn his footsteps thither again. He explained
to his mother — with a vagueness which she found
somewhat puzzling, but ascribed to her own femi-
nine obtuseness in matters of business — the reasons that imperatively demanded his presence in
Patesville. With an early start he could drive
there in one day, — he had an excellent roadster,
a light buggy, and a recent rain had left the road
in good condition, — a day would suffice for the
transaction of his business, and the third day

would bring him home again. He set out on
his journey on Thursday morning, with this pro-
gramme very clearly outlined.

Tryon would not at first have admitted even to
himself that Rena's presence in Patesville had any
bearing whatever upon his projected visit. The
matter about which Judge Straight had written
might, it was clear, be viewed in several aspects.
The judge had written him concerning the one of
immediate importance. It would be much easier
to discuss the subject in all its bearings, and clean
up the whole matter, in one comprehensive personal interview.

The importance of this business, then, seemed
very urgent for the first few hours of Tryon's
journey. Ordinarily a careful driver and merciful to his beast, his eagerness to reach Patesville
increased gradually until it became necessary to
exercise some self-restraint in order not to urge
his faithful mare beyond her powers; and soon he
could no longer pretend obliviousness of the fact
that some attraction stronger than the whole
amount of Duncan McSwayne's note was urging
him irresistibly toward his destination. The old
town beyond the distant river, his heart told him
clamorously, held the object in all the world to
him most dear. Memory brought up in vivid detail every moment of his brief and joyous courtship, — each tender word, each enchanting smile,
every fond caress. He lived his past happiness
over again down to the moment of that fatal dis-

covery. What horrible fate was it that had involved him — nay, that had caught this sweet delicate girl in such a blind alley ? A wild hope flashed across his mind : perhaps the ghastly story might not be true ; perhaps, after all, the girl was no more a negro than she seemed. He had heard sad stories of white children, born out of wedlock, abandoned by sinful parents to the care or adoption of colored women, who had reared them as their own, the children's future basely sacrificed to hide the parents' shame. He would confront this reputed mother of his darling and wring the truth from her. He was in a state of mind where any sort of a fairy tale would have seemed reasonable. He would almost have bribed some one to tell him that the woman he had loved, the woman he still loved (he felt a thrill of lawless pleasure in the confession), was not the descendant of slaves, — that he might marry her, and not have before his eyes the gruesome fear that some one of their children might show even the faintest mark of the despised race.

At noon he halted at a convenient hamlet, fed and watered his mare, and resumed his journey after an hour's rest. By this time he had well-nigh forgotten about the legal business that formed the ostensible occasion for his journey, and was conscious only of a wild desire to see the woman whose image was beckoning him on to Patesville as fast as his horse could take him.

At sundown he stopped again, about ten miles

from the town, and cared for his now tired beast.
He knew her capacity, however, and calculated
that she could stand the additional ten miles without injury.   The mare set out with reluctance,
but soon settled resignedly down into a steady jog.

Memory had hitherto assailed Tryon with the
vision of past joys.   As he neared the town,
imagination attacked him with still more moving
images.   He had left her, this sweet flower of
womankind — white or not, God had never made
a fairer! — he had seen her fall to the hard pavement, with he knew not what resulting injury.
He had left her tender frame — the touch of her
finger-tips had made him thrill with happiness —
to be lifted by strange hands, while he with heartless pride had driven deliberately away, without a
word of sorrow or regret.   He had ignored her as
completely as though she had never existed.   That
he had been deceived was true.   But had he not
aided in his own deception?   Had not Warwick
told him distinctly that they were of no family,
and was it not his own fault that he had not followed up the clue thus given him?   Had not Rena
compared herself to the child's nurse, and had
he not assured her that if she were the nurse, he
would marry her next day?   The deception had
been due more to his own blindness than to any
lack of honesty on the part of Rena and her
brother.   In the light of his present feelings they
seemed to have been absurdly outspoken.   He
was glad that he had kept his discovery to him-

self. He had considered himself very magnanimous not to have exposed the fraud that was being perpetrated upon society: it was with a very comfortable feeling that he now realized that the matter was as profound a secret as before.

"She ought to have been born white," he muttered, adding weakly, "I would to God that I had never found her out!"

Drawing near the bridge that crossed the river to the town, he pictured to himself a pale girl, with sorrowful, tear-stained eyes, pining away in the old gray house behind the cedars for love of him, dying, perhaps, of a broken heart. He would hasten to her; he would dry her tears with kisses; he would express sorrow for his cruelty.

The tired mare had crossed the bridge and was slowly toiling up Front Street; she was near the limit of her endurance, and Tryon did not urge her.

They might talk the matter over, and if they must part, part at least they would in peace and friendship. If he could not marry her, he would never marry any one else; it would be cruel for him to seek happiness while she was denied it, for, having once given her heart to him, she could never, he was sure, — so instinctively fine was her nature, — she could never love any one less worthy than himself, and would therefore probably never marry. He knew from a Clarence acquaintance, who had written him a letter, that Rena had not reappeared in that town.

If he should discover — the chance was one in a thousand — that she was white ; or if he should find it too hard to leave her — ah, well ! he was a white man, one of a race born to command.   He would make her white ; no one beyond the old town would ever know the difference. If, perchance, their secret should be disclosed, the world was wide ; a man of courage and ambition, inspired by love, might make a career anywhere.   Circumstances made weak men ; strong men mould circumstances to do their bidding.   He would not let his darling die of grief, whatever the price must be paid for her salvation. She was only a few rods away from him now.   In a moment he would see her ; he would take her tenderly in his arms, and heart to heart they would mutually forgive and forget, and, strengthened by their love, would face the future boldly and bid the world do its worst.

XXIII

THE evening of the party arrived. The house had been thoroughly cleaned in preparation for the event, and decorated with the choicest treasures of the garden. By eight o'clock the guests had gathered. They were all mulattoes, — all people of mixed blood were called " mulattoes " in North Carolina. There were dark mulattoes and bright mulattoes. Mis' Molly's guests were mostly of the bright class, most of them more than half white, and few of them less. In Mis' Molly's small circle, straight hair was the only palliative of a dark complexion. Many of the guests would not have been casually distinguishable from white people of the poorer class. Others bore unmistakable traces of Indian ancestry, — for Cherokee and Tuscarora blood was quite widely diffused among the free negroes of North Carolina, though well-nigh lost sight of by the curious custom of the white people to ignore anything but the negro blood in those who were touched by its potent current. Very few of those present had been slaves. The free colored people of Patesville were numerous enough before the war to have their own " society," and human enough to despise those who did not possess advantages equal to their own; and at this time they still looked down upon those who had once been held in bondage. The only black man present occupied a chair which stood on a broad chest in one corner, and extracted melody from a fiddle to which a whole generation of the best people of Patesville had danced and made merry. Uncle Needham seldom played for colored gatherings, but made an exception in Mis' Molly's case; she was not white, but he knew her past; if she was not the rose, she had at least been near the rose. When the company had gathered, Mary B., as mistress of ceremonies, whispered to Uncle Needham, who tapped his violin sharply with the bow.

" Ladies an' gent'emens, take yo' pa'dners fer a Fuhginny reel! "

Mr. Wain, as the guest of honor, opened the ball with his hostess. He wore a broadcloth coat and trousers, a heavy glittering chain across the spacious front of his white waistcoat, and a large red rose in his buttonhole. If his boots were slightly run down at the heel, so trivial a detail passed unnoticed in the general splendor of his attire. Upon a close or hostile inspection there would have been some features of his ostensibly good-natured face — the shifty eye, the full and slightly drooping lower lip — which might have given a student of physiognomy food for reflection. But whatever the latent defects of Wain's character, he proved himself this evening a model of

geniality, presuming not at all upon his reputed
wealth, but winning golden opinions from those
who came to criticise, of whom, of course, there
were a few, the company being composed of human
beings.

When the dance began, Wain extended his
large, soft hand to Mary B., yellow, buxom, thirty,
with white and even teeth glistening behind her
full red lips. A younger sister of Mary B.'s was
paired with Billy Oxendine, a funny little tailor,
a great gossip, and therefore a favorite among the
women. Mis' Molly graciously consented, after
many protestations of lack of skill and want of
practice, to stand up opposite Homer Pettifoot,
Mary B.'s husband, a tall man, with a slight stoop,
a bald crown, and full, dreamy eyes, — a man of
much imagination and a large fund of anecdote.
Two other couples completed the set ; others were
restrained by bashfulness or religious scruples,
which did not yield until later in the evening.

The perfumed air from the garden without and
the cut roses within mingled incongruously with the
alien odors of musk and hair oil, of which several
young barbers in the company were especially redolent. There was a play of sparkling eyes and
glancing feet. Mary B. danced with the languor-
ous grace of an Eastern odalisque, Mis' Molly with
the mincing, hesitating step of one long out of practice. Wain performed saltatory prodigies. This
was a golden opportunity for the display in which
his soul found delight. He introduced variations

hitherto unknown to the dance. His skill and suppleness brought a glow of admiration into the eyes of the women, and spread a cloud of jealousy over the faces of several of the younger men, who saw themselves eclipsed.

Rena had announced in advance her intention to take no active part in the festivities. " I don't feel like dancing, mamma — I shall never dance again."

" Well, now, Rena," answered her mother, " of co'se you 're too dignified, sence you 've be'n 'sociatin' with white folks, to be hoppin' roun' an' kickin' up like Ma'y B. an' these other yaller gals; but of co'se, too, you can't slight the comp'ny entirely, even ef it ain't jest exac'ly our party, — you 'll have to pay 'em some little attention, 'specially Mr. Wain, sence you 're goin' down yonder with 'im."

Rena conscientiously did what she thought politeness required. She went the round of the guests in the early part of the evening and exchanged greetings with them. To several requests for dances she replied that she was not dancing. She did not hold herself aloof because of pride; any instinctive shrinking she might have felt by reason of her recent association with persons of greater refinement was offset by her still more newly awakened zeal for humanity; they were her people, she must not despise them. But the occasion suggested painful memories of other and different scenes in which she had lately participated. Once or twice

these memories were so vivid as almost to over-
power her. She slipped away from the company,
and kept in the background as much as possible
without seeming to slight any one.

The guests as well were dimly conscious of a
slight barrier between Mis' Molly's daughter and
themselves. The time she had spent apart from
these friends of her youth had rendered it impossible for her ever to meet them again upon the plane
of common interests and common thoughts. It
was much as though one, having acquired the ver-
nacular of his native country, had lived in a foreign
land long enough to lose the language of his childhood without acquiring fully that of his adopted
country. Miss Rowena Warwick could never again
become quite the Rena Walden who had left the
house behind the cedars no more than a year and
a half before. Upon this very difference were
based her noble aspirations for usefulness, — one
must stoop in order that one may lift others. Any
other young woman present would have been impor-
tuned beyond her powers of resistance. Rena's
reserve was respected.

When supper was announced, somewhat early in
the evening, the dancers found seats in the hall or
on the front piazza. Aunt Zilphy, assisted by Mis'
Molly and Mary B., passed around the refresh-
ments, which consisted of fried chicken, buttered
biscuits, pound-cake, and eggnog. When the first
edge of appetite was taken off, the conversation
waxed animated. Homer Pettifoot related, with

minute detail, an old, threadbare hunting lie, dat-
ing, in slightly differing forms, from the age of
Nimrod, about finding twenty-five partridges sitting in a row on a rail, and killing them all with a
single buckshot, which passed through twenty-four
and lodged in the body of the twenty-fifth, from
which it was extracted and returned to the shot-
pouch for future service.

This story was followed by a murmur of in-
credulity — of course, the thing was possible, but
Homer's faculty for exaggeration was so well
known that any statement of his was viewed with
suspicion. Homer seemed hurt at this lack of
faith, and was disposed to argue the point; but
the sonorous voice of Mr. Wain on the other side
of the room cut short his protestations, in much
the same way that the rising sun extinguishes the
light of lesser luminaries.

" I wuz a member er de fus' legislatur' after de
wah," Wain was saying. " When I went up f'm
Sampson in de fall, I had to pass th'ough Smithfiel'. I got in town in de afternoon, an' put up at
de bes' hotel. De lan'lo'd did n' have no s'picion
but what I wuz a white man, an' he gimme a room,
an' I had supper an' breakfas', an' went on ter
Rolly nex' mornin'. W'en de session wuz over,
I come along back, an' w'en I got ter Smithfiel', I
driv' up ter de same hotel. I noticed, as soon as I
got dere, dat de place had run down consid'able —
dere wuz weeds growin' in de yard, de winders wuz
dirty, an' ev'ything roun' dere looked kinder lone-

some an' shif'less. De lan'lo'd met me at de do';
he looked mighty down in de mouth, an' sezee : —

" ' Look a-here, w'at made you come an' stop at
my place widout tellin' me you wuz a black man?
Befo' you come th'ough dis town I had a fus'-class
business. But w'en folks found out dat a nigger had put up here, business drapped right off,
an' I 've had ter shet up my hotel. You oughter
be 'shamed er yo'se'f fer ruinin' a po' man w'at
had n' never done no harm ter you. You 've done
a mean, low-lived thing, an' a jes' God 'll punish
you fer it.'

" De po' man acshully bust inter tears," continued Mr. Wain magnanimously, " an' I felt so
sorry fer 'im — he wuz a po' white man tryin' ter
git up in de worl' — dat I hauled out my purse
an' gin 'im ten dollars, an' he 'peared monst'ous
glad ter git it."

" How good-hearted ! How kin' ! " murmured
the ladies. " It done credit to yo' feelin's."

" Don't b'lieve a word er dem lies," muttered
one young man to another sarcastically. " He
could n' pass fer white, 'less'n it wuz a mighty dark
night."

Upon this glorious evening of his life, Mr.
Jefferson Wain had one distinctly hostile critic,
of whose presence he was blissfully unconscious.
Frank Fowler had not been invited to the party, —
his family did not go with Mary B.'s set. Rena
had suggested to her mother that he be invited,
but Mis' Molly had demurred on the ground that

it was not her party, and that she had no right to
issue invitations.   It is quite likely that she would
have sought an invitation for Frank from Mary
B. ; but Frank was black, and would not harmonize
with the rest of the company, who would not have
Mis' Molly's reasons for treating him well.   She
had compromised the matter by stepping across the
way in the afternoon and suggesting that Frank
might come over and sit on the back porch and
look at the dancing and share in the supper.

Frank was not without a certain honest pride.
He was sensitive enough, too, not to care to go
where he was not wanted.   He would have curtly
refused any such maimed invitation to any other
place.   But would he not see Rena in her best
attire, and might she not perhaps, in passing, speak
a word to him ?

"Thank y', Mis' Molly," he replied, " I 'll
prob'ly come over."

" You 're a big fool, boy," observed his father after
Mis' Molly had gone back across the street, " ter
be stickin' roun' dem yaller niggers 'cross de street,
an' slobb'rin' an' slav'rin' over 'em, an' hangin'
roun' deir back do' wuss 'n ef dey wuz w'ite folks.
I 'd see 'em dead fus' ! "

Frank himself resisted the temptation for half
an hour after the music began, but at length he
made his way across the street and stationed himself at the window opening upon the back piazza.
When Rena was in the room, he had eyes for her
only, but when she was absent, he fixed his at-

tention mainly upon Wain. With jealous clair-
voyance he observed that Wain's eyes followed
Rena when she left the room, and lit up when she
returned. Frank had heard that Rena was going
away with this man, and he watched Wain closely,
liking him less the longer he looked at him. To
his fancy, Wain's style and skill were affectation,
his good-nature mere hypocrisy, and his glance at
Rena the eye of the hawk upon his quarry. He
had heard that Wain was unmarried, and he could
not see how, this being so, he could help wishing
Rena for a wife. Frank would have been content
to see her marry a white man, who would have
raised her to a plane worthy of her merits. In
this man's shifty eye he read the liar — his wealth
and standing were probably as false as his seeming good-humor.

"Is that you, Frank?" said a soft voice near at
hand.

He looked up with a joyful thrill. Rena was
peering intently at him, as if trying to distinguish
his features in the darkness. It was a bright
moonlight night, but Frank stood in the shadow of
the piazza.

"Yas 'm, it's me, Miss Rena. Yo' mammy said
I could come over an' see you-all dance. You ain'
be'n out on de flo' at all, ter-night."

"No, Frank, I don't care for dancing. I shall
not dance to-night."

This answer was pleasing to Frank. If he could
not hope to dance with her, at least the men inside

— at least this snake in the grass from down the country — should not have that privilege.

" But you must have some supper, Frank," said Rena. " I 'll bring it myself."

" No, Miss Rena, I don' keer fer nothin' — I did n' come over ter eat — r'al'y I did n't."

" Nonsense, Frank, there 's plenty of it. I have no appetite, and you shall have my portion."

She brought him a slice of cake and a glass of eggnog. When Mis' Molly, a minute later, came out upon the piazza, Frank left the yard and walked down the street toward the old canal. Rena had spoken softly to him; she had fed him with her own dainty hands. He might never hope that she would see in him anything but a friend; but he loved her, and he would watch over her and protect her, wherever she might be. He did not believe that she would ever marry the grinning hypocrite masquerading back there in Mis' Molly's parlor; but the man would bear watching.

Mis' Molly had come to call her daughter into the house. " Rena," she said, " Mr. Wain wants ter know if you won't dance just one dance with him."

" Yas, Rena," pleaded Mary B., who followed Miss Molly out to the piazza, " jes' one dance. I don't think you 're treatin' my comp'ny jes' right, Cousin Rena."

" You 're goin' down there with 'im," added her mother, " an' it 'd be just as well to be on friendly terms with 'im."

Wain himself had followed the women. "Sho'ly, Miss Rena, you 're gwine ter honah me wid one dance? I 'd go 'way f'm dis pa'ty sad at hea't ef I had n' stood up oncet wid de young lady er de house."

As Rena, weakly persuaded, placed her hand on Wain's arm and entered the house, a buggy, coming up Front Street, paused a moment at the corner, and then turning slowly, drove quietly up the nameless by-street, concealed by the intervening cedars, until it reached a point from which the occupant could view, through the open front window, the interior of the parlor.

XXIV

SWING YOUR PARTNERS

Moved by tenderness and thoughts of self-sacrifice, which had occupied his mind to the momentary exclusion of all else, Tryon had scarcely
noticed, as he approached the house behind the
cedars, a strain of lively music, to which was added,
as he drew still nearer, the accompaniment of other
festive sounds. He suddenly awoke, however, to
the fact that these signs of merriment came from
the house at which he had intended to stop; —
he had not meant that Rena should pass another
sleepless night of sorrow, or that he should himself
endure another needless hour of suspense.

He drew rein at the corner. Shocked surprise,
a nascent anger, a vague alarm, an insistent curiosity, urged him nearer. Turning the mare into
the side street and keeping close to the fence, he
drove ahead in the shadow of the cedars until he
reached a gap through which he could see into the
open door and windows of the brightly lighted
hall.

There was evidently a ball in progress. The
fiddle was squeaking merrily to a tune that he
remembered well, — it was associated with one of

the most delightful evenings of his life, that of
the tournament ball. A mellow negro voice was
calling with a rhyming accompaniment the figures
of a quadrille. Tryon, with parted lips and slowly
hardening heart, leaned forward from the buggy-
seat, gripping the rein so tightly that his nails
cut into the opposing palm. Above the clatter of
noisy conversation rose the fiddler's voice : —

> "Swing yo' pa'dners ; doan be shy,
> Look yo' lady in de eye !
> Th'ow yo' ahm aroun' huh wais' ;
> Take yo' time — dey ain' no has'e ! "

To the middle of the floor, in full view through
an open window, advanced the woman who all day
long had been the burden of his thoughts — not
pale with grief and hollow-eyed with weeping, but
flushed with pleasure, around her waist the arm
of a burly, grinning mulatto, whose face was offensively familiar to Tryon.

With a muttered curse of concentrated bitterness, Tryon struck the mare a sharp blow with
the whip. The sensitive creature, spirited even
in her great weariness, resented the lash and
started off with the bit in her teeth. Perceiving
that it would be difficult to turn in the narrow
roadway without running into the ditch at the
left, Tryon gave the mare rein and dashed down
the street, scarcely missing, as the buggy crossed
the bridge, a man standing abstractedly by the old
canal, who sprang aside barely in time to avoid
being run over.

Meantime Rena was passing through a trying ordeal.   After the first few bars, the fiddler plunged into a well-known air, in which Rena, keenly susceptible to musical impressions, recognized the tune to which, as Queen of Love and Beauty, she had opened the dance at her entrance into the world of life and love, for it was there she had met George Tryon.   The combination of music and movement brought up the scene with great distinctness.   Tryon, peering angrily through the cedars, had not been more conscious than she of the external contrast between her partners on this and the former occasion.   She perceived, too, as Tryon from the outside had not, the difference between Wain's wordy flattery (only saved by his cousin's warning from pointed and fulsome adulation), and the tenderly graceful compliment, couched in the romantic terms of chivalry, with which the knight of the handkerchief had charmed her ear.   It was only by an immense effort that she was able to keep her emotions under control until the end of the dance, when she fled to her chamber and burst into tears.   It was not the cruel Tryon who had blasted her love with his deadly look that she mourned, but the gallant young knight who had worn her favor on his lance and crowned her Queen of Love and Beauty.

Tryon's stay in Patesville was very brief.   He drove to the hotel and put up for the night.   During many sleepless hours his mind was in a turmoil

with a very different set of thoughts from those
which had occupied it on the way to town. Not
the least of them was a profound self-contempt for
his own lack of discernment. How had he been
so blind as not to have read long ago the character of this wretched girl who had bewitched him?
To-night his eyes had been opened — he had seen
her with the mask thrown off, a true daughter of
a race in which the sensuous enjoyment of the moment took precedence of taste or sentiment or any
of the higher emotions. Her few months of boarding-school, her brief association with white people,
had evidently been a mere veneer over the underlying negro, and their effects had slipped away as
soon as the intercourse had ceased. With the mon-
key-like imitativeness of the negro she had copied
the manners of white people while she lived among
them, and had dropped them with equal facility
when they ceased to serve a purpose. Who but
a negro could have recovered so soon from what
had seemed a terrible bereavement? — she herself
must have felt it at the time, for otherwise she
would not have swooned. A woman of sensibility,
as this one had seemed to be, should naturally feel
more keenly, and for a longer time than a man,
an injury to the affections; but he, a son of the
ruling race, had been miserable for six weeks about
a girl who had so far forgotten him as already to
plunge headlong into the childish amusements of
her own ignorant and degraded people. What
more, indeed, he asked himself savagely, — what

more could be expected of the base-born child of
the plaything of a gentleman's idle hour, who to
this ignoble origin added the blood of a servile
race? And he, George Tryon, had honored her
with his love; he had very nearly linked his fate
and joined his blood to hers by the solemn sanc-
tions of church and state. Tryon was not a devout
man, but he thanked God with religious fervor
that he had been saved a second time from a mistake which would have wrecked his whole future.
If he had yielded to the momentary weakness of
the past night, — the outcome of a sickly sentimentality to which he recognized now, in the light
of reflection, that he was entirely too prone, — he
would have regretted it soon enough. The black
streak would have been sure to come out in some
form, sooner or later, if not in the wife, then in
her children. He saw clearly enough, in this hour
of revulsion, that with his temperament and training such a union could never have been happy.
If all the world had been ignorant of the dark
secret, it would always have been in his own
thoughts, or at least never far away. Each fault
of hers that the close daily association of husband
and wife might reveal, — the most flawless of
sweethearts do not pass scathless through the long
test of matrimony, — every wayward impulse of
his children, every defect of mind, morals, temper,
or health, would have been ascribed to the dark
ancestral strain. Happiness under such conditions
would have been impossible.

When Tryon lay awake in the early morning,
after a few brief hours of sleep, the business which
had brought him to Patesville seemed, in the cold
light of reason, so ridiculously inadequate that he
felt almost ashamed to have set up such a pretext
for his journey. The prospect, too, of meeting
Dr. Green and his family, of having to explain
his former sudden departure, and of running a
gauntlet of inquiry concerning his marriage to the
aristocratic Miss Warwick of South Carolina;
the fear that some one at Patesville might have
suspected a connection between Rena's swoon and
his own flight, — these considerations so moved
this impressionable and impulsive young man that
he called a bell-boy, demanded an early breakfast,
ordered his horse, paid his reckoning, and started
upon his homeward journey forthwith. A certain
distrust of his own sensibility, which he felt to
be curiously inconsistent with his most positive
convictions, led him to seek the river bridge by a
roundabout route which did not take him past the
house where, a few hours before, he had seen the
last fragment of his idol shattered beyond the hope
of repair.

The party broke up at an early hour, since most
of the guests were working-people, and the travelers were to make an early start next day. About
nine in the morning, Wain drove round to Mis'
Molly's. Rena's trunk was strapped behind the
buggy, and she set out, in the company of Wain,

for her new field of labor. The school term was only two months in length, and she did not expect to return until its expiration. Just before taking her seat in the buggy, Rena felt a sudden sinking of the heart.

"Oh, mother," she whispered, as they stood wrapped in a close embrace, "I 'm afraid to leave you. I left you once, and it turned out so miserably."

"It 'll turn out better this time, honey," replied her mother soothingly. "Good-by, child. Take care of yo'self an' yo'r money, and write to yo'r mammy."

One kiss all round, and Rena was lifted into the buggy. Wain seized the reins, and under his skillful touch the pretty mare began to prance and curvet with restrained impatience. Wain could not resist the opportunity to show off before the party, which included Mary B.'s entire family and several other neighbors, who had gathered to see the travelers off.

"Good-by ter Patesville! Good-by, folkses all!" he cried, with a wave of his disengaged hand.

"Good-by, mother! Good-by, all!" cried Rena, as with tears in her heart and a brave smile on her face she left her home behind her for the second time.

When they had crossed the river bridge, the travelers came to a long stretch of rising ground, from the summit of which they could look back over the white sandy road for nearly a mile.

Neither Rena nor her companion saw Frank Fowler behind the chinquapin bush at the foot of the hill, nor the gaze of mute love and longing with which he watched the buggy mount the long incline. He had not been able to trust himself to bid her farewell. He had seen her go away once before with every prospect of happiness, and come back, a dove with a wounded wing, to the old nest behind the cedars. She was going away again, with a man whom he disliked and distrusted. If she had met misfortune before, what were her prospects for happiness now?

The buggy paused at the top of the hill, and Frank, shading his eyes with his hand, thought he could see her turn and look behind. Look back, dear child, towards your home and those who love you! For who knows more than this faithful worshiper what threads of the past Fate is weaving into your future, or whether happiness or misery lies before you?

XXV

BALANCE ALL

THE road to Sampson County lay for the most part over the pine-clad sandhills, — an alternation of gentle rises and gradual descents, with now and then a swamp of greater or less extent. Long stretches of the highway led through the virgin forest, for miles unbroken by a clearing or sign of human habitation.

They traveled slowly, with frequent pauses in shady places, for the weather was hot. The journey, made leisurely, required more than a day, and might with slight effort be prolonged into two. They stopped for the night at a small village, where Wain found lodging for Rena with an acquaintance of his, and for himself with another, while a third took charge of the horse, the accommodation for travelers being limited. Rena's appearance and manners were the subject of much comment. It was necessary to explain to several curious white people that Rena was a woman of color. A white woman might have driven with Wain without attracting remark, — most white ladies had negro coachmen. That a woman of Rena's complexion should eat at a negro's table, or sleep beneath a negro's roof, was a seeming breach of caste which only black blood could excuse. The explanation was never questioned. No white person of sound mind would ever claim to be a negro.

They resumed their journey somewhat late in the morning. Rena would willingly have hastened, for she was anxious to plunge into her new work; but Wain seemed disposed to prolong the pleasant drive, and beguiled the way for a time with stories of wonderful things he had done and strange experiences of a somewhat checkered career. He was shrewd enough to avoid any subject which would offend a modest young woman, but too obtuse to perceive that much of what he said would not commend him to a person of refinement. He made little reference to his possessions, concerning which so much had been said at Patesville; and this reticence was a point in his favor. If he had not been so much upon his guard and Rena so much absorbed by thoughts of her future work, such a drive would have furnished a person of her discernment a very fair measure of the man's character. To these distractions must be added the entire absence of any idea that Wain might have amorous designs upon her; and any shortcomings of manners or speech were excused by the broad mantle of charity which Rena in her new-found zeal for the welfare of her people was willing to throw over all their faults. They were the victims of oppression; they were not responsible for its results.

Toward the end of the second day, while nearing their destination, the travelers passed a large white house standing back from the road at the foot of a lane. Around it grew widespreading trees and well-kept shrubbery. The fences were in good repair. Behind the house and across the road stretched extensive fields of cotton and waving corn. They had passed no other place that showed such signs of thrift and prosperity.

"Oh, what a lovely place!" exclaimed Rena. "That is yours, is n't it?"

"No; we ain't got to my house yet," he answered. "Dat house b'longs ter de riches' people roun' here. Dat house is over in de nex' county. We 're right close to de line now."

Shortly afterwards they turned off from the main highway they had been pursuing, and struck into a narrower road to the left.

"De main road," explained Wain, "goes on to Clinton, 'bout five miles er mo' away. Dis one we 're turnin' inter now will take us to my place, which is 'bout three miles fu'ther on. We 'll git dere now in an hour er so."

Wain lived in an old plantation house, somewhat dilapidated, and surrounded by an air of neglect and shiftlessness, but still preserving a remnant of dignity in its outlines and comfort in its interior arrangements. Rena was assigned a large room on the second floor. She was somewhat surprised at the make-up of the household. Wain's mother — an old woman, much darker than her son — kept

house for him. A sister with two children lived
in the house. The element of surprise lay in the
presence of two small children left by Wain's wife,
of whom Rena now heard for the first time. He
had lost his wife, he informed Rena sadly, a couple
of years before.

" Yas, Miss Rena," she sighed, " de Lawd give
her, an' de Lawd tuck her away. Blessed be de
name er de Lawd." He accompanied this senten-
tious quotation with a wicked look from under his
half-closed eyelids that Rena did not see.

The following morning Wain drove her in his
buggy over to the county town, where she took the
teacher's examination. She was given a seat in a
room with a number of other candidates for cer-
tificates, but the fact leaking out from some remark
of Wain's that she was a colored girl, objection
was quietly made by several of the would-be teachers to her presence in the room, and she was requested to retire until the white teachers should
have been examined. An hour or two later she
was given a separate examination, which she passed
without difficulty. The examiner, a gentleman of
local standing, was dimly conscious that she might
not have found her exclusion pleasant, and was
especially polite. It would have been strange,
indeed, if he had not been impressed by her sweet
face and air of modest dignity, which were all the
more striking because of her social disability. He
fell into conversation with her, became interested
in her hopes and aims, and very cordially offered

to be of service, if at any time he might, in connection with her school.

" You have the satisfaction," he said, " of receiving the only first-grade certificate issued to-day. You might teach a higher grade of pupils than you will find at Sandy Run, but let us hope that you may in time raise them to your own level."

" Which I doubt very much," he muttered to himself, as she went away with Wain. " What a pity that such a woman should be a nigger! If she were anything to me, though, I should hate to trust her anywhere near that saddle-colored scoundrel. He's a thoroughly bad lot, and will bear watching."

Rena, however, was serenely ignorant of any danger from the accommodating Wain. Absorbed in her own thoughts and plans, she had not sought to look beneath the surface of his somewhat overdone politeness. In a few days she began her work as teacher, and sought to forget in the service of others the dull sorrow that still gnawed at her heart.

XXVI

THE SCHOOLHOUSE IN THE WOODS

BLANCHE LEARY, closely observant of Tryon's
moods, marked a decided change in his manner
after his return from his trip to Patesville. His
former moroseness had given way to a certain
defiant lightness, broken now and then by an
involuntary sigh, but maintained so well, on the
whole, that his mother detected no lapses whatever.
The change was characterized by another feature
agreeable to both the women: Tryon showed
decidedly more interest than ever before in Miss
Leary's society. Within a week he asked her
several times to play a selection on the piano, dis-
playing, as she noticed, a decided preference for
gay and cheerful music, and several times suggesting a change when she chose pieces of a sentimental
cast. More than once, during the second week
after his return, he went out riding with her; she
was a graceful horsewoman, perfectly at home in
the saddle, and appearing to advantage in a riding-
habit. She was aware that Tryon watched her now
and then, with an eye rather critical than indulgent.

"He is comparing me with some other girl,"
she surmised. "I seem to stand the test very well,

I wonder who the other is, and what was the trouble?"

Miss Leary exerted all her powers to interest and amuse the man she had set out to win, and who seemed nearer than ever before. Tryon, to his pleased surprise, discovered in her mind depths that he had never suspected. She displayed a singular affinity for the tastes that were his — he could not, of course, know how carefully she had studied them. The old wound, recently reopened, seemed to be healing rapidly, under conditions more conducive than before to perfect recovery. No longer, indeed, was he pursued by the picture of Rena discovered and unmasked — this he had definitely banished from the realm of sentiment to that of reason. The haunting image of Rena loving and beloved, amid the harmonious surroundings of her brother's home, was not so readily displaced. Nevertheless, he reached in several weeks a point from which he could consider her as one thinks of a dear one removed by the hand of death, or smitten by some incurable ailment of mind or body. Erelong, he fondly believed, the recovery would be so far complete that he could consign to the tomb of pleasant memories even the most thrilling episodes of his ill-starred courtship.

"George," said Mrs. Tryon one morning while her son was in this cheerful mood, "I'm sending Blanche over to Major McLeod's to do an errand for me. Would you mind driving her over? The road may be rough after the storm last night, and

Blanche has an idea that no one drives so well as you."

"Why, yes, mother, I'll be glad to drive Blanche over. I want to see the major myself."

They were soon bowling along between the pines, behind the handsome mare that had carried Tryon so well at the Clarence tournament. Presently he drew up sharply.

"A tree has fallen squarely across the road," he exclaimed. "We shall have to turn back a little way and go around."

They drove back a quarter of a mile and turned into a by-road leading to the right through the woods. The solemn silence of the pine forest is soothing or oppressive, according to one's mood. Beneath the cool arcade of the tall, overarching trees a deep peace stole over Tryon's heart. He had put aside indefinitely and forever an unhappy and impossible love. The pretty and affectionate girl beside him would make an ideal wife. Of her family and blood he was sure. She was his mother's choice, and his mother had set her heart upon their marriage. Why not speak to her now, and thus give himself the best possible protection against stray flames of love?

"Blanche," he said, looking at her kindly.

"Yes, George?" Her voice was very gentle, and slightly tremulous. Could she have divined his thought? Love is a great clairvoyant.

"Blanche, dear, I"—

A clatter of voices broke upon the stillness of

the forest and interrupted Tryon's speech. A
sudden turn to the left brought the buggy to a
little clearing, in the midst of which stood a small
log schoolhouse.   Out of the schoolhouse a swarm
of colored children were emerging, the suppressed
energy of the school hour finding vent in vocal
exercise of various sorts.   A group had already
formed a ring, and were singing with great volume
and vigor : —

> " Miss Jane, she loves sugar an' tea,
> Miss Jane, she loves candy.
> Miss Jane, she can whirl all around
> An' kiss her love quite handy.

> " De oak grows tall,
> De pine grows slim,
> So rise you up, my true love,
> An' let me come in."

" What a funny little darkey ! " exclaimed Miss
Leary, pointing to a diminutive lad who was walking on his hands, with his feet balanced in the air.
At sight of the buggy and its occupants this sable
acrobat, still retaining his inverted position, moved
toward the newcomers, and, reversing himself with
a sudden spring, brought up standing beside the
buggy.

" Hoddy, Mars Geo'ge ! " he exclaimed, bobbing
his head and kicking his heel out behind in approved plantation style.

" Hello, Plato," replied the young man, " what
are you doing here ? "

" Gwine ter school, Mars Geo'ge," replied the

lad; "larnin' ter read an' write, suh, lack de w'ite folks."

"Wat you callin' dat w'ite man marster fur?" whispered a tall yellow boy to the acrobat addressed as Plato. "You don' b'long ter him no mo'; you 're free, an' ain' got sense ernuff ter know it."

Tryon threw a small coin to Plato, and holding another in his hand suggestively, smiled toward the tall yellow boy, who looked regretfully at the coin, but stood his ground; he would call no man master, not even for a piece of money.

During this little colloquy, Miss Leary had kept her face turned toward the schoolhouse.

"What a pretty girl!" she exclaimed. "There," she added, as Tryon turned his head toward her, "you are too late. She has retired into her castle. Oh, Plato!"

"Yas, missis," replied Plato, who was prancing round the buggy in great glee, on the strength of his acquaintance with the white folks.

"Is your teacher white?"

"No, ma'm, she ain't w'ite; she 's black. She looks lack she 's w'ite, but she 's black."

Tryon had not seen the teacher's face, but the incident had jarred the old wound; Miss Leary's description of the teacher, together with Plato's characterization, had stirred lightly sleeping memories. He was more or less abstracted during the remainder of the drive, and did not recur to the conversation that had been interrupted by coming upon the schoolhouse.

The teacher, glancing for a moment through the open door of the schoolhouse, had seen a handsome young lady staring at her, — Miss Leary had a curiously intent look when she was interested in anything, with no intention whatever to be rude, — and beyond the lady the back and shoulder of a man, whose face was turned the other way. There was a vague suggestion of something familiar about the equipage, but Rena shrank from this close scrutiny and withdrew out of sight before she had had an opportunity to identify the vague resemblance to something she had known.

Miss Leary had missed by a hair's-breadth the psychological moment, and felt some resentment toward the little negroes who had interrupted her lover's train of thought. Negroes have caused a great deal of trouble among white people. How deeply the shadow of the Ethiopian had fallen upon her own happiness, Miss Leary of course could not guess.

XXVII

A FEW days later, Rena looked out of the window near her desk and saw a low basket phaeton, drawn by a sorrel pony, driven sharply into the clearing and drawn up beside an oak sapling. The occupant of the phaeton, a tall, handsome, well-preserved lady in middle life, with slightly gray hair, alighted briskly from the phaeton, tied the pony to the sapling with a hitching-strap, and advanced to the schoolhouse door.

Rena wondered who the lady might be. She had a benevolent aspect, however, and came forward to the desk with a smile, not at all embarrassed by the wide-eyed inspection of the entire school.

"How do you do?" she said, extending her hand to the teacher. "I live in the neighborhood and am interested in the colored people — a good many of them once belonged to me. I heard something of your school, and thought I should like to make your acquaintance."

"It is very kind of you, indeed," murmured Rena respectfully.

"Yes," continued the lady, "I am not one of

those who sit back and blame their former slaves
because they were freed. They are free now, — it
is all decided and settled, — and they ought to be
taught enough to enable them to make good use of
their freedom. But really, my dear, — you must n't
feel offended if I make a mistake, — I am going
to ask you something very personal." She looked
suggestively at the gaping pupils.

" The school may take the morning recess now,"
announced the teacher. The pupils filed out in
an orderly manner, most of them stationing themselves about the grounds in such places as would
keep the teacher and the white lady in view. Very
few white persons approved of the colored schools ;
no other white person had ever visited this one.

" Are you really colored ? " asked the lady, when
the children had withdrawn.

A year and a half earlier, Rena would have met
the question by some display of self-consciousness.
Now, she replied simply and directly.

" Yes, ma'am, I am colored."

The lady, who had been studying her as closely
as good manners would permit, sighed regretfully.

" Well, it 's a shame. No one would ever think
it. If you chose to conceal it, no one would ever
be the wiser. What is your name, child, and where
were you brought up? You must have a romantic
history."

Rena gave her name and a few facts in regard
to her past. The lady was so much interested,
and put so many and such searching questions,

that Rena really found it more difficult to suppress
the fact that she had been white, than she had
formerly had in hiding her African origin.   There
was about the girl an air of real refinement that
pleased the lady, — the refinement not merely of
a fine nature, but of contact with cultured people;
a certain reserve of speech and manner quite
inconsistent with Mrs. Tryon's experience of colored women. The lady was interested and slightly
mystified.   A generous, impulsive spirit, — her
son's own mother, — she made minute inquiries
about the school and the pupils, several of whom
she knew by name. Rena stated that the two
months' term was nearing its end, and that she
was training the children in various declamations
and dialogues for the exhibition at the close.

" I shall attend it," declared the lady positively.
" I 'm sure you are doing a good work, and it 's
very noble of you to undertake it when you might
have a very different future. If I can serve you
at any time, don't hesitate to call upon me.   I
live in the big white house just before you turn
out of the Clinton road to come this way.   I 'm
only a widow, but my son George lives with me
and has some influence in the neighborhood.   He
drove by here yesterday with the lady he is going
to marry. It was she who told me about you."

Was it the name, or some subtle resemblance
in speech or feature, that recalled Tryon's image
to Rena's mind? It was not so far away — the
image of the loving Tryon — that any powerful

witchcraft was required to call it up. His mother
was a widow; Rena had thought, in happier days,
that she might be such a kind lady as this. But
the cruel Tryon who had left her — his mother
would be some hard, cold, proud woman, who
would regard a negro as but little better than a
dog, and who would not soil her lips by addressing
a colored person upon any other terms than as a
servant. She knew, too, that Tryon did not live
in Sampson County, though the exact location of
his home was not clear to her.

"And where are you staying, my dear?" asked
the good lady.

"I'm boarding at Mrs. Wain's," answered
Rena.

"Mrs. Wain's?"

"Yes, they live in the old Campbell place."

"Oh, yes — Aunt Nancy. She's a good enough
woman, but we don't think much of her son Jeff.
He married my Amanda after the war — she used
to belong to me, and ought to have known better.
He abused her most shamefully, and had to be
threatened with the law. She left him a year or
so ago and went away; I haven't seen her lately.
Well, good-by, child; I'm coming to your exhibition. If you ever pass my house, come in and
see me."

The good lady had talked for half an hour, and
had brought a ray of sunshine into the teacher's
monotonous life, heretofore lighted only by the
uncertain lamp of high resolve. She had satisfied

a pardonable curiosity, and had gone away without mentioning her name.

Rena saw Plato untying the pony as the lady climbed into the phaeton.

" Who was the lady, Plato ? " asked the teacher when the visitor had driven away.

" Dat 'uz my ole mist'iss, ma'm," returned Plato proudly, — " ole Mis' 'Liza."

" Mis' 'Liza who ? " asked Rena.

" Mis' 'Liza Tryon.   I use' ter b'long ter her. Dat 'uz her son, my young Mars Geo'ge, w'at driv pas' hyuh yistiddy wid 'is sweetheart."

XXVIII

THE LOST KNIFE

RENA had found her task not a difficult one so far as discipline was concerned. Her pupils were of a docile race, and school to them had all the charm of novelty. The teacher commanded some awe because she was a stranger, and some, perhaps, because she was white; for the theory of blackness as propounded by Plato could not quite counterbalance in the young African mind the evidence of their own senses. She combined gentleness with firmness; and if these had not been sufficient, she had reserves of character which would have given her the mastery over much less plastic material than these ignorant but eager young people. The work of instruction was simple enough, for most of the pupils began with the alphabet, which they acquired from Webster's blue-backed spelling-book, the palladium of Southern education at that epoch. The much abused carpet-baggers had put the spelling-book within reach of every child of school age in North Carolina, — a fact which is often overlooked when the carpet-baggers are held up to public odium. Even the devil should have his due, and is not so black as he is painted.

At the time when she learned that Tryon lived
in the neighborhood, Rena had already been subjected for several weeks to a trying ordeal. Wain
had begun to persecute her with marked attentions.
She had at first gone to board at his house, — or,
by courtesy, with his mother. For a week or two
she had considered his attentions in no other light
than those of a member of the school committee
sharing her own zeal and interested in seeing the
school successfully carried on. In this character
Wain had driven her to the town for her examination; he had busied himself about putting the
schoolhouse in order, and in various matters affect-
ing the conduct of the school. He had jocularly
offered to come and whip the children for her, and
had found it convenient to drop in occasionally,
ostensibly to see what progress the work was
making.

"Dese child'en," he would observe sonorously,
in the presence of the school, "oughter be monst'ous glad ter have de chance er settin' under
yo' instruction, Miss Rena. I'm sho' eve'body in
dis neighbo'hood 'preciates de priv'lege er havin'
you in ou' mids'."

Though slightly embarrassing to the teacher,
these public demonstrations were endurable so long
as they could be regarded as mere official appreciation of her work. Sincerely in earnest about
her undertaking, she had plunged into it with
all the intensity of a serious nature which love
had stirred to activity. A pessimist might have

sighed sadly or smiled cynically at the notion that a poor, weak girl, with a dangerous beauty and a sensitive soul, and troubles enough of her own, should hope to accomplish anything appreciable toward lifting the black mass still floundering in the mud where slavery had left it, and where emancipation had found it, — the mud in which, for aught that could be seen to the contrary, her little feet, too, were hopelessly entangled. It might have seemed like expecting a man to lift himself by his boot-straps.

But Rena was no philosopher, either sad or cheerful. She could not even have replied to this argument, that races must lift themselves, and the most that can be done by others is to give them opportunity and fair play. Hers was a simpler reasoning, — the logic by which the world is kept going onward and upward when philosophers are at odds and reformers are not forthcoming. She knew that for every child she taught to read and write she opened, if ever so little, the door of opportunity, and she was happy in the consciousness of performing a duty which seemed all the more imperative because newly discovered. Her zeal, indeed, for the time being was like that of an early Christian, who was more willing than not to die for his faith. Rena had fully and firmly made up her mind to sacrifice her life upon this altar. Her absorption in the work had not been without its reward, for thereby she had been able to keep at a distance the spectre of her lost love. Her dreams she could not control, but she banished Tryon as far as possible from her waking thoughts.

When Wain's attentions became obviously personal, Rena's new vestal instinct took alarm, and she began to apprehend his character more clearly. She had long ago learned that his pretensions to wealth were a sham. He was nominal owner of a large plantation, it is true; but the land was worn out, and mortgaged to the limit of its security value. His reputed droves of cattle and hogs had dwindled to a mere handful of lean and listless brutes.

Her clear eye, when once set to take Wain's measure, soon fathomed his shallow, selfish soul, and detected, or at least divined, behind his mask of good-nature a lurking brutality which filled her with vague distrust, needing only occasion to develop it into active apprehension, — occasion which was not long wanting. She avoided being alone with him at home by keeping carefully with the women of the house. If she were left alone, — and they soon showed a tendency to leave her on any pretext whenever Wain came near, — she would seek her own room and lock the door. She preferred not to offend Wain; she was far away from home and in a measure in his power, but she dreaded his compliments and sickened at his smile. She was also compelled to hear his relations sing his praises.

" My son Jeff," old Mrs. Wain would say, " is de bes' man you ever seed. His fus' wife had de easies' time an' de happies' time er ary woman in dis settlement. He's grieve' fer her a long time, but I reckon he's gittin' over it, an' de nex' 'oman w'at marries him 'll git a box er pyo' gol', ef I does say it as is his own mammy."

Rena had thought Wain rather harsh with his household, except in her immediate presence. His mother and sister seemed more or less afraid of him, and the children often anxious to avoid him.

One day, he timed his visit to the schoolhouse so as to walk home with Rena through the woods. When she became aware of his purpose, she called to one of the children who was loitering behind the others, " Wait a minute, Jenny. I 'm going your way, and you can walk along with me."

Wain with difficulty hiu a scowl behind a smiling front. When they had gone a little distance along the road through the woods, he clapped his hand upon his pocket.

" I declare ter goodness," he exclaimed, "ef I ain't dropped my pocket-knife! I thought I felt somethin' slip th'ough dat hole in my pocket jes' by the big pine stump in the schoolhouse ya'd. Jinny, chile, run back an' hunt fer my knife, an' I 'll give yer five cents ef yer find it. Me an' Miss Rena 'll walk on slow 'tel you ketches us."

Rena did not dare to object, though she was afraid to be alone with this man. If she could have had a moment to think, she would have volunteered to go back with Jenny and look for the knife, which, although a palpable subterfuge on her part, would

have been one to which Wain could not object;
but the child, dazzled by the prospect of reward,
had darted back so quickly that this way of escape
was cut off. She was evidently in for a declaration of love, which she had taken infinite pains to
avoid. Just the form it would assume, she could
not foresee. She was not long left in suspense.
No sooner was the child well out of sight than
Wain threw his arms suddenly about her waist
and smilingly attempted to kiss her.

Speechless with fear and indignation, she tore
herself from his grasp with totally unexpected
force, and fled incontinently along the forest path.
Wain — who, to do him justice, had merely meant
to declare his passion in what he had hoped might
prove a not unacceptable fashion — followed in
some alarm, expostulating and apologizing as he
went. But he was heavy and Rena was light, and
fear lent wings to her feet. He followed her until
he saw her enter the house of Elder Johnson, the
father of several of her pupils, after which he
sneaked uneasily homeward, somewhat apprehen-
sive of the consequences of his abrupt wooing,
which was evidently open to an unfavorable construction. When, an hour later, Rena sent one of
the Johnson children for some of her things, with
a message explaining that the teacher had been
invited to spend a few days at Elder Johnson's,
Wain felt a pronounced measure of relief. For an
hour he had even thought it might be better to
relinquish his pursuit. With a fatuousness born of

vanity, however, no sooner had she sent her excuse than he began to look upon her visit to Johnson's as a mere exhibition of coyness, which, together with her conduct in the woods, was merely intended to lure him on.

Right upon the heels of the perturbation caused by Wain's conduct, Rena discovered that Tryon lived in the neighborhood; that not only might she meet him any day upon the highway, but that he had actually driven by the schoolhouse. That he knew or would know of her proximity there could be no possible doubt, since she had freely told his mother her name and her home. A hot wave of shame swept over her at the thought that George Tryon might imagine she were following him, throwing herself in his way, and at the thought of the construction which he might place upon her actions. Caught thus between two emotional fires, at the very time when her school duties, owing to the approaching exhibition, demanded all her energies, Rena was subjected to a physical and mental strain that only youth and health could have resisted, and then only for a short time.

XXIX

PLATO EARNS HALF A DOLLAR

TRYON'S first feeling, when his mother at the dinner-table gave an account of her visit to the schoolhouse in the woods, was one of extreme annoyance. Why, of all created beings, should this particular woman be chosen to teach the colored school at Sandy Run? Had she learned that he lived in the neighborhood, and had she sought the place hoping that he might consent to renew, on different terms, relations which could never be resumed upon their former footing? Six weeks before, he would not have believed her capable of following him; but his last visit to Patesville had revealed her character in such a light that it was difficult to predict what she might do. It was, however, no affair of his. He was done with her; he had dismissed her from his own life, where she had never properly belonged, and he had filled her place, or would soon fill it, with another and worthier woman. Even his mother, a woman of keen discernment and delicate intuitions, had been deceived by this girl's specious exterior. She had brought away from her interview of the morning the impression that Rena was a fine, pure spirit, born out of place, through

some freak of Fate, devoting herself with heroic
self-sacrifice to a noble cause.   Well, he had
imagined her just as pure and fine, and she had
deliberately, with a negro's low cunning, deceived
him into believing that she was a white girl.   The
pretended confession of the brother, in which he
had spoken of the humble origin of the family, had
been, consciously or unconsciously, the most disin-
genuous feature of the whole miserable performance.   They had tried by a show of frankness to
satisfy their own consciences, — they doubtless had
enough of white blood to give them a rudimentary
trace of such a moral organ, — and by the same
act to disarm him against future recriminations, in
the event of possible discovery.   How was he to
imagine that persons of their appearance and pretensions were tainted with negro blood ?   The more
he dwelt upon the subject, the more angry he became with those who had surprised his virgin heart
and deflowered it by such low trickery.   The man
who brought the first negro into the British colonies
had committed a crime against humanity and a
worse crime against his own race.   The father of
this girl had been guilty of a sin against society
for which others — for which he, George Tryon —
must pay the penalty.   As slaves, negroes were tol-
erable.   As freemen, they were an excrescence, an
alien element incapable of absorption into the body
politic of white men.   He would like to send them
all back to the Africa from which their forefathers
had come, — unwillingly enough, he would admit,

— and he would like especially to banish this girl from his own neighborhood ; not indeed that her presence would make any difference to him, except as a humiliating reminder of his own folly and weakness with which he could very well dispense.

Of this state of mind Tryon gave no visible manifestation beyond a certain taciturnity, so much at variance with his recent liveliness that the ladies could not fail to notice it. No effort upon the part of either was able to affect his mood, and they both resigned themselves to await his lordship's pleasure to be companionable.

For a day or two, Tryon sedulously kept away from the neighborhood of the schoolhouse at Sandy Run. He really had business which would have taken him in that direction, but made a detour of five miles rather than go near his abandoned and discredited sweetheart.

But George Tryon was wisely distrustful of his own impulses. Driving one day along the road to Clinton, he overhauled a diminutive black figure trudging along the road, occasionally turning a handspring by way of diversion.

" Hello, Plato," called Tryon, " do you want a lift ? "

" Hoddy, Mars Geo'ge. Kin I ride wid you ? "

" Jump up."

Plato mounted into the buggy with the agility to be expected from a lad of his acrobatic accomplishments. The two almost immediately fell into conversation upon perhaps the only subject of common interest between them. Before the town was reached, Tryon knew, so far as Plato could make it plain, the estimation in which the teacher was held by pupils and parents. He had learned the hours of opening and dismissal of the school, where the teacher lived, her habits of coming to and going from the schoolhouse, and the road she always followed.

"Does she go to church or anywhere else with Jeff Wain, Plato?" asked Tryon.

"No, suh, she don' go nowhar wid nobody ex- cep'n' ole Elder Johnson er Mis' Johnson, an' de child'en. She use' ter stop at Mis' Wain's, but she's stayin' wid Elder Johnson now. She alluz makes some er de child'en go home wid er f'm school," said Plato, proud to find in Mars Geo'ge an appreciative listener, — "sometimes one an' sometimes anudder. I's be'n home wid 'er twice, an' it 'll be my tu'n ag'in befo' long."

"Plato," remarked Tryon impressively, as they drove into the town, "do you think you could keep a secret?"

"Yas, Mars Geo'ge, ef you says I shill."

"Do you see this fifty-cent piece?" Tryon displayed a small piece of paper money, crisp and green in its newness.

"Yas, Mars Geo'ge," replied Plato, fixing his eyes respectfully on the government's promise to pay. Fifty cents was a large sum of money. His acquaintance with Mars Geo'ge gave him the privi- lege of looking at money. When he grew up, he would be able, in good times, to earn fifty cents a day.

" I am going to give this to you, Plato."

Plato's eyes opened wide as saucers. " Me, Mars Geo'ge? " he asked in amazement.

" Yes, Plato. I 'm going to write a letter while I 'm in town, and want you to take it. Meet me here in half an hour, and I 'll give you the letter. Meantime, keep your mouth shut."

" Yas, Mars Geo'ge," replied Plato with a grin that distended that organ unduly. That he did not keep it shut may be inferred from the fact that within the next half hour he had eaten and drunk fifty cents' worth of candy, ginger-pop, and other available delicacies that appealed to the youthful palate. Having nothing more to spend, and the high prices prevailing for some time after the war having left him capable of locomotion, Plato was promptly on hand at the appointed time and place.

Tryon placed a letter in Plato's hand, still sticky with molasses candy, — he had inclosed it in a second cover by way of protection. " Give that letter," he said, " to your teacher ; don't say a word about it to a living soul ; bring me an answer, and give it into my own hand, and you shall have another half dollar."

Tryon was quite aware that by a surreptitious correspondence he ran some risk of compromising Rena. But he had felt, as soon as he had indulged his first opportunity to talk of her, an irre-

sistible impulse to see her and speak to her again.
He could scarcely call at her boarding-place, —
what possible proper excuse could a young white
man have for visiting a colored woman? At the
schoolhouse she would be surrounded by her pupils,
and a private interview would be as difficult, with
more eyes to remark and more tongues to comment upon it. He might address her by mail, but
did not know how often she sent to the nearest
post-office. A letter mailed in the town must pass
through the hands of a postmaster notoriously inquisitive and evil-minded, who was familiar with
Tryon's handwriting and had ample time to attend
to other people's business. To meet the teacher
alone on the road seemed scarcely feasible, according to Plato's statement. A messenger, then, was
not only the least of several evils, but really the
only practicable way to communicate with Rena.
He thought he could trust Plato, though miserably
aware that he could not trust himself where this
girl was concerned.

The letter handed by Tryon to Plato, and by
the latter delivered with due secrecy and precau-
tion, ran as follows : —

DEAR MISS WARWICK, — You may think it
strange that I should address you after what has
passed between us ; but learning from my mother
of your presence in the neighborhood, I am constrained to believe that you do not find my proximity embarrassing, and I cannot resist the wish

to meet you at least once more, and talk over the circumstances of our former friendship. From a practical point of view this may seem superfluous, as the matter has been definitely settled. I have no desire to find fault with you ; on the contrary, I wish to set myself right with regard to my own actions, and to assure you of my good wishes. In other words, since we must part, I would rather we parted friends than enemies. If nature and society — or Fate, to put it another way — have decreed that we cannot live together, it is nevertheless possible that we may carry into the future a pleasant though somewhat sad memory of a past friendship. Will you not grant me one interview? I appreciate the difficulty of arranging it; I have found it almost as hard to communicate with you by letter. I will suit myself to your convenience and meet you at any time and place you may designate. Please answer by bearer, who I think is trustworthy, and believe me, whatever your answer may be,

Respectfully yours,

G. T.

The next day but one Tryon received through the mail the following reply to his letter : —

GEORGE TRYON, ESQ.

Dear Sir, — I have requested your messenger to say that I will answer your letter by mail, which I shall now proceed to do. I assure you that

I was entirely ignorant of your residence in this neighborhood, or it would have been the last place on earth in which I should have set foot.

As to our past relations, they were ended by your own act. I frankly confess that I deceived you; I have paid the penalty, and have no complaint to make. I appreciate the delicacy which has made you respect my brother's secret, and thank you for it. I remember the whole affair with shame and humiliation, and would willingly forget it.

As to a future interview, I do not see what good it would do either of us. You are white, and you have given me to understand that I am black. I accept the classification, however unfair, and the consequences, however unjust, one of which is that we cannot meet in the same parlor, in the same church, at the same table, or anywhere, in social intercourse; upon a steamboat we would not sit at the same table; we could not walk together on the street, or meet publicly anywhere and converse, without unkind remark. As a white man, this might not mean a great deal to you; as a woman, shut out already by my color from much that is desirable, my good name remains my most valuable possession. I beg of you to let me alone. The best possible proof you can give me of your good wishes is to relinquish any desire or attempt to see me. I shall have finished my work here in a few days. I have other troubles, of which you know nothing, and any meeting with you would

only add to a burden which is already as much as
I can bear.   To speak of parting is superfluous —
we have already parted.   It were idle to dream of
a future friendship between people so widely different in station.   Such a friendship, if possible
in itself, would never be tolerated by the lady
whom you are to marry, with whom you drove by
my schoolhouse the other day.   A gentleman so
loyal to his race and its traditions as you have
shown yourself could not be less faithful to the
lady to whom he has lost his heart and his memory
in three short months.

No, Mr. Tryon, our romance is ended, and better so.   We could never have been happy.   I have
found a work in which I may be of service to
others who have fewer opportunities than mine
have been.   Leave me in peace, I beseech you,
and I shall soon pass out of your neighborhood as
I have passed out of your life, and hope to pass
out of your memory.

Yours very truly,
ROWENA WALDEN.

XXX

AN UNUSUAL HONOR

To Rena's high-strung and sensitive nature, already under very great tension from her past experience, the ordeal of the next few days was a severe one. On the one hand, Jeff Wain's infatuation had rapidly increased, in view of her speedy departure. From Mrs. Tryon's remark about Wain's wife Amanda, and from things Rena had since learned, she had every reason to believe that this wife was living, and that Wain must be aware of the fact. In the light of this knowledge, Wain's former conduct took on a blacker significance than, upon reflection, she had charitably clothed it with after the first flush of indignation. That he had not given up his design to make love to her was quite apparent, and, with Amanda alive, his attentions, always offensive since she had gathered their import, became in her eyes the expression of a villainous purpose, of which she could not speak to others, and from which she felt safe only so long as she took proper precautions against it. In a week her school would be over, and then she would get Elder Johnson, or some one else than Wain, to take her back to Patesville. True, she might

abandon her school and go at once; but her work
would be incomplete, she would have violated her
contract, she would lose her salary for the month,
explanations would be necessary, and would not be
forthcoming. She might feign sickness, — indeed,
it would scarcely be feigning, for she felt far from
well; she had never, since her illness, quite recovered her former vigor — but the inconvenience
to others would be the same, and her self-sacrifice
would have had, at its very first trial, a lame and
impotent conclusion. She had as yet no fear of
personal violence from Wain; but, under the circumstances, his attentions were an insult. He was
evidently bent upon conquest, and vain enough to
think he might achieve it by virtue of his personal attractions. If he could have understood
how she loathed the sight of his narrow eyes, with
their puffy lids, his thick, tobacco-stained lips, his
doubtful teeth, and his unwieldy person, Wain,
a monument of conceit that he was, might have
shrunk, even in his own estimation, to something
like his real proportions. Rena believed that, to
defend herself from persecution at his hands, it
was only necessary that she never let him find her
alone. This, however, required constant watch-
fulness. Relying upon his own powers, and upon
a woman's weakness and aversion to scandal, from
which not even the purest may always escape
unscathed, and convinced by her former silence
that he had nothing serious to fear, Wain made it
a point to be present at every public place where

she might be. He assumed, in conversation with her which she could not avoid, and stated to others, that she had left his house because of a previous promise to divide the time of her stay between Elder Johnson's house and his own. He volunteered to teach a class in the Sunday-school which Rena conducted at the colored Methodist church, and when she remained to service, occupied a seat conspicuously near her own. In addition to these public demonstrations, which it was impossible to escape, or, it seemed, with so thick-skinned an individual as Wain, even to discourage, she was secretly and uncomfortably conscious that she could scarcely stir abroad without the risk of encountering one of two men, each of whom was on the lookout for an opportunity to find her alone.

The knowledge of Tryon's presence in the vicinity had been almost as much as Rena could bear. To it must be added the consciousness that he, too, was pursuing her, to what end she could not tell. After his letter to her brother, and the feeling therein displayed, she found it necessary to crush once or twice a wild hope that, her secret being still unknown save to a friendly few, he might return and claim her. Now, such an outcome would be impossible. He had become engaged to another woman, — this in itself would be enough to keep him from her, if it were not an index of a vastly more serious barrier, a proof that he had never loved her. If he had loved her truly, he

would never have forgotten her in three short
months, — three long months they had heretofore
seemed to her, for in them she had lived a lifetime
of experience. Another impassable barrier lay in
the fact that his mother had met her, and that she
was known in the neighborhood. Thus cut off
from any hope that she might be anything to
him, she had no wish to meet her former lover;
no possible good could come of such a meeting;
and yet her fluttering heart told her that if he
should come, as his letter foreshadowed that he
might, — if he should come, the loving George of
old, with soft words and tender smiles and specious talk of friendship — ah! then, her heart
would break! She must not meet him — at any
cost she must avoid him.

But this heaping up of cares strained her endurance to the breaking-point. Toward the middle of
the last week, she knew that she had almost reached
the limit, and was haunted by a fear that she
might break down before the week was over. Now
her really fine nature rose to the emergency, though
she mustered her forces with a great effort. If she
could keep Wain at his distance and avoid Tryon
for three days longer, her school labors would be
ended and she might retire in peace and honor.

"Miss Rena," said Plato to her on Tuesday,
"ain't it 'bout time I wuz gwine home wid you
ag'in?"

"You may go with me to-morrow, Plato,"
answered the teacher.

After school Plato met an anxious-eyed young man in the woods a short distance from the school-house.

"Well, Plato, what news?"

"I's gwine ter see her home ter-morrer, Mars Geo'ge."

"To-morrow!" replied Tryon; "how very unfortunate! I wanted you to go to town to-morrow to take an important message for me. I'm sorry, Plato — you might have earned another dollar."

To lie is a disgraceful thing, and yet there are times when, to a lover's mind, love dwarfs all ordinary laws. Plato scratched his head disconsolately, but suddenly a bright thought struck him.

"Can't I go ter town fer you atter I've seed her home, Mars Geo'ge?"

"N-o, I'm afraid it would be too late," returned Tryon doubtfully.

"Den I'll haf ter ax 'er ter lemme go nex' day," said Plato, with resignation. The honor might be postponed or, if necessary, foregone; the opportunity to earn a dollar was the chance of a lifetime and must not be allowed to slip.

"No, Plato," rejoined Tryon, shaking his head, "I shouldn't want to deprive you of so great a pleasure." Tryon was entirely sincere in this characterization of Plato's chance; he would have given many a dollar to be sure of Plato's place and Plato's welcome. Rena's letter had re-inflamed his smouldering passion; only opposition was needed to fan it to a white heat. Wherein lay the great superiority of his position, if he was denied the right to speak to the one person in the world whom he most cared to address? He felt some dim realization of the tyranny of caste, when he found it not merely pressing upon an inferior people who had no right to expect anything better, but barring his own way to something that he desired. He meant her no harm — but he must see her. He could never marry her now — but he must see her. He was conscious of a certain relief at the thought that he had not asked Blanche Leary to be his wife. His hand was unpledged. He could not marry the other girl, of course, but they must meet again. The rest he would leave to Fate, which seemed reluctant to disentangle threads which it had woven so closely.

"I think, Plato, that I see an easier way out of the difficulty. Your teacher, I imagine, merely wants some one to see her safely home. Don't you think, if you should go part of the way, that I might take your place for the rest, while you did my errand?"

"Why, sho'ly, Mars Geo'ge, you could take keer er her better 'n I could — better 'n anybody could — co'se you could!"

Mars Geo'ge was white and rich, and could do anything. Plato was proud of the fact that he had once belonged to Mars Geo'ge. He could not conceive of any one so powerful as Mars Geo'ge, unless it might be God, of whom Plato had heard more or less, and even here the com-

parison might not be quite fair to Mars Geo'ge,
for Mars Geo'ge was the younger of the two. It
would undoubtedly be a great honor for the teacher
to be escorted home by Mars Geo'ge. The teacher
was a great woman, no doubt, and looked white;
but Mars Geo'ge was the real article. Mars
Geo'ge had never been known to go with a black
woman before, and the teacher would doubtless
thank Plato for arranging that so great an honor
should fall upon her. Mars Ge'oge had given him
fifty cents twice, and would now give him a dollar.
Noble Mars Geo'ge! Fortunate teacher! Happy
Plato!

"Very well, Plato. I think we can arrange it
so that you can kill the two rabbits at one shot.
Suppose that we go over the road that she will
take to go home."

They soon arrived at the schoolhouse. School
had been out an hour, and the clearing was deserted. Plato led the way by the road through
the woods to a point where, amid somewhat thick
underbrush, another path intersected the road they
were following.

"Now, Plato," said Tryon, pausing here, "this
would be a good spot for you to leave the teacher
and for me to take your place. This path leads
to the main road, and will take you to town very
quickly. I should n't say anything to the teacher
about it at all; but when you and she get here,
drop behind and run along this path until you
meet me, — I 'll be waiting a few yards down the

road, — and then run to town as fast as your legs will carry you. As soon as you are gone, I 'll come out and tell the teacher that I 've sent you away on an errand, and will myself take your place. You shall have a dollar, and I 'll ask her to let you go home with her the next day. But you must n't say a word about it, Plato, or you won't get the dollar, and I 'll not ask the teacher to let you go home with her again."

" All right, Mars Geo'ge, I ain't gwine ter say no mo' d'n ef de cat had my tongue."

XXXI

IN DEEP WATERS

RENA was unusually fatigued at the close of her school on Wednesday afternoon. She had been troubled all day with a headache, which, beginning with a dull pain, had gradually increased in intensity until every nerve was throbbing like a trip-hammer. The pupils seemed unusually stupid. A discouraging sense of the insignificance of any part she could perform towards the education of three million people with a school term of two months a year hung over her spirit like a pall. As the object of Wain's attentions, she had begun to feel somewhat like a wild creature who hears the pursuers on its track, and has the fear of capture added to the fatigue of flight. But when this excitement had gone too far and had neared the limit of exhaustion came Tryon's letter, with the resulting surprise and consternation. Rena had keyed herself up to a heroic pitch to answer it; but when the inevitable reaction came, she was overwhelmed with a sickening sense of her own weakness. The things which in another sphere had constituted her strength and shield were now her undoing, and exposed her to dangers from which they lent her no protection. Not only was this her position in

theory, but the pursuers were already at her heels.
As the day wore on, these dark thoughts took on
an added gloom, until, when the hour to dismiss
school arrived, she felt as though she had not a
friend in the world. This feeling was accentu-
ated by a letter which she had that morning
received from her mother, in which Mis' Molly
spoke very highly of Wain, and plainly expressed
the hope that her daughter might like him so well
that she would prefer to remain in Sampson
County.

Plato, bright-eyed and alert, was waiting in the
school-yard until the teacher should be ready to
start. Having warned away several smaller children who had hung around after school as though
to share his prerogative of accompanying the
teacher, Plato had swung himself into the low
branches of an oak at the edge of the clearing,
from which he was hanging by his legs, head downward. He dropped from this reposeful attitude
when the teacher appeared at the door, and took
his place at her side.

A premonition of impending trouble caused the
teacher to hesitate. She wished that she had kept
more of the pupils behind. Something whispered
that danger lurked in the road she customarily
followed. Plato seemed insignificantly small and
weak, and she felt miserably unable to cope with
any difficult or untoward situation.

" Plato," she suggested, " I think we 'll go round
the other way to-night, if you don't mind."

Visions of Mars Geo'ge disappointed, of a dollar unearned and unspent, flitted through the narrow brain which some one, with the irony of ignorance or of knowledge, had mocked with the name of a great philosopher. Plato was not an untruthful lad, but he seldom had the opportunity to earn a dollar. His imagination, spurred on by the instinct of self-interest, rose to the emergency.

" I's feared you mought git snake-bit gwine roun' dat way, Miss Rena. My brer Jim kill't a water-moccasin down dere yistiddy 'bout ten feet long."

Rena had a horror of snakes, with which the swamp by which the other road ran was infested. Snakes were a vivid reality; her presentiment was probably a mere depression of spirits due to her condition of nervous exhaustion. A cloud had come up and threatened rain, and the wind was rising ominously. The old way was the shorter; she wanted above all things to get to Elder Johnson's and go to bed. Perhaps sleep would rest her tired brain — she could not imagine herself feeling worse, unless she should break down altogether.

She plunged into the path and hastened forward so as to reach home before the approaching storm. So completely was she absorbed in her own thoughts that she scarcely noticed that Plato himself seemed preoccupied. Instead of capering along like a playful kitten or puppy, he walked by her side unusually silent. When they had gone a short distance and were approaching a path which intersected their road at something near a right angle, the teacher missed Plato. He had dropped behind a moment before ; now he had disappeared entirely. Her vague alarm of a few moments before returned with redoubled force.

" Plato ! " she called ; " Plato ! "

There was no response, save the soughing of the wind through the swaying treetops. She stepped hastily forward, wondering if this were some childish prank. If so, it was badly timed, and she would let Plato feel the weight of her displeasure.

Her forward step had brought her to the junction of the two paths, where she paused doubtfully. The route she had been following was the most direct way home, but led for quite a distance through the forest, which she did not care to traverse alone. The intersecting path would soon take her to the main road, where she might find shelter or company, or both. Glancing around again in search of her missing escort, she became aware that a man was approaching her from each of the two paths. In one she recognized the eager and excited face of George Tryon, flushed with anticipation of their meeting, and yet grave with uncertainty of his reception. Advancing confidently along the other path she saw the face of Jeff Wain, drawn, as she imagined in her anguish, with evil passions which would stop at nothing.

What should she do ? There was no sign of Plato — for aught she could see or hear of him,

the earth might have swallowed him up. Some
deadly serpent might have stung him. Some
wandering rabbit might have tempted him aside.
Another thought struck her. Plato had been
very quiet — there had been something on his conscience — perhaps he had betrayed her! But to
which of the two men, and to what end?

The problem was too much for her overwrought
brain. She turned and fled. A wiser instinct
might have led her forward. In the two conflicting dangers she might have found safety. The
road after all was a public way. Any number of
persons might meet there accidentally. But she
saw only the darker side of the situation. To
turn to Tryon for protection before Wain had by
some overt act manifested the evil purpose which
she as yet only suspected would be, she imagined,
to acknowledge a previous secret acquaintance
with Tryon, thus placing her reputation at Wain's
mercy, and to charge herself with a burden of
obligation toward a man whom she wished to avoid
and had refused to meet. If, on the other hand,
she should go forward to meet Wain, he would
undoubtedly offer to accompany her homeward.
Tryon would inevitably observe the meeting, and
suppose it prearranged. Not for the world would
she have him think so — why she should care
for his opinion, she did not stop to argue. She
turned and fled, and to avoid possible pursuit,
struck into the underbrush at an angle which she
calculated would bring her in a few rods to an-

other path which would lead quickly into the main road. She had run only a few yards when she found herself in the midst of a clump of prickly shrubs and briars. Meantime the storm had burst; the rain fell in torrents. Extricating herself from the thorns, she pressed forward, but instead of coming out upon the road, found herself penetrating deeper and deeper into the forest.

The storm increased in violence. The air grew darker and darker. It was near evening, the clouds were dense, the thick woods increased the gloom. Suddenly a blinding flash of lightning pierced the darkness, followed by a sharp clap of thunder. There was a crash of falling timber. Terror-stricken, Rena flew forward through the forest, the underbrush growing closer and closer as she advanced. Suddenly the earth gave way beneath her feet and she sank into a concealed morass. By clasping the trunk of a neighboring sapling she extricated herself with an effort, and realized with a horrible certainty that she was lost in the swamp.

Turning, she tried to retrace her steps. A flash of lightning penetrated the gloom around her, and barring her path she saw a huge black snake, — harmless enough, in fact, but to her excited imagination frightful in appearance. With a wild shriek she turned again, staggered forward a few yards, stumbled over a projecting root, and fell heavily to the earth.

When Rena had disappeared in the underbrush,

Tryon and Wain had each instinctively set out in
pursuit of her, but owing to the gathering darkness, the noise of the storm, and the thickness of
the underbrush, they missed not only Rena but
each other, and neither was aware of the other's
presence in the forest. Wain kept up the chase
until the rain drove him to shelter. Tryon, after
a few minutes, realized that she had fled to escape
him, and that to pursue her would be to defeat
rather than promote his purpose. He desisted,
therefore, and returning to the main road, stationed
himself at a point where he could watch Elder
Johnson's house, and having waited for a while
without any signs of Rena, concluded that she had
taken refuge in some friendly cabin. Turning
homeward disconsolately as night came on, he in-
tercepted Plato on his way back from town, and
pledged him to inviolable secrecy so effectually
that Plato, when subsequently questioned, merely
answered that he had stopped a moment to gather
some chinquapins, and when he had looked around
the teacher was gone.

Rena not appearing at supper-time nor for an
hour later, the elder, somewhat anxious, made inquiries about the neighborhood, and finding his
guest at no place where she might be expected to
stop, became somewhat alarmed. Wain's house
was the last to which he went. He had surmised
that there was some mystery connected with her
leaving Wain's, but had never been given any
definite information about the matter. In response

to his inquiries, Wain expressed surprise, but betrayed a certain self-consciousness which did not
escape the elder's eye. Returning home, he organized a search-party from his own family and several near neighbors, and set out with dogs and
torches to scour the woods for the missing teacher.
A couple of hours later, they found her lying
unconscious in the edge of the swamp, only a few
rods from a well-defined path which would soon
have led her to the open highway. Strong arms
lifted her gently and bore her home. Mrs. Johnson undressed her and put her to bed, adminis-
tering a homely remedy, of which whiskey was
the principal ingredient, to counteract the effects
of the exposure. There was a doctor within five
miles, but no one thought of sending for him, nor
was it at all likely that it would have been possible
to get him for such a case at such an hour.

Rena's illness, however, was more deeply seated
than her friends could imagine. A tired body,
in sympathy with an overwrought brain, had left
her peculiarly susceptible to the nervous shock of
her forest experience. The exposure for several
hours in her wet clothing to the damps and miasma
of the swamp had brought on an attack of brain
fever. The next morning, she was delirious. One
of the children took word to the schoolhouse that
the teacher was sick and there would be no school
that day. A number of curious and sympathetic
people came in from time to time and suggested
various remedies, several of which old Mrs. John-

son, with catholic impartiality, administered to the helpless teacher, who from delirium gradually sunk into a heavy stupor scarcely distinguishable from sleep.   It was predicted that she would probably be well in the morning ; if not, it would then be time to consider seriously the question of sending for a doctor.

XXXII

THE POWER OF LOVE

AFTER Tryon's failure to obtain an interview with Rena through Plato's connivance, he decided upon a different course of procedure. In a few days her school term would be finished. He was not less desirous to see her, was indeed as much more eager as opposition would be likely to make a very young man who was accustomed to having his own way, and whose heart, as he had discovered, was more deeply and permanently involved than he had imagined. His present plan was to wait until the end of the school; then, when Rena went to Clinton on the Saturday or Monday to draw her salary for the month, he would see her in the town, or, if necessary, would follow her to Patesville. No power on earth should keep him from her long, but he had no desire to interfere in any way with the duty which she owed to others. When the school was over and her work completed, then he would have his innings. Writing letters was too unsatisfactory a method of communication — he must see her face to face.

The first of his three days of waiting had passed, when, about ten o'clock on the morning of the second day, which seemed very long in prospect, while driving along the road toward Clinton, he met Plato, with a rabbit trap in his hand.

"Well, Plato," he asked, "why are you absent from the classic shades of the academy to-day?"

"Hoddy, Mars Geo'ge. W'at wuz dat you say?"

"Why are you not at school to-day?"

"Ain' got no teacher, Mars Geo'ge. Teacher's gone!"

"Gone!" exclaimed Tryon, with a sudden leap of the heart. "Gone where? What do you mean?"

"Teacher got los' in de swamp, night befo' las', 'cause Plato wa'n't dere ter show her de way out'n de woods. Elder Johnson foun' 'er wid dawgs and tawches, an' fotch her home an' put her ter bed. No school yistiddy. She wuz out'n her haid las' night, an' dis mawnin' she wuz gone."

"Gone where?"

"Dey don' nobody know whar, suh."

Leaving Plato abruptly, Tryon hastened down the road toward Elder Johnson's cabin. This was no time to stand on punctilio. The girl had been lost in the woods in the storm, amid the thunder and lightning and the pouring rain. She was sick with fright and exposure, and he was the cause of it all. Bribery, corruption, and falsehood had brought punishment in their train, and the innocent had suffered while the guilty escaped. He must learn at once what had become of her.

Reaching Elder Johnson's house, he drew up by the front fence and gave the customary halloa, which summoned a woman to the door.

" Good-morning," he said, nodding unconsciously, with the careless politeness of a gentleman to his inferiors. " I 'm Mr. Tryon. I have come to inquire about the sick teacher."

" Why, suh," the woman replied respectfully, " she got los' in de woods night befo' las', an' she wuz out'n her min' most er de time yistiddy. Las' night she must 'a' got out er bed an' run away w'en eve'ybody wuz soun' asleep, fer dis mawnin' she wuz gone, an' none er us knows whar she is."

" Has any search been made for her ? "

" Yas, suh, my husban' an' de child'en has been huntin' roun' all de mawnin', an' he 's gone ter borry a hoss now ter go fu'ther. But Lawd knows dey ain' no tellin' whar she 'd go, 'less'n she got her min' back sence she lef'."

Tryon's mare was in good condition. He had money in his pocket and nothing to interfere with his movements. He set out immediately on the road to Patesville, keeping a lookout by the roadside, and stopping each person he met to inquire if a young woman, apparently ill, had been seen traveling along the road on foot. No one had met such a traveler. When he had gone two or three miles, he drove through a shallow branch that crossed the road. The splashing of his horse's hoofs in the water prevented him from hearing a low groan that came from the woods by the road-side.

He drove on, making inquiries at each farm-house and of every person whom he encountered. Shortly after crossing the branch, he met a young negro with a cartload of tubs and buckets and piggins, and asked him if he had seen on the road a young white woman with dark eyes and hair, apparently sick or demented. The young man answered in the negative, and Tryon pushed for-ward anxiously.

At noon he stopped at a farmhouse and swal-lowed a hasty meal. His inquiries here elicited no information, and he was just leaving when a young man came in late to dinner and stated, in response to the usual question, that he had met, some two hours before, a young woman who answered Tryon's description, on the Lillington road, which crossed the main road to Patesville a short distance beyond the farmhouse. He had spoken to the woman. At first she had paid no heed to his question. When addressed a second time, she had answered in a rambling and disconnected way, which indicated to his mind that there was some-thing wrong with her.

Tryon thanked his informant and hastened to the Lillington road. Stopping as before to inquire, he followed the woman for several hours, each mile of the distance taking him farther away from Patesville. From time to time he heard of the woman. Toward nightfall he found her. She

was white enough, with the sallowness of the sand-
hill poor white. She was still young, perhaps, but
poverty and a hard life made her look older than
she ought. She was not fair, and she was not
Rena. When Tryon came up to her, she was sitting
on the doorsill of a miserable cabin, and held in
her hand a bottle, the contents of which had never
paid any revenue tax. She had walked twenty
miles that day, and had beguiled the tedium of the
journey by occasional potations, which probably
accounted for the incoherency of speech which several of those who met her had observed. When
Tryon drew near, she tendered him the bottle with
tipsy cordiality. He turned in disgust and retraced his steps to the Patesville road, which he
did not reach until nightfall. As it was too dark
to prosecute the search with any chance of success,
he secured lodging for the night, intending to
resume his quest early in the morning.

XXXIII

A MULE AND A CART

FRANK FOWLER's heart was filled with longing for a sight of Rena's face. When she had gone away first, on the ill-fated trip to South Carolina, her absence had left an aching void in his life; he had missed her cheerful smile, her pleasant words, her graceful figure moving about across the narrow street. His work had grown monotonous during her absence; the clatter of hammer and mallet, that had seemed so merry when punctuated now and then by the strains of her voice, became a mere humdrum rapping of wood upon wood and iron upon iron. He had sought work in South Carolina with the hope that he might see her. He had satisfied this hope, and had tried in vain to do her a service; but Fate had been against her; her castle of cards had come tumbling down. He felt that her sorrow had brought her nearer to him. The distance between them depended very much upon their way of looking at things. He knew that her experience had dragged her through the valley of humiliation. His unselfish devotion had reacted to refine and elevate his own spirit. When he heard the suggestion, after her second departure, that she might marry Wain, he could not but compare himself with this new aspirant. He, Frank, was a man, an honest man — a better man than the shifty scoundrel with whom she had ridden away. She was but a woman, the best and sweetest and loveliest of all women, but yet a woman. After a few short years of happiness or sorrow, — little of joy, perhaps, and much of sadness, which had begun already, — they would both be food for worms. White people, with a deeper wisdom perhaps than they used in their own case, regarded Rena and himself as very much alike. They were certainly both made by the same God, in much the same physical and mental mould; they breathed the same air, ate the same food, spoke the same speech, loved and hated, laughed and cried, lived and would die, the same. If God had meant to rear any impassable barrier between people of contrasting complexions, why did He not express the prohibition as He had done between other orders of creation?

When Rena had departed for Sampson County, Frank had reconciled himself to her absence by the hope of her speedy return. He often stepped across the street to talk to Mis' Molly about her. Several letters had passed between mother and daughter, and in response to Frank's inquiries his neighbor uniformly stated that Rena was well and doing well, and sent her love to all inquiring friends. But Frank observed that Mis' Molly, when pressed as to the date of Rena's return, grew more and more indefinite; and finally the mother, in a burst of confidential friendship, told Frank of all her hopes with reference to the stranger from down the country.

"Yas, Frank," she concluded, " it 'll be her own fault ef she don't become a lady of proputty, fer Mr. Wain is rich, an' owns a big plantation, an' hires a lot of hands, and is a big man in the county. He's crazy to git her, an' it all lays in her own han's."

Frank did not find this news reassuring. He believed that Wain was a liar and a scoundrel. He had nothing more than his intuitions upon which to found this belief, but it was none the less firm. If his estimate of the man's character were correct, then his wealth might be a fiction, pure and simple. If so, the truth should be known to Mis' Molly, so that instead of encouraging a marriage with Wain, she would see him in his true light, and interpose to rescue her daughter from his importunities. A day or two after this conversation, Frank met in the town a negro from Sampson County, made his acquaintance, and inquired if he knew a man by the name of Jeff Wain.

"Oh, Jeff Wain!" returned the countryman slightingly; "yas, I knows 'im, an' don' know no good of 'im. One er dese yer biggity, braggin' niggers — talks lack he own de whole county, an' ain't wuth no mo' d'n I is — jes' a big bladder wid a handful er shot rattlin' roun' in it. Had a wife,

when I wuz dere, an' beat her an' 'bused her so
she had ter run away."

This was alarming information. Wain had
passed in the town as a single man, and Frank had
had no hint that he had ever been married. There
was something wrong somewhere. Frank determined that he would find out the truth and, if
possible, do something to protect Rena against the
obviously evil designs of the man who had taken
her away. The barrel factory had so affected the
cooper's trade that Peter and Frank had turned
their attention more or less to the manufacture of
small woodenware for domestic use. Frank's mule
was eating off its own head, as the saying goes. It
required but little effort to persuade Peter that
his son might take a load of buckets and tubs and
piggins into the country and sell them or trade
them for country produce at a profit.

In a few days Frank had his stock prepared, and
set out on the road to Sampson County. He went
about thirty miles the first day, and camped by
the roadside for the night, resuming the journey
at dawn. After driving for an hour through the
tall pines that overhung the road like the stately
arch of a cathedral aisle, weaving a carpet for the
earth with their brown spines and cones, and soothing the ear with their ceaseless murmur, Frank
stopped to water his mule at a point where the
white, sandy road, widening as it went, sloped
downward to a clear-running branch. On the
right a bay-tree bending over the stream mingled

the heavy odor of its flowers with the delicate perfume of a yellow jessamine vine that had overrun
a clump of saplings on the left.   From a neighboring tree a silver-throated mocking-bird poured
out a flood of riotous melody.   A group of minnows,
startled by the splashing of the mule's feet, darted
away into the shadow of the thicket, their quick
passage leaving the amber water filled with laugh-
ing light.

The mule drank long and lazily, while over
Frank stole thoughts in harmony with the peaceful
scene, — thoughts of Rena, young and beautiful,
her friendly smile, her pensive dark eyes.   He
would soon see her now, and if she had any cause
for fear or unhappiness, he would place himself at
her service — for a day, a week, a month, a year,
a lifetime, if need be.

His reverie was broken by a slight noise from
the thicket at his left.   " I wonder who dat is?"
he muttered.   " It soun's mighty quare, ter say de
leas'."

He listened intently for a moment, but heard
nothing further.   " It must 'a' be'n a rabbit er
somethin' scamp'in' th'ough de woods.   G'long
dere, Cæsar ! "

As the mule stepped forward, the sound was
repeated.   This time it was distinctly audible, the
long, low moan of some one in sickness or distress.

" Dat ain't no rabbit," said Frank to himself.
" Dere 's somethin' wrong dere.   Stan' here, Cæsar, till I look inter dis matter."

Pulling out from the branch, Frank sprang from the saddle and pushed his way cautiously through the outer edge of the thicket.

"Good Lawd!" he exclaimed with a start, "it's a woman — a w'ite woman!"

The slender form of a young woman lay stretched upon the ground in a small open space a few yards in extent. Her face was turned away, and Frank could see at first only a tangled mass of dark brown hair, matted with twigs and leaves and cockleburs, and hanging in wild profusion around her neck.

Frank stood for a moment irresolute, debating the serious question whether he should investigate further with a view to rendering assistance, or whether he should put as great a distance as possible between himself and this victim, as she might easily be, of some violent crime, lest he should himself be suspected of it — a not unlikely contingency, if he were found in the neighborhood and the woman should prove unable to describe her assailant. While he hesitated, the figure moved restlessly, and a voice murmured : —

"Mamma, oh, mamma!"

The voice thrilled Frank like an electric shock. Trembling in every limb, he sprang forward toward the prostrate figure. The woman turned her head, and he saw that it was Rena. Her gown was torn and dusty, and fringed with burs and briars. When she had wandered forth, half delirious, pursued by imaginary foes, she had not stopped to put on her shoes, and her little feet were blistered and

swollen and bleeding. Frank knelt by her side
and lifted her head on his arm. He put his hand
upon her brow; it was burning with fever.

"Miss Rena! Rena! don't you know me?"

She turned her wild eyes on him suddenly.
"Yes, I know you, Jeff Wain. Go away from
me! Go away!"

Her voice rose to a scream; she struggled in
his grasp and struck at him fiercely with her
clenched fists. Her sleeve fell back and disclosed
the white scar made by his own hand so many
years before.

"You 're a wicked man," she panted. "Don't
touch me! I hate you and despise you!"

Frank could only surmise how she had come
here, in such a condition. When she spoke of
Wain in this manner, he drew his own conclusions.
Some deadly villainy of Wain's had brought her
to this pass. Anger stirred his nature to the
depths, and found vent in curses on the author of
Rena's misfortunes.

"Damn him!" he groaned. "I 'll have his
heart's blood fer dis, ter de las' drop!"

Rena now laughed and put up her arms ap-
pealingly. "George," she cried, in melting tones,
"dear George, do you love me? How much do
you love me? Ah, you don't love me!" she
moaned; "I 'm black; you don't love me; you
despise me!"

Her voice died away into a hopeless wail.
Frank knelt by her side, his faithful heart break-

ing with pity, great tears rolling untouched down
his dusky cheeks.

"Oh, my honey, my darlin'," he sobbed, "Frank
loves you better 'n all de worl'."

Meantime the sun shone on as brightly as before, the mocking-bird sang yet more joyously.
A gentle breeze sprang up and wafted the odor of
bay and jessamine past them on its wings. The
grand triumphal sweep of nature's onward march
recked nothing of life's little tragedies.

When the first burst of his grief was over,
Frank brought water from the branch, bathed
Rena's face and hands and feet, and forced a few
drops between her reluctant lips. He then pitched
the cartload of tubs, buckets, and piggins out into
the road, and gathering dried leaves and pine-
straw, spread them in the bottom of the cart. He
stooped, lifted her frail form in his arms, and laid
it on the leafy bed. Cutting a couple of hickory
withes, he arched them over the cart, and gathering an armful of jessamine quickly wove it into
an awning to protect her from the sun. She was
quieter now, and seemed to fall asleep.

"Go ter sleep, honey," he murmured caressingly,
— "go ter sleep, an' Frank 'll take you home ter
yo' mammy!"

Toward noon he was met by a young white man,
who peered inquisitively into the canopied cart.

"Hello!" exclaimed the stranger, "who 've you
got there?"

"A sick woman, suh."

" Why, she 's white, as I 'm a sinner! " he cried, after a closer inspection. " Look a-here, nigger, what are you doin' with this white woman?"

" She 's not w'ite, boss, — she 's a bright mulatter."

" Yas, mighty bright," continued the stranger suspiciously. " Where are you goin' with her ? "

" I 'm takin' her ter Patesville, ter her mammy."

The stranger passed on. Toward evening Frank heard hounds baying in the distance. A fox, weary with running, brush drooping, crossed the road ahead of the cart. Presently, the hounds straggled across the road, followed by two or three hunters on horseback, who stopped at sight of the strangely canopied cart. They stared at the sick girl and demanded who she was.

"I don't b'lieve she 's black at all," declared one, after Frank's brief explanation. " This nigger has a bad eye, — he 's up ter some sort of devilment. What ails the girl?"

" 'Pears ter be some kind of a fever," replied Frank; adding diplomatically, " I don't know whether it 's ketchin' er no — she 's be'n out er her head most er de time."

They drew off a little at this. " I reckon it 's all right," said the chief spokesman. The hounds were baying clamorously in the distance. The hunters followed the sound and disappeared in the woods.

Frank drove all day and all night, stopping only

for brief periods of rest and refreshment. At
dawn, from the top of the long white hill, he
sighted the river bridge below. At sunrise he
rapped at Mis' Molly's door.

Upon rising at dawn, Tryon's first step, after
a hasty breakfast, was to turn back toward Clinton. He had wasted half a day in following the
false scent on the Lillington road. It seemed,
after reflection, unlikely that a woman seriously
ill should have been able to walk any considerable distance before her strength gave out. In her
delirium, too, she might have wandered in a wrong
direction, imagining any road to lead to Patesville.
It would be a good plan to drive back home,
continuing his inquiries meantime, and ascertain
whether or not she had been found by those who
were seeking her, including many whom Tryon's
inquiries had placed upon the alert. If she should
prove still missing, he would resume the journey
to Patesville and continue the search in that direction. She had probably not wandered far from
the highroad ; even in delirium she would be likely
to avoid the deep woods, with which her illness
was associated.

He had retraced more than half the distance
to Clinton when he overtook a covered wagon.
The driver, when questioned, said that he had met
a young negro with a mule, and a cart in which
lay a young woman, white to all appearance, but
claimed by the negro to be a colored girl who

had been taken sick on the road, and whom he was conveying home to her mother at Patesville. From a further description of the cart Tryon recognized it as the one he had met the day before. The woman could be no other than Rena. He turned his mare and set out swiftly on the road to Patesville.

If anything could have taken more complete possession of George Tryon at twenty-three than love successful and triumphant, it was love thwarted and denied. Never in the few brief delirious weeks of his courtship had he felt so strongly drawn to the beautiful sister of the popular lawyer, as he was now driven by an aching heart toward the same woman stripped of every adventitious advantage and placed, by custom, beyond the pale of marriage with men of his own race. Custom was tyranny. Love was the only law. Would God have made hearts to so yearn for one another if He had meant them to stay forever apart? If this girl should die, it would be he who had killed her, by his cruelty, no less surely than if with his own hand he had struck her down. He had been so dazzled by his own superiority, so blinded by his own glory, that he had ruthlessly spurned and spoiled the image of God in this fair creature, whom he might have had for his own treasure, — whom, please God, he would yet have, at any cost, to love and cherish while they both should live. There were difficulties — they had seemed insuperable, but love would surmount them. Sacrifices must be made, but if the world without love would be nothing, then why not give up the world for love? He would hasten to Patesville. He would find her; he would tell her that he loved her, that she was all the world to him, that he had come to marry her, and take her away where they might be happy together. He pictured to himself the joy that would light up her face; he felt her soft arms around his neck, her tremulous kisses upon his lips. If she were ill, his love would woo her back to health, — if disappointment and sorrow had contributed to her illness, joy and gladness should lead to her recovery.

He urged the mare forward; if she would but keep up her present pace, he would reach Patesville by nightfall.

Dr. Green had just gone down the garden path to his buggy at the gate. Mis' Molly came out to the back piazza, where Frank, weary and haggard, sat on the steps with Homer Pettifoot and Billy Oxendine, who, hearing of Rena's return, had come around after their day's work.

"Rena wants to see you, Frank," said Mis' Molly, with a sob.

He walked in softly, reverently, and stood by her bedside. She turned her gentle eyes upon him and put out her slender hand, which he took in his own broad palm.

"Frank," she murmured, "my good friend — my best friend — you loved me best of them all."

The tears rolled untouched down his cheeks. "I'd 'a' died, fer you, Miss Rena," he said brokenly.

Mary B. threw open a window to make way for the passing spirit, and the red and golden glory of the setting sun, triumphantly ending his daily course, flooded the narrow room with light.

Between sunset and dark a traveler, seated in a dusty buggy drawn by a tired horse, crossed the long river bridge and drove up Front Street. Just as the buggy reached the gate in front of the house behind the cedars, a woman was tying a piece of crape upon the door-knob. Pale with apprehension, Tryon sat as if petrified, until a tall, side-whiskered mulatto came down the garden walk to the front gate.

"Who's dead?" demanded Tryon hoarsely, scarcely recognizing his own voice.

"A young cullud 'oman, suh," answered Homer Pettifoot, touching his hat, "Mis' Molly Walden's daughter Rena."